John Ryan

ALAN GLYNN is a graduate of Trinity College, Dublin. His first novel, *The Dark Fields,* was republished as *Limitless* and simultaneously released as a film of the same name in March 2011, which has since been developed into a TV series by CBS. He is also the author of *Winterland; Bloodland,* a finalist for the Edgar Award for Best Paperback Original; and *Graveland.* He lives in Ireland.

ALSO BY ALAN GLYNN

Graveland
Bloodland
Winterland
Limitless

PRAISE FOR ALAN GLYNN

"[Glynn] has a knack for depicting a shifting reality, partly by introducing us to characters who are already at their mental and emotional limits. . . . His heroes exist in contemporary free fall, bracing themselves against whatever surface is available. . . . Remarkable."
—*The Los Angeles Review of Books*

"*Graveland* is an excellent novel—smart and edgy yet possessing real substance and depth. Glynn is fast becoming one of the best contemporary thriller writers around."
—R. J. Ellory

"Ripped from tomorrow's headlines, *Bloodland* is irresistible."
—Val McDermid

"Glynn plays out these grand themes—the global economic crisis, America's battle with China for dominance in Africa, the human costs of illegal mining—on a very personal scale, through a group of deeply flawed but compelling characters."
—NPR on *Bloodland*

"A terrific read . . . Completely involving."
—George Pelecanos on *Winterland*

"A noir masterpiece."
—Ken Bruen on *Winterland*

"Alan Glynn has created enough twists and thrills to keep readers up late—even without resorting to illegal and dangerous substances."
—*The New York Times Book Review* on *Limitless*

PARADIME

PARADIME

A NOVEL

ALAN GLYNN

PICADOR   NEW YORK

This is a work of fiction. All of the characters, organizations, and events portrayed in this novel are either products of the author's imagination or are used fictitiously.

PARADIME. Copyright © 2016 by Alan Glynn. All rights reserved. Printed in the United States of America. For information, address Picador, 175 Fifth Avenue, New York, N.Y. 10010.

picadorusa.com • picadorbookroom.tumblr.com
twitter.com/picadorusa • facebook.com/picadorusa

Picador® is a U.S. registered trademark and is used by St. Martin's Press under license from Pan Books Limited.

For book club information, please visit facebook.com/picadorbookclub or e-mail marketing@picadorusa.com.

Designed by Anna Gorovoy

Library of Congress Cataloging-in-Publication Data

Names: Glynn, Alan, 1960– author.
Title: Paradime : a novel / Alan Glynn.
Description: First U.S. Edition. | New York : Picador, 2016.
Identifiers: LCCN 2015044497 (print) | LCCN 2015047112 (e-book) |
    ISBN 978-1-250-06182-9 (trade paperback) | ISBN 978-1-250-06183-6
    (e-book)
Subjects: | BISAC: FICTION / Thrillers. | GSAFD: Suspense fiction.
Classification: LCC PR6107.L93 P37 2016 (print) | LCC PR6107.L93 (e-book) |
    DDC 823'.92—dc23
LC record available at http://lccn.loc.gov/2015044497

Our books may be purchased in bulk for promotional, educational, or business use. Please contact your local bookseller or the Macmillan Corporate and Premium Sales Department at 1-800-221-7945, extension 5442, or by e-mail at MacmillanSpecialMarkets@macmillan.com.

Originally published in Great Britain by Faber and Faber Ltd.

First U.S. Edition: August 2016

10 9 8 7 6 5 4 3 2 1

For John Schoenfelder

I

1

There's no app for this.

Though I seem to have one for nearly everything else. I can track my movements over the course of a day, every footstep, every heart-beat. I can monitor my stress levels, boost productivity, enhance cognition.

But relieve anxiety? Eliminate dread? Not a chance.

As the R train rattles towards 59th Street, I look down at my phone and swipe to the right.

Start your free seven-day trial now . . .

I'll never use any of these. I put my phone away.

The green I-beam columns and ceramic wall tiles of the station flicker into view. I get up and wait by the car door. It's 11:30 a.m., the platform not particularly crowded—a lull between surges, the secret hour for tourists, junkies, and unemployed people.

Up on 59th Street, it's bright and sunny, the sky almost aggres-sively blue. Just ahead, vast and constipated as always, looms the Plaza Hotel. At the curb, waiting to cross, I gaze for a moment down Fifth at the flow of traffic and buildings—parallel lines that trail towards a meeting point at the blistering horizon. I turn and look the other way, over at the huddled expanse of Central Park, and then, a little farther to the right, at the deck of sidewalk awnings fanning north— the ones fronting the granite and marble mansions that line this side of Fifth, what used to be called, quaintly, Millionaire's Row.

This morning, up here, the specific anxiety, the specific dread, is easy to identify. It's simply that I don't belong. I'm not a tourist en route to Tiffany's, or an addled junkie wandering lost through the canyons of Midtown. I belong to that third group, the unemployed, and consequently have no real business being here. Every person I see reinforces this—every silk-suited alpha dog barking into his cell phone, every skinny society hostess dripping in jewelry and laden down with designer shopping bags, every map-consulting European family of four, immaculate in their ironed jeans and matching Oxford-blue Windbreakers.

But I have to go somewhere, right? I can't be *no*where. And that's the problem. No matter where I end up, there'll be a local supply of reasons to feel shitty and out of place. If I go into the park, for example, all those bright, determined people in Lycra running towards a better future . . . well, they'll crush any semblance of hope *I* might have. If I go too far west, Tenth Avenue and beyond, the gradual disintegration I'll see all around me won't do my mood any good.

If I go back to the apartment . . .

Can't really do that though, not until late afternoon, not until Kate has put in however many hours she needs to put in. And even then . . .

If I leave New York?

If I go back to Asheville?

It doesn't matter. When it comes to anxiety and dread, there'll always be location-specific reasons. But it's when *they* run out that the existential shit really hits the fan—because even if I found the perfect location, where conditions were ideal, guess what . . . *I'd* still be there.

How do you escape that?

I cross Fifth, walk past the Plaza and on towards Sixth, where I turn left.

The Avenue of the Americas.

I could walk down to Greenwich Village from here, block after block, passing through several Americas in the process and certainly ending up in one that's different from the one I'm in right now. But what then? Another cappuccino in some dingy café? Another hour or two in the Strand? How long will it be before I start shouting at people—from a park bench, say, or in the street, or on a subway platform?

Hey, you!

Hey, buddy!

Hey, gorgeous!

The prospects aren't good. I need something to occupy my time. I need something to occupy my *mind*. I need a job. And I need one fast.

Three weeks ago I was a civilian contractor in Afghanistan.

Working in a chow hall.

All my life, on and off, I've worked in kitchens. My old man had a restaurant—*restaurant*, it was a steakhouse—and I spent a lot of time there, first as a kid running around the place, then as a teenager washing pots, bringing out the garbage, even doing some basic prep, but always, as I remember—and no disrespect to the old man here—always dreaming of what it'd be like to work in a proper kitchen. By this I think I probably meant the kitchen of some place like the Four Seasons on 52nd Street, which I'd once seen an article about in a trade magazine. But with visions of pristine chef whites and brushed-steel surfaces etched in my mind, sustaining me, I never thought I'd end up working in a place that served food you'd be embarrassed to feed to a dog—food that was tasteless, highly processed, and basically inedible. The stuff still had to be cooked, though, and the job of doing that, it turns out, was an actual job, and a well-paying one—something that at the time I really needed.

The chow hall was at Forward Operating Base Sharista in Nangarhar Province and was one of countless food-service facilities privately operated by Gideon Logistics. That meant production-line industrial food shipped in frozen, then cooked (for lack of a better word) and served up to exhausted, bored, jangly nerved, hot, and, above all, hungry servicemen. Described as a "global provider of integrated supply-chain solutions," Gideon was in Afghanistan as part of the LOGCAP IV program and had a hand in pretty much everything over there. Security, transportation, freight management, food and laundry services, sanitation—you name it, they were doing it, squeezing every last dollar out of the war before the fucking thing ground to a halt.

I'd only been there for four months, shipped over myself like a box of frozen burger patties after I answered an ad and signed up for what promised to be a lucrative two-year contract with above-average benefits and good rotation cycles. They were looking for food-service managers, chefs, line cooks, whatever, to help run their various overseas facilities, most of which were located in environments ranging, the ad said, from "potentially hostile" to "extremely dangerous." In short, the work would be "demanding, but rewarding." Kate was dead set against it, of course—why would you put yourself in that position when you didn't have to—but all I could see were the numbers. I'd already been in Iraq—done two tours there—so I wasn't intimidated by the war-zone thing, and I had sufficient food-industry experience to qualify for the job. The math was simple. Two short years over there and I could earn what it would take me five or six to earn here. Which, given our financial circumstances at the time, made it a no-brainer.

It's just that, I suppose, go figure, things didn't exactly work out as planned.

Every few blocks or so, stopped at the lights, I almost resolve to quit this charade and head back to the apartment. It's Kate's, a one-bedroom sublet in a rent-stabilized walk-up on 10th Street, so it's small and cramped—but still, I could lie quietly on the bed, laid out like a corpse waiting to be embalmed, and she wouldn't even have to know I was there. How different would that be from what I'm doing now, which is, supposedly—and at Kate's gentle insistence—out looking for a job?

Or meeting people, at the very least.

Networking.

Her word.

Sometimes I wonder if Kate has met *me*.

To be fair, though, she's doing her best. Equipped with a BA in political science from Atherton College, Kate moved to Manhattan five years ago with high hopes of . . . I don't know, going to law school, eventually getting into public service, something, whatever, but after only a few months it became obvious that her chief asset, the one thing she had going for her, was this rent-stabilized sublet, because without it, bottom line, she wouldn't be living in Manhattan, probably not even in Brooklyn. More than likely, in fact, with today's rents, she'd be back living with her parents in Baltimore. She got the sublet through a connection of her old man's, an ex-colleague who'd also promised to show her the ropes, even pave the way to a possible job, something decent, but unfortunately this same guy got sick, lost *his* job, and had to skip town, leaving Kate with the just-about-affordable apartment and the dawning realization that she had little or no prospect of getting into law school, little or no prospect of getting anything like a "decent" job, and little or no prospect of paying back her student-loan debts, which amounted to more than thirty-three thousand dollars and were probably now set to become the defining fact of her life.

And then—let there be no doubt—she met me.

I resolve once more to quit this charade and head back to the apartment, but again don't quite manage it.

It's like each day now is its own little tour of duty, and in that context there's no scenario where you can just say *Fuck it*, let's return to base. Think I'll de-enlist. Don't want to do this anymore.

I come to the lights at 42nd, stop, and look around. The big difference here is that I'm on my own. There's no command structure, no one barking orders, no exit strategy either, or even talk of one. My four months in Afghanistan might be only just behind me, but I find that my memory, if left on autopilot, drifts more readily to Iraq. Those impressions are bigger, louder, stickier. But that's just what they are, impressions, because I can't pinpoint specific incidents, I don't have recurring nightmares, there are no indelible images in my head. Other guys have stories to tell, this happened, that happened, shit they'll never forget as long as they live, but *some* guys (like me, I suppose), while never really able to stop thinking about it, can't actually fucking remember the experience in any relatable detail at all.

My days at Sharista, on the other hand, they're in high def. It's just that I really, *really* don't want to remember them—wholesale, retail, it doesn't matter.

On the far side of 42nd, past Bryant Park, I have what amounts to a mild panic attack, a sudden, razor-blade swipe to the gut . . . a constriction in the chest, then difficulty breathing. It threatens to become overwhelming, but I know from experience that it won't. I keep walking, wrestling the sensations down, folding them into my stride.

To look at me you wouldn't think anything was wrong. To look at me you'd think I was normal. Which I am. But isn't that the point? People have interior lives—I do, you do, everyone walking around me here on the street does—but the sad truth is we're all riddled with fear and insecurity. And me acting like a crazy person on the sidewalk, clutching my chest and hyperventilating—that's not going to help anyone, it's not going to move the situation along. Besides, I'm used to stress, and I take a certain amount of pride in being able to handle it. Not only have I spent time working in high-pressure kitchens, I've done basic military training, I've served in a war zone.

This, on the other hand . . . this is Midtown on a quiet, sunny morning in early spring. I have to believe I'm capable of holding it together here. Because what's the alternative? I go apeshit? Pull a gun out?

Discharge it randomly? Then what, a cop or a security guard shoots *me*? And that's *it*? Game over for Danny Lynch—thirty-three-year-old Iraq War veteran, unemployed, disaffected, and with a history of mental health problems? *That's* my fifteen minutes? "He frequently skipped his meds," a psychiatrist I hadn't seen in five years would be quoted as saying on Fox News. "He pretty much kept to himself," someone else would tell Gawker. And then it would come out, the big reveal, that just three weeks earlier I had been fired by Gideon Logistics in Afghanistan after an "altercation" at the base involving some TCNs—third country nationals—and that two people had died as a result.

It'd be the perfect narrative—rounded, cautionary, easy to digest. Just not entirely true.

Confirmation bias would take a serious hit when it emerged that I wasn't some lone-wolf type acting out a paranoid fantasy, that I had merely witnessed the incident at Sharista, and that furthermore, several hundred other employees had been let go at the same time not due to the altercation but to the fact that Gideon was embroiled in a multibillion-dollar billing dispute with the Department of Defense and needed to implement drastic cuts.

But who would care? Who would even listen? The only thing anyone would *hear* is the reference to mental health problems—which is a fairly broad stroke of the brush . . . but let's face it, a little ADD as a kid and some standard-issue PTSD after Iraqi Freedom, and they've got you on their books, marked and labeled forever.

To them, that's who you are.

And how do you escape that? I'm not sure you can, but the thing is, when Kate and I are together . . . I don't feel like I *am* that person. I'm more grounded. I'm less likely to spiral out of control. I have space to breathe. And that's one of the reasons I clear out of the apartment every day. To give her some space. In fact, she's back there right now sitting at the kitchen table with her laptop open in front of her, learning how to code, doing an intensive online course in it. I'm not even

sure I know what coding is exactly, but Kate has read that it's the ab-
solute must-have skillset of the future, that knowledge of HTML and
CSS is the new literacy. It may not get her into law school, but she
thinks it'll be a passport to a job market one or two notches above
the one she's been in for the past few years—service positions that
are themselves becoming harder to get, and if you have one, harder to
hold on to, not to mention less well paid and with practically no benefits. It used to be that you could fake the necessary enthusiasm to
secure one of these jobs and use it as a stepping stone to your preferred
career path. But not anymore.

Over the past few years, Kate has been a waitress (at Mouzon,
where we met), a legal proofreader, a temp, she's worked at a call center, in retail, she's babysat, walked dogs, done all sorts of stuff, and
never once (in my hearing) complained about it. She hasn't relin-
quished her dreams, either, and that's saying something. For my part,
I don't have dreams. You might think I'd aspire to be a chef, or to have
my own restaurant, or to be out pushing the boundaries of molecular
gastronomy, but it's just work to me, a paycheck, and I guess I've got
the old man to thank for that. If I'm a kitchen lifer it's because of him,
but at the same time he ruined it for me by the way he let it grind
him down, so whatever ambition I have now is vicarious, it's for Kate—
it's so *she* doesn't end up getting ground down. Which is what the
Gideon contract was about. I'd go over to Afghanistan, do the work,
put in the time, stockpile the cash, and get out. Then I'd head back to
my job at Mouzon and Kate would clear her student-loan debts. We'd
get some breathing space out of it—a chance to slow down, to look
around, to look forward.

At least, that was the plan.

As I approach 38th Street, my cell phone vibrates. I answer it. "Hi,
Kate."

"Hi, honey, where are you?"

"Uh . . . Midtown," I say quickly. "Just ran into a guy I knew from before, Sheldon Wu. He's got an Asian fusion place in Chelsea, and one in Park Slope, but . . . he's not hiring at the moment."

Fine, that's a lie, but it's not as if I'm drinking shots here and playing pool—I *want* to have just met a guy with two fusion restaurants who almost gave me a job. That'd be awesome. Or almost awesome. I mean, what was the first thing I did when I got back from Afghanistan? Head over to Mouzon, where I'd been a line cook for nearly two years, that's what, fully confident that they'd rehire me, but I turned the corner at Hudson and there was the place all boarded up, paint peeling off the sign, zombie-apocalypse style.

I'd only been away four months.

"It's this economy," the guy who owned the place told me later when I called him. "I don't know, the customer base just isn't there anymore."

So I'm not exactly psyched about hustling for work. And the problem isn't the work itself, I could do that all day, set me up at a station and I'll zen out, but really, do I have to deal with other people?

"Well," she says, "at least you're putting yourself out there, right?"

"Yeah." I slow down, stop at a store window, and study the busy display of cameras, tripods, and binoculars. "Something'll turn up."

"I know, but for your sake, Danny, pray it doesn't involve writing code. Anyway, listen, I just picked up the mail and there's a letter for you, it's from Gideon."

I freeze. "What does it say?"

"I don't know. It's addressed to you."

"Well, go ahead," I say, pressing the phone against my ear. "Open it."

I hear her tearing the envelope, pulling out the letter, silence for a moment, then a barely audible intake of breath.

I close my eyes. "What?"

"Fuck."

"*What?*"

"They're . . . they're withholding your last check."

"Jesus." I open my eyes. "On what grounds?"

She doesn't answer.

"Kate, on what grounds?"

"Wait a sec, I'm trying to read it. Uh . . . suspected violation of . . . GO-1C? Does that make any sense?"

"General order number one, yeah it makes sense, except that it fucking doesn't." I turn from the window display and gaze out across Sixth. My final paycheck from Gideon Logistics is due next week and I need it. We need it. What are these pricks up to? "Does it say anything else?"

"There's a long bit about . . . termination of contract, stipulations, regulatory something, pursuant to . . . I don't know, it's all legalese, I'd need to read it closely. But Jesus, can they really do this?"

I swallow hard, the ground beneath my feet beginning to melt, the avenue itself beginning to spin. I lean back against the window.

"Look," I say, almost in a whisper—and conscious that I'm speaking to a person who believes in the legal system, who actually wants to some day *be* a lawyer—"the truth is, these people can do whatever the fuck they want."

Once she's established that I don't have any other "appointments" set up for the rest of the day, Kate insists that I come back to the apartment.

I get an F train to 14th Street, an L over to Third Avenue, and walk the remaining few blocks to our building, slowing down the closer I get.

I've never been good at looking for work, but in a weird way that's never mattered because work has always found me. After the old man died, and the place closed, plenty of other kitchen opportunities opened up for me in Asheville—which was maybe why it took me three more years to get the fuck out of there and why my route out was the recruiting station.

After Iraq—two fifteen-month tours with six months in between—I spent a whole year doing nothing, living in a cousin's house, smoking weed, going through a box of old paperbacks that I found in the basement, and trying to figure out who or what I was. Then one day a guy from my old company called up and said, if memory served, I was a kitchen guy, right, and did I want a job in New York, that he and his brother were opening a place and needed to build a crew. So I figured that's what I was, a kitchen guy, and why fight it? Anyway, that particular venture didn't work out, but it did lead, in turn, to the Mouzon gig and two years of steady employment. The money was lousy, though, so when I saw an ad for the position with Gideon, I jumped at it.

I get to the entrance of our building on 10th Street and suddenly feel sick, like I'm going to puke right there on the sidewalk. I haven't eaten, so there's nothing *to* puke, but the feeling persists. I go inside, along the narrow hallway, and up the stairs, hoping I don't run into anybody. I don't like this place, and although it made sense for me to move in, which I did about a year ago, I half suspect that one of the attractions of shipping out to Afghanistan was to get away from here—not away from Kate, away from this damp and cluttered little apartment of hers. I don't have nightmares about Iraq, go figure, but I do have nightmares about this place, about still having to trudge up these stairs when I'm forty, or about being trapped here, say, with a baby.

Which is something we've discussed.

With my key out, I get to our door and open it. Kate looks up from the table, a smile on her face. It quickly fades. She's out of the chair in an instant, but in the next I'm in the bathroom, retching into the toilet bowl. Not long after this, we're both at the table, poring over the letter, dissecting it, parsing the language—one minute convinced it's nothing more than a stalling tactic, the next that Gideon doesn't just intend to withhold my last paycheck but might actually be threatening me with some form of legal action as well.

After a while I stand up and walk over to the refrigerator. I take out a bottle of water and knock a third of it back in one go. Screwing the cap on again, I look at Kate. She's small and slim, with bright blue eyes and shoulder-length red hair. At times, in her black-rimmed glasses and plain black T-shirt, she can seem fairly intense, but she's also thoughtful and circumspect, good qualities, I'm sure, for a lawyer—at least the kind she wants to be. Speaking of which, there's a conversation we haven't had since I got back, an interrogation she hasn't conducted, and I have to say I admire her restraint in not initiating it. *What really happened over there?* That's all she'd have to say to get the ball rolling. And I'd tell her. I wouldn't lie. But she hasn't asked. When I spoke to her on the phone a couple of days before I shipped back, I tried to explain how these staff cuts were the result of a massive lawsuit Gideon was involved in and that, because of an early release clause in my contract, there was nothing I could do about it. Besides— I was at pains to add—maybe my timing hadn't been so great. The war was winding down, after all, and troops were coming home.

This was greeted with the kind of silence that told me she knew I was full of shit.

Since there were more important things to focus on when I got back, such as what to do next, there didn't seem to be much point in conducting a postmortem, in trying to pick apart a decision that couldn't be reversed, so it became the official line, and nothing more was said about it.

But with this letter now and its veiled threat of litigation, I won't have any choice *but* to talk about it. There's pride in the mix too. Kate never liked the idea of me going to Afghanistan, never approved of Gideon Logistics, and I sort of ended up defending them, being all hard-nosed and pragmatic about it. I don't usually have a problem admitting that I'm wrong, but when it's this spectacularly wrong? You need a little lead time.

It's been three weeks, though. How much longer do I need?

Kate holds up the letter, and shakes her head. "I just . . . I don't understand this, Danny."

I put the water back in the fridge. I close the door and lean against it. "That's because there's something I haven't told you."

She stares at me, her eyes widening.

If the fridge behind me didn't have such a loud hum, she'd probably be able to hear my heart beating from the other side of the table.

"There was an incident at the base," I say, "something pretty horrible, something that I witnessed, and I wasn't the only one, but for some reason they're trying to implicate me in it, with this letter, and . . . the thing is, I don't understand it either."

Any lawyerly composure Kate has falls away and, for a brief moment, the look on her face displays a nervousness, a reluctance to hear what I have to say that almost equals my own reluctance to say it.

But then her composure returns.

"What is it, Danny?" she says in a whisper, leaning back in the chair. "What happened?"

2

This might be the most Kate has ever heard me speak at any one time since the day we met.

The Forward Operating Base at Sharista, I tell her, was huge—a maze of shipping containers, Humvees, and B huts. It was an insanely elaborate ecosystem teeming within a heavily fortified perimeter of Hesco barriers and wire-mesh fencing. My job as an assistant kitchen coordinator at the main DFAC was to oversee a turnover of between five hundred to a thousand covers on any given day. This meant working twelve-hour shifts, six days a week, sometimes seven. It meant rotating crews in a mechanized system that was less about real cooking and more about defrosting, heating, and reheating, about moving shit along a conveyor belt and making sure that the ex-flow of meals and the in-flow of diners aligned, like some sort of celestial eclipse.

There were a few other guys, nearly all ex-servicemen, doing the same thing I was, which was basically shift supervision, but since we were also on rotation there wasn't much time for hanging out or getting to know each other. The vast majority of the kitchen staff—the preppers, line cooks, servers, cleaners—these were all TCNs, i.e. Filipinos, Nepalese, Bangladeshis, Kenyans, Nigerians, most of them with no English, most of them trafficked in by small recruiting agencies that wouldn't know a basic wage or welfare regulation if it came up and bit them in the ass.

Now, I was exhausted most of the time, so it took me a while to start paying attention to this stuff and to realize that these people working under me were being treated like shit. Their living conditions were awful, they weren't paid anything like what they'd been promised, and some of the women (if I understood correctly what I was hearing) had routinely been victims of sexual harassment, if not outright assault. And something else: there often wasn't enough food to go around their compound at designated mealtimes.

I look at Kate directly now. She's staring back at me with a shocked expression in her eyes, one that tells me I need to explain this, I need to make it make sense, and *fast*.

But I can't.

Because apart from anything else, I haven't told her what happened yet.

During my time in Afghanistan, Kate and I kept our communications to one quick phone call a week. It was easier that way. Long e-mails or Facebook posts aren't my thing, and in a five-minute call I could keep it breezy. Even if conditions at the FOB had been ideal, hearing about my routine there still would have been depressing, or at the very least boring, so I tended to let Kate do most of the talking.

What she's hearing now, therefore, is definitely new to her, and if she's wondering why I've kept it to myself for the past three weeks, she doesn't let on.

"There was this one guy," I tell her, "from Nepal, Sajit something. He was skinny, like a stick insect. He worked one of the walk-in freezer units, loaded it, unloaded it, twelve hours a day. He spoke English, enough anyway to hold a decent conversation, and he was funny too—I liked him. It was Sajit who told me what was going on in the compound, Gideon security guys showing up at night, picking out girls, then stories about a trade in fake documents, about intimidation, about people getting cheated out of whatever small amounts of cash they'd managed to save. I brought this up one day with a Gideon manager. I asked him if he knew what conditions were like for the TCNs, but he laughed in my face, told me to shut the fuck up and get back to work. An hour later, as if he'd been thinking about it, he showed up again, walked right over to me, and said I needed to mind my own business if I knew what was good for me. Then, like a good cop-bad cop rolled into one, he tried to confide in me, saying, 'Look, what do you want, these people are animals, you know, you should see how they live, how they choose to live, it's disgusting.' Before I could come up with an answer, he'd moved on, but I don't know if there'd've been much point in speaking up anyway. I don't think Sajit would have thanked me, or any of the others. Conditions were bad enough without dragging my stupid shit into the equation. But let me tell you, with two months down, and nearly twenty-two to go, I was sick to my stomach of the whole fucking place."

"Jesus, Danny . . ."

I say nothing for a moment. Funny how two little words can be so loaded, so nuanced, so ambiguous—there is sympathy in them, of course, but also confusion, and not a little dread. Kate isn't going to judge me for not speaking up, not yet. She knows how to hold her own counsel. It's in her head, though. I can see it in her eyes.

"It went on the same way for a while," I say, "weeks and weeks. Sajit would talk to me, or I'd hear stuff from some of the others, a couple of the line cooks, Kenyan guys I'd bullshit around with when there was a break in service. Technically, it was none of my business, and there wasn't much I could do about it anyway, but it bugged me. I suppose it's naive to think of war as anything other than a form of business, but this particular war seemed to be run exclusively by pricks at head office with boxes to tick and targets to meet—like how many people you can fit into a fucking shipping container at night, for instance, or what's the least amount of rice you can distribute to the maximum number of mouths." I pause at this point, and glance down at my shoes. I guess I'm stalling. "So about a month ago," I go on, looking up again, "there was . . . well, there was a riot at the base."

"A *riot*?"

"Yeah, more or less. No other word for it. Three hundred people were lined up for dinner in this compound at the rear of the base, and about halfway through they just ran out of food—that was it, there was nothing left, and it was apparently the second or third time it had happened in the space of a few weeks, so . . . empty plates, empty bellies, no prize for guessing what comes next."

Kate leans forward, eyebrows furrowed. "Let me get this straight, this wasn't the main dining place, right, where you worked, this was their—"

"Yeah, it was a separate facility, a separate arrangement, but that's what it's like there, the whole base, it's a fucking patchwork of subcontracts and outsourcing. What probably happened is that someone at a computer terminal somewhere three thousand miles away basically made a mistake filling out an order form for supplies. Now we had plenty of food in *our* stores, it's just that—"

"Oh Jesus."

"—Gideon weren't about to simply hand their shit out like they were a relief agency or something. So about eight or ten of the TCNs—to start with, anyway—stormed into the manager's office and demanded more rice, or bread, or whatever the fuck was available. The manager flipped, said they had no right to demand anything. He started screaming, soon *they* were screaming, it went back and forth, then someone got pushed, and it just erupted. In less than a minute, half a dozen young guys were smashing the place up, furniture, desks, filing cabinets, windows, computers. More joined in, and it spilled outside, where there were now at least a hundred others lined up waiting. Then it spread throughout the camp, all of these hungry fucking people rampaging around, throwing rocks and swinging lead pipes they'd found. A bunch of them, including Sajit, broke into the main DFAC storerooms and started taking stuff and passing it along a chain to the outside. Then Sajit, with two others, managed to get one of the big walk-in freezers open, which didn't make any sense, because all the stuff in there was frozen, obviously, by definition, so what use was *that* going to be, but I guess by this stage it was more frustration and rage running the show than actual hunger."

"Where were *you* during this? Did you see everything?"

"At the start of it I was half asleep in my little B hut listening to music. Then I heard noises outside, screams, glass breaking. I got up, headed out and made straight for the kitchens, and just as I was getting there, to the storerooms, to the walk-in freezer, several heavily armed guards, Gideon security guys, were also showing up. At first, it was chaotic and confusing, but with Sajit and the other two now more or less cornered, backed all the way into this freezer, the situation very quickly got *very* fucking tense."

Standing now in our small apartment on 10th Street, looking directly into Kate's eyes, I feel something pulse through my body—a mild electric current, like a push notification on vibrate.

Am I really going to do this?

"Sajit . . ." I say, and hesitate, but there's no turning back. "Sajit was the freezer guy, okay, and because it was, I don't know, his domain, he stood out a little from the other two, like he was a ringleader or something. He definitely wasn't, though, and in fact at the end there, I'm not sure, he may even have been trying to protect the place."

But suddenly this seems implausible to me, like a self-serving rationalization, and I hope Kate doesn't pick up on it. "Anyway, I was standing there at the entrance to the freezer, all these security guys in front of me, in pairs, three deep, with M4s and body armor on, full battle rattle, and there was this thick odor, as well, Kevlar and refrigerator coolant . . . it was awful." I exhale loudly at this point, and shake my head. "I couldn't catch Sajit's eye from where I was standing, and when I eventually called out his name, one of the Gideon security guys turned to look at me like I was insane. And after that, with a terrible inevitability to it, there was this lightning-quick sequence of movements that just played out in front of everyone's eyes . . ."

Avoiding Kate's gaze now, I stare at the floor, my voice barely above a whisper.

"One of the two guys with Sajit lifted a box of frozen burger patties from a pallet next to him and raised it above his head. There was a lot of shouting. Sajit turned as if he was going to pick up another of the frozen boxes, at which point two of the security guys rushed him. There was more pushing and shoving, and it was hard to make out what was going on, to make out who had the frozen box in their hands at any given moment, but then suddenly I had this clear view for a few seconds of the first Gideon guy bringing the box down right onto Sajit's head, knocking him to the floor, raising the box and hitting him with it again and again."

"Oh *fuck*." Kate covers her face with her hands.

I swallow hard, my throat dry and raspy. "When the two Gideon guys stood up and moved back, you could see it, everything, Sajit and the second guy on the floor, both dead, skulls cracked, Sajit's totally smashed in on one side . . . and his face . . ."

"*STOP*."

I do, but only for a moment. "The third guy was against the back wall of the freezer unit, cowering between two pallets. The guards quickly cleared everyone out of the storerooms, herding us out with their rifle butts, and then they sealed the whole place off. When word of what happened spread throughout the camp, instead of inflaming the situation, as it might have done, it knocked the riot stone cold dead. A lot of damage had been inflicted, mainly to property, and in a very short space of time, but no one had been hurt, not physically." I hear myself saying this, and then add, "Well, no one *else,* that is . . . apart from . . ."

But this time I really can't go on.

What I do instead is pick the letter up from the table and reread it, study it line by line, not because I didn't understand it the first time but as a way of avoiding eye contact with Kate.

There wasn't anything I could have done to prevent what happened, so maybe the guilt I'm feeling over it is irrational, like a form of survivor guilt, but it's certainly real, and it's all I've been able to think about since I got back. It's also very clear to me that even though there really wasn't anything I could have done, it'd be hard for someone who wasn't there to see it that way.

So I guess I'm surprised at how Kate eventually reacts. No indictment is handed down, nor does she say "I told you so." She reaches across the table, puts her hand on mine, and squeezes gently.

I feel like a jerk for having expected anything different. At the same time, I hope what I've just told her goes some way towards explaining why I've been so moody and difficult these past three weeks. Or at least moodier and more difficult than usual. Not to mention distant and unavailable. I know it's been hard on her, there's been a lot of tension. We had sex the night I got back, but not since. I don't particularly care right now (which has to indicate something), but I know for sure that Kate does. She's had to put up with a lot of things from me in our time, but withholding has never been one of them. Sex means something as far as she's concerned, it's a form of communication, it's a language. And when we're not talking, we're not talking.

She squeezes my hand again now. "Danny. My God. Why didn't you tell me about this?" I try to formulate an answer, but before I can get a word out, she's shaking her head. "You know what, don't answer that. It's a stupid question. Anyway, you did tell me. You told me just now. And it can't have been easy." She runs a hand through her hair. *"Jesus."*

She goes silent for a bit, staring into space, and I can see what she's doing, what she can't help doing—visualizing it, a human skull being bashed in with something like a solid block of ice, the repeated blows, the cracking of bone, the crunching sounds, the blood, the tissue . . .

"Kate, please . . . don't."

She gets up, comes around to where I'm sitting, and we embrace, tightly, taking in each other's tension, neutralizing it. This is a relief, and a step forward—but I know we're not done yet. There are still unanswered questions, things to be explained. There is still this letter from Gideon Logistics.

Kate pulls away, flicks her hair back and adjusts her glasses. Then, as if on cue, she points at the letter. "So I still don't get it. I don't get what they're up to. You were a witness to this murder, right, this *double* murder. Presumably they're going to need you for that, to testify. Why are they threatening you?"

I take a deep breath. "I don't really know, but I think it's because, okay, yes, I was a witness to what happened, but . . . maybe that's the problem."

"What do you mean?"

"This riot went unreported, Kate, completely. Did you read anything about it, hear any mention of it online? Anywhere? *No.* Which means it didn't happen, which means no one is getting charged."

"*What?*"

I look at a granola box on the shelf behind Kate, focus on it as I speak. "They emptied the place out. They removed the bodies. They cleaned up. The next morning it was as if nothing had happened. So I went and asked around, asked where the bodies were being *kept,* what the arrangements were, who was going to inform the families. Then I asked about the two security guys, the ones who did it. And you know what? I was met with a brick fucking wall. About all of it. They told me to go back to work. To mind my own business."

"I don't—" Kate throws her hands up. "This is unbelievable. What did you *do?*"

24

Here comes the hard part.

"I stood there like an idiot for ten minutes and then went back to work."

"*What?*"

"Kate, this is a military base. In a war zone. Mortar shells are going off. There's artillery fire. Meanwhile, *I* work in the kitchen."

This elicits an elaborate gesture of incredulity. "*So?*"

"I was powerless. There were no authorities I could go to, because I was already talking to them. You want a definition of powerless, that's it right there." I look at her now. "So tell me, what was I supposed to do? What was my next move?"

She shrugs. "I . . . but—"

"What I did . . ." I pause here for a second to catch my breath. "What I did, and without delay, was go and speak to some of the line cooks, some of the servers and cleaners. I was expecting real anger, and plans for . . . I don't know, a fucking armed rebellion or something, but what I got instead, weirdly, was another wall of silence. They were too scared to speak, because already, within hours, the intimidation had kicked in, the checking of papers, talk of visa irregularities, breaches of contract, fines, deportation, this, that, whatever. Then, after a couple of days, word came through that there was going to be a huge Gideon shake-up *anyway,* that a thousand people at Sharista and a second base nearby were being let go. It was a numbers thing and had to do with this pending DoD case. Supposedly. But anyone connected to Sajit and the other two? Sent off back to wherever. That meant me as well, and God knows who else. It was a clean sweep."

Kate just stares at me.

I stare back.

"I tried again," I continue after a bit. "Couple of times. Once at the base, before shipping out, but all I got was, 'What are you talking about? We don't know what you're talking about.' And then at the airport, at Kandahar. There was a congressman, in the departure lounge, Jack Gwynne, a New Jersey guy, I recognized him from a thing I saw once on TV. He was with a delegation, I think, and had quite an entourage, aides and personal assistants and shit, but I just walked right up and started talking to him." I pause here, remembering the incident. "I talked for maybe twenty seconds, really fast, trying to get it out, with him just looking at me, before I realized, damn, he's not listening to a word I'm saying, all he's doing is waiting for one of his fucking aides to come and rescue him, because I'm that guy, *I'm the nutjob*, the deranged person that people like him have to put up with all the time, but that he can't be rude to in case I have a vote. Well, one of his aides, big guy in an Italian suit, did rescue him, and was subsequently *very* rude to me. This was five minutes later in the men's room, when he had me pinned against a wall. 'Pull something like that again, cocksucker,' he told me, 'and my Christ, the fucking shit that will rain down on you.'"

Kate flinches. "Oh my God, Danny."

"I know. And all this guy was referring to was me talking to his stupid boss without an appointment. It was insane. Anyway, fifteen hours later and I'm back in JFK."

"But . . . Danny . . ."

She doesn't know where to begin is my guess. "Yeah?"

I guessed wrong.

"We can't let these bastards get away with this. We have to do something, we have to fight them."

"Jesus . . . fight them with *what*?"

"I don't know, how about," she waves a speculative hand in the air, "how about *with everything we've got.*"

"Come on, Kate, we're not in Zuccotti Park now."

She glares at me. "I'm a little confused here, Danny, you don't think this is awful, what you saw, what these people are doing?"

"Of course I do. But—"

"But *what*?"

"I'm not in a position to do anything about it. I can't prove it happened, there's no record of it, no evidence, and even if there was, how would *I* get access to that? Gideon has closed ranks." I point at the letter on the table. "And it's pretty clear they're now on the attack as well. This is a massive corporation, Kate, with massive financial resources."

"All the more reason why they shouldn't be allowed get away with this."

"Yeah, but,"—it's hard not to bang my fist on the table here—"shouldn't be allowed *how*?"

Kate gets up, stands at the window looking out. There's nothing to see except the back of another apartment building—other windows, other lives.

"This shit's been in my head since it happened, Kate, every single day. I've replayed it a thousand times, rearranged it. I have versions where I intervene, versions where it still plays out but afterwards I'm listened to, versions where what *you* want to happen happens. They're not real, though. What's real is that I'm actually powerless to do anything."

She turns around. "But the law, Danny—"

"The *law*? The law is what shuts it all down. Let's say I go to someone with these accusations, the cops, a media outlet even. Fine. But they're going to bring in legal counsel, and believe me, ten minutes of that and we're *done*. Sajit? Sajit *who*? I don't know the guy's full name, don't know anything about him. End of story. Say it goes further, though. How long you think before Gideon comes out with claims that I'm unstable, that I have a history of so-called mental problems?" I pick the letter up again from the table. "This is the law. I mean, look, GO-1C? You know what that is? Prohibited activities for military personnel within a US Central Command zone. But it also applies to civilian contractors. And that's *me*. So participating in a fucking riot? Which I guarantee is how they'll frame it. I wouldn't stand a chance.

The law is all on their side, Kate." I shake the letter. "And *this* is a preemptive strike."

"What . . . you mean *you* could face charges?"

"In theory."

"Jesus."

"If they push it. If *I* push *them*. Which is probably what this is really about."

"Well . . . couldn't . . ."

I wait, but she caves in, sits down again. She puts her head in her hands and sighs. "This is fucking horrible, Danny."

"I know."

I look at the open laptop in front of her, the notebook beside it, her neat handwriting, the coffee mug. I shouldn't have come back and disturbed her. I should have just let her be.

"Look, Kate," I say, "losing my last paycheck is bad enough, but if I get tied up in legal shit with these people, I'll never get out from under it. And if I get charged? There's no telling where that goes, and no fucking end to the collateral consequences either—if I ever need to take out a mortgage, or look for certain kinds of work, or, I don't know, apply for stuff . . ." I pause, feeling anxious about everything now, even the pronouns I'm using. "So, maybe . . ."

She looks up. "Yeah?"

"So maybe what I have to do is make contact here, and . . . let them know I'm not a threat."

There it is. Capitulation, surrender, the exact opposite of what Kate was proposing two minutes ago.

But I've said it, and now it's out in the open.

I lay the letter on the table and smooth the edges flat with my hand. "There's a phone number," I say. "They have offices on Third Avenue. I could call them. I might not get through to anyone who'll talk to me, but it's worth a shot."

Kate is struggling. I can see it. She wants to be sympathetic, to be reasonable, but she can't quite get there—can't quite get with the capitulation and the surrender. And I don't blame her. I was never in Zuccotti Park, but she actually was, and although that's a long time ago now, and she's been through a lot since, the experience of being down there left its mark. To a certain degree, it still informs the way she thinks.

So it's hardly a surprise if she finds *this* shit hard to take.

I get my phone out and stand up. I take the letter from the table. "Okay," I say, not looking at her. "I'll do it in the bedroom."

3

I sit on the side of the bed—my side—facing the window, phone in one hand, letter in the other. I stall for a bit, thinking there might be a way out of this, then just enter the number really fast. I get through to someone who puts me on hold for five minutes. Is this a display of indifference on their part, I wonder, contempt for the client, or have I set an alarm bell ringing? Do I stew in irritation or paranoia? I don't know, but either way, it's a long five minutes.

I look around, a tinny "Windmills of Your Mind" ringing in my ear. The bedroom, like our whole apartment, is oppressive. What little space remains, when you discount the bed itself, is cluttered with shoes, clothes, and books. There's also a strong scent in the room, a mix of candles, perfume, soap, and stray lingerie. When I moved in over a year ago, living here was supposed to be temporary. I had a lease in Williamsburg that was nearly up and the timing seemed right. I didn't have much stuff with me, and, besides, before we knew it we'd be getting our shit together and moving on to a bigger apartment.

"Sir?"

"Yes."

"Um, okay . . . this afternoon at four. Mr. Galansky will see you then. Do you have the address?"

"Yes, I do, and I'd—"

But that's it, she's gone. No have a nice day, no thank you for calling, no fuck you, loser.

Whatever.

So who is this Mr. Galansky? I study the letter again. It was signed by Abe Porter, assistant to the vice president of Legal Affairs and the person I'd asked to speak to before I was put on hold. I google Galansky on my phone and find out that he's the *actual* vice president of Legal Affairs. Which could mean I'm moving up in the world.

Or about to leave it.

My first interview with Gideon Logistics was in a building downtown, and although they had a suite of offices on the third floor, the rest of the building seemed to be virtually deserted. Subsequent interviews and orientation sessions took place in a remote and very basic facility in Pennsylvania. Their corporate HQ on Third Avenue was never really on my radar. But now, out of the blue, I'm headed there for a sit-down with—I look at my phone again—Arthur P. Galansky?

Holy *fuck*.

So, irritation or paranoia? There's no contest. Not anymore.

By the time I come out of the bedroom, Kate's ambivalence has evaporated. She's able to speak again, able to express both outrage at what I told her and a keen desire for me to be free of any fallout. I mention Galansky and the appointment at 4 p.m. She doesn't think it's a good idea.

Nodding at her laptop, I tell her I'm going to go outside to clear my head for a bit, give her a chance to get back to her coding thing. She looks at me, eyebrows raised, about to object it seems, but in a flash I'm out the door and down the stairs.

I check the time, and then put my phone on silent. I have about two hours. It probably would have made sense for me to stick around, have a shower and change my clothes, even shave, but another part of me thinks, *fuck it*, I should go into this meeting as scruffy and disheveled as possible. Who are these people? Legal Affairs? They're going to walk all over me anyway, so what do I care? What difference does it make?

I hit Second Avenue and head uptown.

What I need to do is make a convincing case to this Arthur Galansky that my time at Sharista is behind me, that I've moved on, and that if they want to withhold my last paycheck for some contractual reason, fine, they can knock themselves out, because what can *I* do about it? I signed the contract, didn't I? And, besides, I've moved on. The idea being that they'll back off and leave me the fuck alone. The thing is, I'm just as outraged as Kate is about all this, and there's nothing I'd like more than to see Gideon Logistics exposed. But I'm not a fool. I don't have any illusions. I know if I make trouble for them, if I start acting the loudmouth, they could—and would—crush me as quickly as they did those two guys in the walk-in freezer.

As I pass a store window, I see my reflection. It occurs to me that maybe I *should* smarten up a bit. No matter how reasonable I sound, if I look like a street person Arthur P. Galansky will more than likely conclude that I am a risk and can't be relied on to play ball. I pass another window and realize that I don't look *that* bad. Besides, my idea of smartened up probably wouldn't register with them as being all that different from how I look now. But something else occurs to me as I cross 14th. Is that what I'm proposing to do here? To play ball? It is, isn't it? Which is why I don't want to go back to the apartment, or look at any of the three text messages (I'm assuming from Kate) that I've already felt vibrating in my pocket. I don't need to be reminded every five minutes that my response to the Gideon letter is craven and spineless. I *know* it is. But whose is the more lawyerly approach in all of this? Mine or Kate's? Who's being more pragmatic?

It occurs to me that I should probably get something to eat. The only thing I've had since I got up this morning is a glass of OJ, and I'm beginning to feel light-headed. After another few blocks I stop at a diner, sit in a booth, and order a BLT. I feel better once I've eaten. I drag my time out with a few refills of coffee. Then I leave and take the train up to Grand Central.

The place where Gideon has its offices, the Wolper & Stone Building, is one I've passed many times but have never given a second glance. It's an anonymous glass box that houses dozens of companies, and there's a constant flow of people in and out of it. I pace the sidewalk for a while, but then just head inside and walk straight over to reception. I'm half an hour early, but I don't care. I give my name. The guy at reception checks my ID, consults his register, and calls up.

A few minutes later I'm in an elevator on the way to the seventeenth floor. Gideon's reception area is spacious and sleek, and, although I'm all too familiar with the company logo, I've never seen it in such an anodyne corporate setting before. I stand at the reception desk as the lady I spoke to on the phone earlier deals with a call and checks something on her screen. Music hums in the background, but it's so low and subtle it might actually be some sort of brain-wave entrainment.

"May I help you?" the receptionist says, her eyes still on the screen. After a beat, she looks at me. Her voice may be neutral, but those eyes tell a different story.

"Danny Lynch," I say, "for Arthur Galansky. I'm a bit early."

She consults a sheet in front of her. "Yes, sir. Indeed."

In my pocket, I feel the pulse of another message alert.

"I'll let Mr. Galansky know you're here. Please take a seat, Mr., uh . . . Lynch."

I move across reception to an area with some seats and a low glass table. As I'm sitting down I take out my phone. Kate's first two messages were basically "Call me." Her third was "Call a lawyer" . . . as in, I might need one, so shouldn't I take care of that before I actually meet with anyone? She has a point—I guess, in theory—but it's too late now. I'm here, I'm on my own, and the last thing I want to do is give these people the impression that I'm even *thinking* of lawyering up. The fourth message, the one that came through just a few moments ago, is longer and somewhat panicky in tone. Kate looked up Galansky too, and got a bit more detail than I did. It seems the guy is something of a legend in corporate legal circles, with an impressive record of crushing it in whistle-blower litigation cases. So basically her message—sent at 3:41—is that I should skip this meeting . . . *that I shouldn't go near Galansky* . . .

I look around reception again.

I could just walk out, but . . . there are surveillance cameras everywhere. If I bolt now, they'll have footage of me behaving like a suspicious lowlife that could be used at some future point—in a courtroom, say, or online. Something else that's bothering me is Kate's use of the word "whistle-blower." Even though this is exactly what I'm proposing *not* to become, it isn't really how I ever thought of myself in the first place. But I suppose when I was confronting the Gideon manager at the base, or attempting to speak with Congressman Jack Gwynne, what the hell did I *think* I was doing?

Sensing movement, I look up and see a man appearing from a hallway over to the left. As he passes the receptionist, he says something I don't catch and then heads over in my direction. I stand up as he gets near. He's midsixties, I'd say, medium height, burly, muscular even, and tanned. He's wearing a suit, but not a tie. There's something about him . . . two things, in fact. One, he doesn't really seem like a buttoned-up corporate type. And two, he looks vaguely familiar.

I stretch out my hand, "Hi. I'm Daniel Lynch."

We shake. His grip is firm, and fairly intense, like his smile.

"How are you, Daniel? Or . . . *Danny*, right? I can call you Danny?"

"Sure. And I'm good. I guess." I pause here and take a deep breath. This is uncomfortable, but better to forge ahead, I reckon, better to get right to it. "Look, Mr. Galansky, I got a letter from you this morning, from Abe Porter actually, that . . . well, that came as something of a shock to me."

"Of course." He nods vigorously and places an outstretched hand on my shoulder. "But listen, Danny, first I owe you an apology, okay? I'm not Mr. Galansky. Artie is otherwise engaged, there's been some development in . . . I don't know *what* in, some case, who knows, but he's pretty much chained to his desk for now. You and I can talk, though, right?" He withdraws his hand from my shoulder. "And you know what?" He glances around, as though someone might be listening. "Frankly, I'm happy to keep legal out of this."

I stare at him, trying to make sense of what I've just heard.

"Look at you," he says, and laughs. "Wondering who the hell *this* guy is. Well, I don't blame you, Danny, to be honest. But let me introduce myself, okay? My name is Phil Coover."

I don't recognize his name, but I do remember where I've seen him before. It was in Afghanistan, at the base, and probably more than once. I would have seen him around the admin offices, is my guess, or in the back of a car coming through the checkpoint, or with a visiting group of military brass. Who the fuck knows. But he radiates a confidence that you don't forget, a looseness. People with serious skin in the game, like high-level corporate execs or four-star generals, tend to be very uptight and locked in to what they're doing. This guy has none of that. It's as if he thinks it really is a game.

But clearly he's with Gideon Logistics, even though you wouldn't think it from the way he's behaving. After supplying his name, for instance, he consults his watch like he's on a golf course and says, "You know what? Enough of this shit, let's go for a drink."

I do an internal double take.

Because right now I'd fucking *love* to go for a drink, but not in these circumstances, not with this guy. Not with a possible lawsuit hanging over me.

I look at him. "A *drink*?"

"Yeah," he says, "why not? There's a little place across the street, it's quiet, they have these exquisite olives. Best in the city."

So, before I know it, we're riding the elevator down to the lobby.

Turns out this is another thing about Phil Coover: he doesn't take no for an answer, and he has the force of personality to back it up.

As we're crossing Third, I picture myself just taking off at a run and heading for the nearest subway station. But, appealing as that might be, it's not a serious option, because at some level I'm being played here—that's what it feels like—and I really need to find out what's going on. Besides, I suspect it'd take more than a few stops on a 6 train to escape the orbit of Coover's attention.

We go into a bar—a cocktail lounge, the Bradbury—and sit in a booth near the back. So far, Coover has done most of the talking, and about nothing really—how busy he is, his travel schedule, even the weather. We could be two guys who just happened to leave work at the same time and decided to grab a drink together.

But we're not.

So I lean forward now and look him in the eye. "Mr. Coover, I don't . . . I don't get this. I don't even know who you *are*. I mean, I recognize you from Sharista, but . . . *this*?" I indicate where we are. "A drink? With some fancy fucking olive in it? Is this supposed to make up for my last paycheck or something?"

Coover shakes his head. "No, Danny, it isn't. And you have every right to ask, but . . . give me a second, will you?"

When I realize he's reaching for his phone, I roll my eyes. He takes it out, and, as he's scanning whatever message is on the screen, he says, half in a whisper, "Call me Phil, by the way."

Our waitress arrives before I can respond.

"Hi there, gentlemen. I'm Cecily. How are you fellas doing today?"

Coover finishes with his phone, puts it on the table and turns his attention to Cecily. Effusing courtly charm, he orders two . . . *something* martinis, I don't catch what he calls them, but I'm assuming they contain olives. The whole time, he doesn't consult or even look at me, so when he's done, I turn to Cecily and say, "And *I'll* have a club soda."

Coover laughs.

When Cecily leaves, he looks at me. "Okay, Danny, okay." He pauses. "I'm a consultant, yeah? These days mainly for Gideon, but I've worked with some of the other PMCs, and on both sides of the fence: direct combat, security details, all of that, but also management, and people."

Where is this going?

"People?"

"Yeah, not human resources exactly, more conflict resolution. In the workplace, and elsewhere. It's funny, but most of these disputes could either be avoided altogether or resolved by the simple application of a bit of basic goddamned common sense." He taps the side of his head. "Psychology. Because it never ceases to amaze me how flat out stupid people can be. For instance, I get called in on some *thing* that has already spun out of control, okay? I look at what they're proposing to do about it, and ninety-five percent of the time you know what my initial response is? I'll tell you. It's me going, holy shit, excuse me, this is your plan, this is what you want to do, you're kidding me, right?" He throws his hands up in despair. "It's unbelievable, because what the 'this' invariably is is fuel they're adding to an already raging fire."

"So . . ."

"So what's *my* solution? I look people in the eye, I hold their attention, and get them to focus for five minutes on the least damaging options they have in front of them. Figuratively speaking, I talk them down from the ledge."

He waves a hand in the air, as if to say *It's that simple,* then sits back and smiles.

All of a sudden my heart is thumping.

"You think *I'm* on a ledge?"

"No, Danny, I don't, not at all. But I think our mutual employer might be. That's the point."

I stare at him for a moment. What am I supposed to make of this? I hate it when people talk to me in riddles. I end up just wanting to punch them in the face.

"I'm sorry, Phil, but you're going to have to explain that to me."

"Fine." He taps the table with his index finger. "Things are very tense at Gideon these days, with the DoD, with the industry in general, with everyone suing everyone else, to the extent that it seems like the whole thing is getting out of control. I mean, Artie Galansky is on a troubleshooting roller coaster right now and he doesn't know how to get off. All he does know is how to escalate shit and make it worse. He's a lawyer, it's what they do, they generate billable hours, but sometimes you have to take a step back, you know what I mean?"

I shrug, half wondering now if Coover has made a mistake, if he might actually think I'm someone else. Because why would he be talking to *me* like this?

"So then," he continues, lowering his voice slightly, "along comes some low-level employee, a food-services guy, say, and there's a situation, there's uncertainty, there's a perceived risk. What does Artie do? What's *his* plan? Crush the little cockroach, that's what. He doesn't give it a moment's thought, doesn't have to, because it's all mapped out in the contract of employment, signed—as Artie sees it—by the cockroach."

I swallow. And loudly.

Coover waits, giving me a moment. "Did you ever *read* your contract, Danny?"

I shrug again. "Yeah, of course, but—"

"I know, who gets beyond page one, right? But interestingly, on page *fifteen* there's a confidentiality clause that effectively prohibits you from speaking to anyone—journalists, investigators, prosecutors, your girlfriend, doesn't matter—about any allegations you might have against Gideon. The declared purpose of the clause is to protect the company's internal review process, but in essence it's a gag order on whistle-blowers. So, put *that* with your GO-1C violation, and you're in a very vulnerable position. In fact, as far as Artie Galansky is concerned, you're not even a problem anymore, because your employment's been terminated, you have your letter of warning, and the next step, if required, is automatic legal action, which—believe me—will be clear-cut, swift, and brutal." He smiles. "You're a ticked box, my friend."

It's not thumping anymore, my heart—it's paralyzed, frozen over. Coover's passive-aggressive style is exhausting, and I'm not sure what to think, let alone what I might even begin to say.

Our drinks show up.

But the time-out is all too brief. Coover doesn't even acknowledge Cecily's presence, which means that Cecily, being the pro that she is, doesn't acknowledge ours. She's gone pretty quick.

For a second or two I look at the martini on my side of the table, then reach for the club soda. I take a sip from it.

"Okay, Phil," I say, "what are you telling me here that isn't in the letter? Why is *this* cockroach getting special attention?"

"Well . . ."—he drags the word out—"that's simple. It's because *I* think Artie Galansky is wrong." He reaches for my Martini and pulls it towards his so that the two glasses are aligned directly in front of him, the large olives hovering below his face now like an extra set of eyeballs. "He's paranoid is what it is, about whistle-blowers, because these days even the *word* is enough to—"

"But I'm not a whistle-blower."

Coover clicks his tongue. "Maybe not technically, Danny, maybe not *yet*—"

"What are you talking about?"

But even as I'm asking him the question, I get an uncomfortable sense of what the answer is going to be, or at least its shape, the contours of it.

"Listen, Danny," he says, "Gideon has its systems, its internal review mechanisms, and they're looking at what happened that night, all of it, the riot, the thing you saw, or *think* you saw, they're investigating it, you can rest assured of that . . . but what they don't need is someone loudly confronting senior officials or approaching a congressman in a goddamned airport lounge. What they really don't need—according to Artie Galansky anyway—is some emotional, guilt-ridden wreck of a guy walking the streets of Manhattan ticking like a goddamned *time bomb*."

"Jesus . . . am I under surveillance?"

"Well, *duh*." Coover takes a sip from the first Martini. "They're watching you like you're a video game, Danny. What did you think?" He takes another sip and puts the glass down. "They're just waiting for you to finally crack and take up where you left off back in Afghanistan, making wild accusations, shooting your mouth off. At which point they'll crush you."

I lean forward now, almost halfway across the table. "Yeah, I *get* that. Jesus. I'm not an idiot. And the reason I've been walking the streets is because I'm looking for a fucking *job*, Phil. Which is something I really need. So I don't have any intention of shooting my mouth off. As you call it. But you know what? If Artie Galansky wants to push things—"

"*Yes*." Coover slaps the palm of his hand on the table. "There, that's it, you see? *That's* what I'm talking about. You're a smart guy, Danny. You get it. But you have your limits too, and if Artie pushes you over some line, all hell's going to break loose, am I right? Though"—he pauses, and holds up a finger—"if that happens, make no mistake, you'll still get crushed. *My* argument is that if it happens, Gideon will suffer too. But in ways they don't foresee."

I lean back again, listening closely, my anger now cut with real confusion.

Coover huddles forward. "Look, Danny, I'm going to be straight with you. Gideon is a fairly dysfunctional outfit . . . and, okay, you know, maybe I don't like the way they run those bases over there, fine, but my job as a strategist is to protect the company, and in this particular situation the most effective way I can do that is actually very simple. It's to make *them* leave *you* alone."

I know I'm being manipulated here, and in a way that I don't fully comprehend, but if this is a possible outcome, does it really even matter?

"I'm not going to argue with that," I say, as I reach across the table, retrieve the second Martini, and bring it to my lips. If the hit I take from it isn't quite a gulp, it's definitely more than a sip.

I put the glass down and add, "But I'm not going to pretend I understand it either."

"Understand it, as in—"

"As in why, and . . . I guess . . . *how*?"

"How is easy. How is I tell them and they do it."

"What, you just tell them to leave me alone?"

"I tell them that in my professional assessment you're a level-headed guy with good judgment, that you're not going to crack, and that they should drop the GO-1C thing and pay up what they owe you. And they listen. End of story."

"But . . . *why* would you do that?"

"Well, that's the thing, isn't it? I wouldn't be doing it for *you*, Danny. I'd be doing it for them." He takes a sip from his Martini. "Because . . . okay, let's say you start shooting your mouth off about Gideon, about these two alleged deaths on the base, and let's say you get some lawyer involved, and Gideon responds by invoking their confidentiality clause, yeah? That's where I see the trouble starting. For *us*. As I said before, *you'd* be buried in a pile of shit regardless, with legal expenses, the GO-1C thing, and a slew of countersuits, all of which you'd lose. But there's a good chance, in the current climate, that Gideon would face a challenge over the legitimacy of the clause itself. Because there *is* an argument to be made that it violates the federal False Claims Act. Just possibly. Now that might not sound like much, but it could have some pretty far-reaching consequences, so why draw attention to it? Especially if you don't have to? Yeah?" He pauses. "It's a can of worms that we don't want to see opened up, is what I'm saying." He pauses again, as though searching for a better way to explain himself. "At the end of the day, it's not anything you need to be concerned with. It's nitpicky lawyer stuff that affects *us*, potentially, but if I can give Artie the assurance that you're a disinterested party, just some guy trying to get on with his life, then . . . I think we can all relax. Artie cuts a check. You tear that letter up. Everyone's happy."

There are several things I could say to this, questions I could ask, remarks I could make, but I think we've reached the endgame. Coover has made his offer. There's really nothing more to discuss.

I look at him and nod. "Okay."

He nods back and gently taps the edge of the table. "Good."

If this was a negotiation, then I've actually come out of it with more than I was looking for going in. Which feels good. But also feels too good to be true. In any case, at this point Coover reverts right back to his earlier, chattier mode and starts asking me questions—Iraq, Asheville, the old man—so that by the time we're finishing our drinks and getting up to leave, he's morphed into my best bud. He even half apologizes for the whole mess and says, you know, the way these corporate types think they can just trample over people is actually sickening. On our way out, he quizzes me about work—what kind of job I'm looking for, what I'm good at. And even though I can't help feeling that he must know most of this stuff already, I tell him anyway.

"You know what," he says, when we're out on the street, "leave it with me, will you? I'm friends with a lot of people in this town, and if I can't scare something up then what am I good for, right?"

Again, there's nothing to argue with here.

He extends his hand and we shake.

"Are you all set?" he says, looking around. "You want me to call a car for you?"

"No, no, I'm fine, thanks."

"Okay, well, I guess I'm done for the day. I'll talk to you soon, Danny."

And with that he takes off.

It's just after five o'clock, and Third Avenue is hopping, offices everywhere letting out, the sidewalk a torrent of humanity. The afternoon has clouded over too, and the air has a dark, strangely oppressive feel to it.

I walk to the next corner, and stop at the curb. As I wait for the light to change, I glance over my shoulder and across the street. Despite the traffic and the crowds on the other side, I catch a glimpse of Phil Coover slipping back in through the revolving doors of the Wolper & Stone Building.

My mind is in knots as I walk home, and for good reason, but it's only as I arrive at the door to our apartment that I understand why.

I'm going to end up lying to Kate—and hating myself for it.

Of course, what makes it a little easier—at first—is that she's pissed at me. Did I go to the meeting? Why didn't I answer her texts? What is the fucking *point* of having a cell phone?

"I'm sorry," I tell her, "I just wanted to get it over with."

She stands there, waiting for more, looking over her glasses at me. "Well?"

The version I give her is accurate as far as it goes, but I leave stuff out—like the fact that I have been, and presumably still am, under surveillance. I don't tell her that my overall impression of the meeting is that Phil Coover pretty much played me like a fiddle. Which is another thing. I don't actually mention Phil Coover by name. What I tell her is that Arthur Galansky was tied up and I spoke to some other guy. I try to focus on the positives. They're going to release my last check. They *might* drop the GO-1C charge.

"I'm confused," she says. "What changed their minds? How did you convince them?"

This is a reasonable question but what do I tell her? "I made a case, I guess. I told them it had nothing to do with *me*."

"As in—"

"As in the *thing*. What happened over there." I clear my throat. "Look, I can barely remember what I said. It was a tense situation. I was nervous."

I'm beginning to feel weird now, on the defensive, as if I'm being cross-examined.

Kate nods. It's clear that her earlier ambivalence hasn't gone away, but she seems to know not to push it.

My own ambivalence hasn't gone away either. I manage to keep a lid on it while I'm awake, but in bed later—unexpected, unbidden—I get to see a human skull being cracked open, then smashed. It happens in a variety of locations—the lobby of the Wolper & Stone Building, my old prep station at Mouzon, our *bedroom*. I wake each time, the transition seamless, whatever chaotic setting of the previous moment giving way in an instant to the oppressive smallness of our actual bedroom.

In the morning I have a thumping headache. I drink lots of black coffee and eat a bowl of cereal. Kate has a coding assignment to finish today, and it's going to require a lot of concentration, so I need to be out of the apartment pretty early. I don't want to be a distraction to her, and, after yesterday, I know I would be. We don't say much as we glide around each other, from bathroom to kitchen to living room, the familiar *pas de deux* of couples who live in small apartments. Sort of inconveniently too, and, in spite of my headache, I find myself actually wanting her. This is something I haven't felt since that first night I got back. And call me obvious or stupid, but it happens as she's emerging from the bathroom after her shower. She's in a loose robe, her pale and lightly freckled skin glowing, her auburn hair wet and glistening. But that's not what this is, not exactly—I see her like that every day. This is more a build-up over time of subtler tensions, of deeper needs, things which are now, suddenly and unexpectedly, uncoiling inside me. But then I realize that it's always this way, that when it comes to Kate my arousal is unique and complex and layered, and that what I'm feeling in this moment is not just desire, it's love.

It still *is* desire, though, and there's empirical (if ephemeral) evidence for it. But there'll be no happy resolution here—not at 8 a.m., not with the caffeine rush and *Morning Edition* on the radio and the screeching baby next door and the looming ones and zeros on Kate's laptop all so determinedly ranged against it. I wish I could transmit something of what I'm feeling to her, but I know it would get too complicated too fast and end up derailing her morning. So I just decamp. I give her a kiss as I leave—a rushed one, little more than a peck— and tell her I hope her assignment goes well.

Outside it's sunny, but there's already a thickening in the air. I walk briskly along 10th Street for several blocks, heading west, and turn right onto Broadway. This isn't anything different from what I've been doing for the past three weeks, but it feels different. It feels like something fundamental has shifted, and I'm now faced with a choice— either I slide further into the shit, or I wake the fuck up and start looking for a job. Because even if I get my last paycheck from Gideon, that's it, there'll be no more money coming in. So it's really quite simple. I have to get my act together. I have to start scouring job sites and sending out copies of my résumé.

And I have to put Afghanistan behind me.

I stop at a bench in Union Square and sit down, the city swirling all around me, noise, traffic, streaks of color . . . honking horns, snippets of conversation, dogs, dog walkers, ringtones, skin tones. Some days you don't even notice this stuff, it washes over you, and others it becomes so dense, so distracting, it's all you see. I close my eyes for a few seconds, dreading the prospect of actually having to look for work. The first time I ever compiled a résumé was for the Gideon job. Any other jobs I've had I got through referrals. That was how I got Mouzon. That was how I got the three or four jobs I'd worked back in Asheville. Someone gives your name out, they vouch for you, you go meet a guy, you talk, next thing you know you're wearing checked pants and dicing carrots.

Old school, which, I guess, is called that for a reason.

I take out my phone and start searching for listings. It'd be easier to do this at home using the laptop, but I'm not at home and I want to get a move on. In any case, I have an app here that can record whatever notes, numbers, or links I might possibly need. Looking down, I try to focus, to shut out all the surrounding distractions, the white noise, but less than a minute in and the fucking phone itself rings.

I stare at it for a moment, annoyed, but also uncertain. It's a blocked number.

I answer it.

"Hello?"

"Danny? Hi, it's Phil Coover."

Union Square tilts a little on its axis.

"Oh . . . Phil."

"Hey, glad I caught you, I'm just heading to the airport and I wanted to talk. So. I sat down with Artie, and that thing? It's sorted, no problem. Last check, plus a little extra thrown in. Call it severance."

"Jesus, Phil . . ."

"It's only fair, am I right? At least, that's how *I* look at it."

My stomach is churning. I glance up and see a small Asian woman gliding by with a dog that's nearly bigger than she is. Then, passing in the other direction, two middle-aged guys in suits.

"Phil, I don't—"

"And something else, Danny. I made a couple of calls. There's a place on 44th Street, Barcadero. Get over there this morning and ask for Stanley. He'll fix you up with some work."

I close my eyes. "Phil, how . . . I don't . . . how do I—"

"No need. It's my job. Which I'll lose if I miss this flight. Okay, so you got that? Stanley. Barcadero. Forty-fourth Street. Best of luck, Danny. Best of luck with everything."

And that's it, he's gone.

Fuck.

Opening my eyes, I lean back on the bench and gaze up at the sky, which is a hazy blue. What just happened? Another job referral? I'm excited about it, my heart is racing, but at the same time I feel uneasy. I sit forward again, and, as I look around, something occurs to me. *Am I still under surveillance?* There were those two guys in suits. And right now, in my direct line of vision, I see someone who could easily be watching me. The whole idea is pretty absurd, though. So maybe Coover had just said that as a way to spook me, to make me think it was true.

In which case it worked.

But again, if the outcome is what he said, if he actually delivers—the check, some form of severance, an actual job—who cares?

Kate, probably, but that's not going to stop me.

I stand up and move away from the bench, then head back onto Broadway.

Next landmark, the Flatiron, but Coover said "this morning," and it's not even nine o'clock yet. I know restaurants, however, I know their circadian rhythms, and for sure there are guys up there right now taking in deliveries—the crates of produce, the sacks of flour, the vacuum-packed slabs of meat. In the kitchen someone is halfway through zesting fifty lemons and someone else is hauling a twenty-quart container of chicken stock out of the walk-in. There's a guy out by the loading dock having a cigarette and another one in the poky little backroom office tearing his hair out over prep lists. But it might still be too early for this Stanley individual. He's probably at the gym doing kettlebell workouts. Either that or he's at home slumped in front of his medicine cabinet, nursing a vicious hangover and trying to decide what pills he needs to get through the day.

I'll stop off someplace, get coffee and a bagel, sit in a booth for a while. Look out the window, read a paper, then show up at around ten, ten thirty.

Stanley. Barcadero. Forty-fourth Street.

I've got this.

4

The first striking thing about Barcadero is how high-end it is. Given its location, this shouldn't come as any surprise, but it does. On my way there, I look it up and find out that it's been open for more than two years. And that's the second thing. Restaurants open and close all the time in New York, but if you pay attention to this stuff a joint like Barcadero would at least be on your radar. And it's definitely not on mine.

Though who am I kidding? Not only have I been out of the loop for months, it's not as if any loop I ever *was* in would mean I'd be hearing about a place like this. Anyway, with executive chef Jacques Marcotte running the kitchen, I'm guessing that Barcadero is conservative and pricy with the kind of atmosphere that food critics feel compelled to call "rarefied."

One of the kitchen guys lets me into the vestibule area, and, as I'm waiting for Stanley to appear, I look out over the main room. Turns out I'm not wrong, and I quickly conclude that I'm wasting my time. I was happy to get the referral, and maybe it'll kick-start something else, but I can't see it—they're not going to hire a guy whose last job was working at a military *chow hall*. Jesus. I mean, Mouzon was a nice

49

place, okay, but it was small and very casual, and before that . . .

"Danny?"

I turn. The man approaching me is short and wiry, though I'd say it's more kettlebells than pills. He radiates such an immediate and intense energy that I'm almost afraid I'll get electrocuted if I shake his hand.

"Stanley Podnick," he says.

We shake. I survive.

"Come on."

He leads me into the dining area, pulls out a chair at the nearest two-seater and sits down. He indicates for me to do the same and places a cloth-bound notebook and a fountain pen in front of him. He looks at his watch.

"Okay, Danny," he says, opening the notebook, "we have a situation this morning. A callout."

I lean forward slightly, and swallow. "A callout?"

"Yeah, one of my prep guys, Yannis, he says it's an ulcer, peptic, perforated, I don't know . . ." He looks at me quickly, rolls his eyes, then goes back to the notebook. "What am I going to do, call him a liar? Anyway, I've tried all my covers, and no dice. Bottom line, I'm in a bit of a pickle." He looks at me again. "So how about it?"

"I . . . I don't—"

"What? Is there somewhere you have to be?"

"No, it's just, I thought there'd be more of an interview process."

Stanley Podnick looks at his watch again and picks up the fountain pen. "I don't have the luxury. Besides, you come highly recommended." He taps his pen at the open page of his notebook. "Two years at Mouzon, the DFAC stuff. It's clear you know your way round a kitchen."

What the fuck? He's got my résumé?

"Yeah," I say, "it's about the only thing I *do* know."

"So?"

I shrug. "Just like that?"

He leans in towards me, and whispers. "Danny, I'm in a bind. Plus, like I said, you come recommended." He pauses, holding my gaze. "What do you want? This is above my pay grade. For *now*. You fuck up in my kitchen, though? That's a different story. Anyway, seeing as how you'd be prepping here but you worked the line at Mouzon, this would actually be a step down for you. In theory." He makes a sweeping gesture with his hand, indicating the grandeur of the room. "Though not in reality, of course. In reality, this would be a fantastic opportunity for you." He flips the notebook closed and puts it under his arm. Shifting sideways in his chair, he looks at me and raises his eyebrows. "Well?"

"Yeah," I say. "Okay. Great. And thanks."

"Let's just hope I'm the one thanking *you* in ten hours." He hops up. "Come on, I'll show you around."

The kitchen at Barcadero is pretty big, not chow-hall big but bigger than any regular place I've ever worked in. When I see the expanse of stainless-steel surfaces, the long station racks, the vent hoods, the enormous ovens, burners, gas ranges, and cooling units, I realize that this is as close as I'll probably ever get to my dream of working at a place like the Four Seasons. Stanley gets me an apron, a jacket, and a pair of clogs. He conducts a lightning-fast tour of the kitchen and then introduces me to Pablo, one of the other prep guys. The place is still pretty quiet, so I have a chance to get my bearings.

I've met a hundred guys like Pablo—he's late twenties, handsome in that chiseled, unshaven way, and barely speaks any English. But it becomes apparent within minutes that he's not an asshole, which is good news for me. Because he easily could have been—protective of Yannis and ready to pound my balls nonstop for the whole shift. Instead, he lends me some knives and sets me up at a station peeling veg, easing me into it. And in his broken English he gives what turns out to be a pretty funny running commentary on the entire place as it slowly comes to life—as the dishwasher moves about, turning on all the equipment, as the sous chef arrives, followed by the line cooks, then the garde-manger, then Jacques Marcotte himself, as the tasks multiply and the real cooking gets under way, and finally—too busy after that—as actual service begins.

Every time he does a pass through the kitchen, Stanley checks up on me, but there's never a problem. If I'm finding it a challenge, it's only in terms of volume and pacing. There's a clear rhythm here, like in any kitchen, and you just have to learn it. But there's nothing I can't do, no task or procedure I'm unsure of or have to ask about.

At one point, I get a ten-minute break and go outside to the loading dock, where I turn on my phone and send a text to Kate: "Hope the assignment's going well. Good news. Found work. Already halfway through my first shift."

I stand there for a while and listen to the hum and roar of the city. I haven't had time to think about any of this, about Phil Coover and the referral and Stanley Podnick having my details, or about the fact that I'm *working*. But it's fine. I'm tired, and relieved, and there'll be plenty of time to dissect all of this later on.

Kate replies: "Amazing!!! Can't wait to hear xo."

Back inside, I go along the narrow hallway and into the kitchen. As I walk by the pick-up window, I glance out at the dining area, which is slammed at the moment, a sea of business suits, tanned faces, and mostly grey hair. What are they all talking about? The food? I doubt it. It'll more likely be money, how you get it, how you multiply it, how you keep it, a hundred variations on *that* conversation—a hundred out of the million that take place in restaurants all over the city every day.

Back at my prep station, I realize that from where I'm standing I have a direct line of sight into the dining area. It's only a sliver; the rest of the view is blocked by a large vent hood on one side and a bank of refrigerators on the other—but still, it's a welcome distraction. I hadn't noticed it earlier, because I was concentrating so hard. It's an angle on the room, a corner of it, one table, three people at the moment, but it could be four, a static shot, medium close, without sound—not much, but something to play around with when the monotony kicks in.

By the time my shift ends, I'm destroyed, mainly because I'm out of the habit—three and a half weeks of idleness is a long time in this game. Without Pablo, it would have been a lot harder, and I thank him.

And then Stanley thanks *me*. "That was impressive. You fit right in."

I nod.

"So, you up for this again tomorrow?"

"Sure."

"And after that I guess it'll depend on how Yannis is doing, but . . . you know, I have your number."

I nod again and tell him I'm available.

Outside on the street, Pablo suggests going for a drink, but I know how that one usually plays out, so I pass and take the subway home.

When I come through the door, I see Kate at the table, laptop open in front of her, papers everywhere. She's slumped forward a bit, her eyes are red, and she looks pretty much the way I feel.

But as I'm closing the door, she pulls her chair back and moves towards me. We meet halfway for a quick hug. Then she sits down again, I stand by the refrigerator, and we talk. For the first few minutes it's all about *my* day—the work, how I came by it, Barcadero, what kind of place it is, what the prospects are.

Tell me, tell me.

And I do.

But not having mentioned anything yesterday about Phil Coover, I decide not to mention anything about him tonight. I have to improvize a detail or two, but I manage to pull it off and once I'm *at* the restaurant it's easy: there's the rarefied atmosphere to describe, there's energetic Stanley, Yannis's ulcer, the kitchen, Pablo, the routine, the food, plus the fact that this could turn out to be what Stanley called a fantastic opportunity . . .

Then I ask how her day went, how she got on with the coding assignment, and, when she looks up at me, I see that she's got tears in her eyes. "Kate? What is it?"

She clenches her fist. "Nothing. It's—"

"*Kate.*" I go over, pull out the chair next to hers and sit directly in front of her. "Kate, what's wrong? Is it the assignment?"

"No, I gave that up after twenty minutes—"

"Well look, who cares, it doesn't—"

"No, I could *do* it, I *will* do it. I just couldn't concentrate. Not today." She uses her sleeve to wipe away the tears. Then she looks straight at me. "I couldn't get it out of my mind, Danny, that image . . ."

"What—"

"Those two guys lying dead on the floor of a freezer. With their heads smashed in? It's . . . it's *insane.*" Her face crumples again.

"Oh Jesus, Kate. I'm sorry."

She takes a deep, gulping breath. "It's not *your* fault. And you had to tell me. It's just that . . . I don't—"

She stops here, uncertain how to proceed, and looks away, over my shoulder, as if the rest of her sentence might be somewhere behind me, on a Post-it note stuck to the fridge, or scrawled across the wall. In blood.

"Kate," I say, feeling sicker with each passing second, "*what?*"

She looks back at me. "I don't think we can just . . . *unknow* this. It happened. You saw it. It was covered up, and that's wrong."

"Kate . . ."

"Kate *nothing.* I mean, you didn't invent it, did you?"

"No, of course not."

"Well, then. We have to *do* something."

"I thought we had this conversation yesterday. I don't have any—"

"Danny, look,"—she reaches for a sheaf of papers beside her laptop—"I've been online all day, looking stuff up, printing articles. It's crazy, I know, but just bear with me."

As she flicks through the pages, I catch a glimpse of the Gideon logo on one of them, and my stomach sinks. She pulls a single page out and studies it for a second.

"Okay, get this," she says. "Over the past fifteen years there have been nine separate whistle-blower cases involving Gideon—and we're talking everything: fraud, contract violations, falsifying accounts, whatever, but also instances of sexual harassment and even human trafficking—*nine,* and those are just the ones that have come to trial. They've got pretty damn good at defending them too, because with the first couple they ended up incurring huge fines, but after that—"

"Kate, stop."

She does, but only for a second. "These people are unbelievable, Danny, and they're getting away with it. I mean, Jesus, from what you told me, they're literally getting away with murder."

"Kate . . ."

She turns to the laptop and clicks something. "Look at this."

I look. It's a YouTube video. She hits play, and as we wait the standard one or two seconds of dead time for it to start, I sigh loudly. But it comes out sounding more like a deep shiver. Of dread. Which is also how it feels. Kate doesn't notice because she's too intently focused on what's about to appear on the screen. This turns out to be a talking head on some studio panel, a middle-aged guy, beardy, academic, bifocals on a chain.

"So, these defense contractors," he's saying, "they've developed quite an attitude. I mean, it's not just that they think they're above the law, which they often *are,* it's that by aggressive lobbying, by packing government advisory committees, and by other frankly less than ethical means, they think they can actually make the laws, shape them, customize them to their own requirements. We're talking about billions of taxpayer dollars being funneled into a sector that isn't accountable, that isn't part of any chain of command, a sector that operates outside the jurisdiction of the United States and is therefore free to formulate what effectively amounts to its own foreign policy. So real reform is needed here, you know, and I think people should start demanding that reform, they should contact their elected representatives, they should get on the phone—"

"Kate, who is this guy?"

"—they should send e-mails, texts, tweets, whatever it takes, in order to—"

She taps the space bar to pause it. The beardy man freezes, silenced mid-sentence. Without looking at me, Kate says, "It's Harold Brunker, he's a law professor at NYU. He represented some of the Occupy people after that thing on the bridge. He's—"

"A law professor?"

She looks at me. "Yeah."

"And what's this?" I nod at the screen. "What's he on? Some kind of news show?"

"It's . . . I don't know, it's just . . . a clip I came across, it's—"

"Great. A clip on the Internet."

"Excuse me?"

"A *clip*. On the *Internet*." If I wasn't so tired, I'm sure I'd be able to do a better job of muffling the contempt in my voice. Shit, if I wasn't so tired, I'm sure I wouldn't even be talking.

"What's that supposed to mean?"

"It means . . . learn how to code on the Internet, Kate, fine, that makes sense, maybe, but the law? You think you're going to learn about the law by looking up random web sites and watching fucking You-Tube clips?"

"*What?*"

"You heard the professor there. This is a private corporation that gets to make up its own foreign policy. So you can be damned sure that at the very least all of their lawyers went to actual *law school*."

The look I get for this is one of momentary incomprehension. It's as if my statement has to be translated from another language. Except that it doesn't.

"Jesus," she whispers, after a long silence.

I'm immediately sorry and want to say so, but I know if I start, the words will catch in my throat.

"Anyway," she goes on, a little shakily, "my ignorance of the law is hardly the point." She turns and flips the laptop closed. "Man, they really did a number on you over there, didn't they?"

She walks past me and goes into the living room.

The next morning things aren't any better, and we're giving each other the silent treatment. I don't know what I can say without making the situation worse. Because the thing is, I really want this job at Barcadero. It'll be a chance to claw our way back a little. But taking it will effectively preclude me—preclude *us*—from voicing any criticism whatsoever of Gideon Logistics. And after last night, how do I break that to Kate?

Though maybe the job won't work out—maybe this Yannis guy chugs down a bottle of Pepto-Bismol, shows up for work, and I'm back at square one. At least in that case I'd no longer feel the need to be so defensive. And hypocritical. And like an asshole.

On the subway, I stare vacantly across at my reflection as it flickers in and out of visibility. I know it's just a job, but I'd like the regular paycheck, and I guess I wouldn't be unhappy with the step up in prestige either. At the same time, I briefly imagine how I'd feel if Stanley were to tell me this morning that Yannis is fine, that he'll be back tomorrow, that two shifts is all I'm getting.

Actually, I'd probably be okay with that. I might even be relieved. It would mean I could look Kate in the eye again. It would mean I could stop lying to her. So, as I walk the three blocks to the restaurant, I convince myself that this is what's going to happen, and that when it does I'll make the necessary adjustments—I'll express disappointment, but be professional about it, I'll use the momentum (and maybe some of Stanley's good will) to try and find a new job elsewhere. And then I'll go home and patch things up with Kate.

I arrive at Barcadero and the place doesn't seem as frenetic as it did yesterday. The atmosphere is a little muted. There's none of the usual banter going on. With Pablo I'm guessing it's a hangover, but they can't all be hungover. So maybe it's that someone is in a mood and the whole kitchen is affected. I've certainly seen that happen, though I'm not familiar enough with everyone here to be able to read the signs with any degree of confidence. Nevertheless, things grind into gear and before long I'm totally focused on precision dicing some pork for a ragù.

After a while, Stanley shows up, catches my eye from across the kitchen and indicates for me to follow him. I wipe up around the prep station before taking off down the dimly lit hallway that leads to the cramped office at the back. It's clear that Stanley is just as downbeat as everyone else is, and when I see him slumped at his little desk I get a weird feeling.

Without looking at me, he says, in a quiet voice, "Nadine, our accountant, will be in later and you can talk details and stuff with her, but I'm just going to go ahead now and slot you in for all of his shifts, okay?"

When I don't respond, Stanley eventually turns to face me. Up close like this, I can see that his eyes are red and slightly raw-looking.

"Stanley, no one has said a word to me this morning. I don't know what—"

"Yannis died," he says, and his face contorts a little. A tear runs down his cheek.

"Oh shit, Stanley. I'm sorry."

"Yeah." He wipes his eyes with his sleeve and sighs loudly. "Two years he worked here, almost from the beginning. He drove us all crazy with his stupid jokes . . . but he was a real sweetheart. Everyone loved him."

I swallow. "Was it . . . the ulcer?" I can't believe I'm even asking him this. People don't *die* of ulcers these days, do they? "Perforated, you said?"

"We don't know. His boyfriend found him last night, in their apartment. He was just . . . lying there." His face contorts again. "It's fucking awful."

I stand in the doorway for a moment, but it's clear we're done.

My walk back along the dim hallway to the kitchen is a long one. Yesterday I was covering for Yannis. I was anonymous, invisible. Today I'm replacing him. Today I'm the new guy.

I feel like I should be sending a text to Kate or something, but what would I say?

And so begins this new work regime in my life, which is not unlike the one I had before I left for Afghanistan—better restaurant, okay, and slightly better pay—but basically the same. It's still kitchen hours, still kitchen *work* . . . nicks, burns, high heat, tempers, ego, shouting, mind-numbing repetition. A bit like a war zone. Unless, that is, you've ever fought in a real war zone.

At home, however, in terms of pre- and post-Afghanistan, things are markedly different. It's my fault, but what's going on between me and Kate is awful. The truth is, I'm losing her, and in a way I'm also losing *me*—losing that version of Danny that she allows me to be, the one who doesn't have a label, who's sane, who's in control. *That* guy. So if I do end up losing Kate, what happens to him? Where does he go?

I have no answer, and with each passing day things just get more complicated. My final check from Gideon comes through, accompanied by a three-month unofficial severance payment, which is fucking great, but I find myself not mentioning this last part to Kate. My hours at Barcadero mean that I have fewer opportunities to mention anything to her, but when I do have a moment, my brain is usually fried and I'm not inclined to—which means it's easier to just let things fester.

How this plays out on a day-to-day basis is that I get home from work in a sort of operational coma, and, depending on which shift cycle I'm on, early or late, Kate is either there at the kitchen table doing her coding stuff, or she's out, or watching TV, or having a bath, or even already in bed. We talk, and are cordial, we deal with the small stuff—shopping for food, cooking, doing the laundry—but day after day the subtext gets buried that little bit deeper. Occasionally, a ripple of anxiety will surface. A violent item on the news will spark an unwelcome association, say, or a phone call from the debt collection agency that now owns Kate's student loan will detonate like an IED in the quiet of our living room. Or a simple sex scene in a movie we're both watching late at night will serve as an uncomfortable reminder of how long it's been for *us*.

The worst thing is that we don't seem capable of going into reverse on any of this. I'm genuinely exhausted on a permanent basis now, and Kate has become more determined than ever to turn her coding MOOC into a job opportunity, so we are busy, we are preoccupied, we do have these brutal demands on our time—but how sustainable is all this over the long term? How compatible is it with the notion of our being in a serious relationship? And how corrosive is it to our periodically expressed desire to have a baby together?

As it turns out, things aren't that much better at work. If I had a honeymoon period at Barcadero, I suppose it was just that first shift—those ten hours when I wasn't the guy who was replacing the guy who died. But ever since then no one has been willing to see my presence in the kitchen as anything other than bad juju—snippy comments are routinely made, looks are exchanged, cooperation is withheld. This makes for a shitty environment. The work still has to get done, though, orders have to be filled. For my part, I can lock into an intense rhythm and hit a flow state.

There is one thing that helps. It's the partial but clear line of sight I have from my prep station out into the dining area. During service, when the atmosphere in the kitchen gets too weird or toxic, I'll glance through the pick-up to see who's out there. I'll go around the table, rotating my attention, filling in imaginary details, names, job titles. I've done it once already this evening, and now, with service in full swing and tempers fraying all around me, I do it again. I glance out and this time see just two people sitting there—a youngish-looking couple. The guy, from what I can make out, is a business type in an expensive suit, but it's *she* who catches my eye. Most of the women who come to this place have that brittle, moneyed look, too tanned and coiffed, too much work done. This woman isn't anything like that. Even from a distance, I can see that she has an ethereal quality, a natural beauty so intense that she looks unreal, out of place, almost like an alien.

In fact, I'm so distracted by her that at one point, chopping asparagus tips, I nearly slice off the top of my left index finger. There's a tiny spurt of blood, but I manage to conceal it. I go over to one of the fridges where we keep a tin of Band-Aids. Taking cover behind the open door, I quickly stick two on my finger in an x formation. On the way back, avoiding eye contact, I decide I'm an idiot and should just keep my head down in the future. Because another slip like that—a more serious one, time spent at the ER, someone having to cover for *me*—all of that could jeopardize my position at Barcadero. But once I'm over at the prep station again, standing there . . . I can't resist.

I raise my head and look through the window.

She's not there anymore.

That's the second thing I notice. The first thing I notice is that *I* am.

The woman's seat is empty, and the guy is sitting at a slightly different angle, looking in my direction, more or less. I have a clear view of his face, and . . . it's the weirdest thing . . . I'm still chopping asparagus tips, but it occurs to me that I should slow down, that I'm not in full control here, that unless I want to lose a finger for real I have to actually pay attention to what I'm doing. So right now that's what I do, I look down at my cutting board, at the kinetic blur of wrist and hand and knife.

I slow my pace, eventually bringing the operation to a complete halt. After a moment, I glance through the window again, but I can't believe my eyes . . .

Which I close.

At this point I become hyperaware of every sound in the kitchen, of Pablo to my left, slicing duck breasts and muttering continuously in Spanish; of Alex, our Australian sous chef over to the right, crucifying one of the line guys for putting too much seasoning in the soubise; of every whoompf and sizzle, every plate clattering, every unit humming and shuddering—and it's in this simultaneously heightened and almost paralyzed state, like some partial form of locked-in syndrome, that I open my eyes again, just a fraction, and look out . . .

And holy shit . . .

He's still there, the guy in the suit, still alone, still facing this way. He's not looking at *me*, not directly, but I'm looking at *him*, and I can see his face, which is just like *my* face, remarkably so—the face that I see when I look in a mirror, or at a photograph.

It gives me a sick, dizzy feeling, and I turn away.

"Danny?"

I glance down at my hands, which are shaking slightly. I'm still holding the knife. I tap the edge of it gently on the cutting board.

"Danny?"

This is Alex. He's standing by the pass now, next to Chef, but staring back at me. "The fuck, mate?"

I ignore him and look out again—I can't not. The likeness is uncanny. I'm a little scruffy and need a shave, I'm pale, I could do with some proper nourishment, whereas this guy is tanned and chiseled and healthy-looking . . . not to mention that suit he's wearing . . . but still—

"Wakey, wakey, over there. Jesus Christ. Someone slip you a fucking roofie?"

It suddenly strikes me—because of the angles and where people are standing—that no one else here can see what I can, that no one else here is looking at what I'm looking at. And I'm glad. I wouldn't want them to. Because this feels very personal.

Tapping the edge of my knife on the board again, I reach for the next handful of asparagus stalks. I then tear my eyes away from the pick-up window and glance over at Alex.

"Quaalude," I whisper, mouthing the word very clearly for him to see. As I start chopping again, I hold his gaze. I wait for him to roll his eyes and turn his attention back to the production line. When he does, *my* eyes dart back out to the dining area.

But the guy in the suit is standing up now, facing away, and moving off to the right. The woman appears from the left, obviously back from the bathroom. She glides across my line of vision, and the two of them disappear.

I feel something next to me, a sudden movement, then hear a sharp intake of breath. I turn to Pablo, who's staring bug-eyed down at my hands.

"Pero ché coño?" he says.

I look down. There are tiny speckles of blood everywhere, not only on my cutting board, but all over Pablo's as well.

It's a measure of the shit storm this causes—shouting, name-calling, a tricky sequence of refires, the ceaseless animosity that ripples down the line at me all night—that it's not until my shift is over and I'm on the subway heading home that I remember the guy in the suit, the guy who . . . who what? Who *looked* just like me?

I gaze down at the floor of the subway car for a moment.

Did he, though? Really?

From this remove, it seems a bit implausible, the image less distinct now, the whole episode sort of blurry in my mind.

Except . . .

I remember the woman all right. She was gorgeous. So was it maybe a little wishful thinking on my part? Instead of peeping at her,

undetected, from a distance, like a deranged creep, my mind decides
it'd be nicer, maybe, to sit across a table from her, with a glass of
wine, and admire those high cheekbones up close?

I don't know.

But if so, it's pathetic.

I look at my finger. At least that's something I'll be able to talk to
Kate about. Maybe I could even get some sympathy. Though without
going into the reason for it, of course. That I got distracted looking at
this beautiful woman and then so caught up in a fantasy about having
dinner with her that I slashed my fucking finger.

She'd love that.

But I needn't have worried. When I get in, Kate is already in bed,
asleep, or pretending to be.

The next morning, the Band-Aid on my finger is just that, a Band-Aid
on my finger, not enough to stimulate an actual conversation. So in
frustration—because I don't know what Kate is thinking—I do something pretty awful. I scroll through her browsing history while she's
in the bathroom. Does it help? I don't know. In among all the course
pages, I find multiple searches for Gideon Logistics, for whistle-blower
cases, and for Afghanistan. There are also a few for PTSD.

Is that, after all, what she thinks I have?

It might explain why she's been putting up with my various
dysfunctions—emotional, social, erectile. But then again it might not.
So I also listen in on phone conversations she's having. I allow myself
to overhear them from the next room. It's a small apartment, and she
can't imagine there's any real privacy when she's on the phone, so on
those occasions when she brings her voice down a notch or two, almost to a whisper sometimes, I have to wonder what she thinks she's
doing, if not inviting me to listen even harder. In which case, what
am I supposed to think when I hear this? ". . . oh, I don't know, Sal,

he's trying . . ." Or this? ". . . they're *so* manipulative, and they have
very deep pockets . . ."

But who? Who has deep pockets? And in what way, I'd like to know,
does she think I'm *trying*?

On my next day off, I take things a step further. Kate says she's
going out to meet a friend for coffee and I decide to follow her. I give
her the impression that I'll be hanging out in the apartment all morning, but the second she's out the door I get dressed and skip down to
the street. I know which direction she's probably headed in, so it
doesn't take me more than thirty seconds to catch up and fall in behind
her. We move in unison down First Avenue, half a block apart.

What am I doing, though? What is it that I expect to find? Evidence
of something? Of *what*? I already have ample evidence that Kate is
big-hearted and kind and extremely patient. So what am I looking for
now, evidence that she's conspiring against me somehow? Am I out
of my fucking mind?

At 4th Street she turns right. I continue behind her, but slow down
and let her pull ahead. I think I know where she's going anyway, a
place she likes on Great Jones. By the time I get onto Second Avenue
and look left, I catch a glimpse of her on the southwest corner disap-
pearing right onto 3rd. By this stage, I've had enough and stay where
I am. I stand there for a few moments, a little tripped out, looking at
people, traffic, yellow cabs—one of which, slowing down now for a
light, comes to a halt directly in front of where I'm standing. It's only
there for maybe five seconds, and all I see is a profile . . . but fuck me
if that isn't . . . Harold Brunker, the guy on the YouTube clip, the law
professor. It's the beard, something about the—or am I mistaken?

When the light changes, and the cab takes off, I watch as it zigzags
across the avenue, deftly maneuvering itself for a right turn onto 3rd
Street.

Fuck.

She's meeting *him*?

I could go down there and . . . what? Storm into a crowded coffee shop? Start shouting? Make a scene?

But what if it's not him?

Of course it's fucking him.

I glance around, irritated now. For some reason, I've never liked this stretch of Second Avenue. It's dark and airless.

I turn and make my way quickly back over to First.

Kate shows up at the apartment again around midday, by which point my irritation has mutated into acute sexual jealousy. Why was she meeting Harold Brunker? To reminisce about Occupy Wall Street? To discuss whistle-blower legislation? Over coffee? And that's it?

Please.

Although the practical details of whatever else might be going on— the where, the *how*—resist coherent formation in my mind, I resolve to confront Kate about it the moment she gets in. But when the door opens, I see an equally determined resolve on *her* face.

"Danny," she says, putting her bag down, "you remember that thing I showed you a while ago, the YouTube clip? The one you were so dismissive of?"

I remain silent and try to look puzzled.

"Come on, you remember. The one of that guy, the law professor? Harold Brunker?"

I nod.

"Well, I actually met with him this morning."

Yeah? Really? This is where I might grab a kitchen knife, swipe the air with it and level insane accusations at her—instead of what I do, which is just offer a blank, "Oh?"

"Yeah, my friend Sally's at NYU, she asked around, and it turns out he's pretty approachable."

"Yeah?"

"Yeah, he's active in the whole protest scene and takes a special interest in, you know, the privatization of the military, all the fallout from that, the human cost. He says it's a form of moral Botox. He says—"

"Jesus, Kate, he *says*. You didn't talk about me, did you? You didn't tell him about Afghanistan, about Sharista?"

"No. *No.* I wouldn't do that. Not without asking you first. I was going to maybe build up to it."

"Build up to it? What does that mean? What *did* you talk about?"

"Oh baby," she says, visibly deflating, "I just . . . I wanted to talk to someone." She hesitates, a pleading look in her eyes. "I mean . . . *you* won't talk to me. And I really want to help, I really want to try and understand all of this."

I swallow, afraid to speak now. Stupid as it was, the jealousy is no longer there, but something else has set in, and I can't quite place it.

"And look," she goes on, "it's okay that you don't want to talk."

From this, it's clear that she has a worked-out and most likely Google-generated theory about why I don't want to talk. It's because I'm hurting, I'm traumatized, and the process of resolving that stuff takes time, it takes effort and commitment.

Nothing to do with how if I *do* talk, I'll have to keep on lying to her.

"Moral Botox?" I say eventually. "Cute. Did he make that up all by himself?"

She stares at me, her big heart obviously weary now, her kindness and patience fraying. "I don't know, Danny. Maybe he did. Maybe he didn't. Maybe he heard it somewhere. Does it matter?"

That night, I dream about Iraq. It's a rush of impressions, the heat and rumble and smell of a Humvee's interior, the stark sound of an ammo feed-tray being slammed shut, the plume of smoke that rises from a distant bend in the road. On approach, this becomes a crash site, where an AH-64 Apache helicopter has just been downed. Strewn everywhere are battered sections of fuselage, and the person they're pulling from the wreckage, it turns out—though I think we're already somewhere else—is my father . . .

That wakes me up.

For a while, I just lie there, in shock, staring up at the ceiling. He was a drunk, my old man, bitter and shouty, and he died of lung cancer, too many Marlboro reds. It was actually my mother who got pulled from a wreck, but that was years earlier, after a car accident—a collision with an oncoming truck, apparently. Beside her was my half brother, Tom . . . who I can't remember anymore, can't even see in my mind's eye . . .

I look at Kate, asleep next to me in the bed. I listen to her as she breathes, and I wonder how long it will be before I can't remember *her*. In a way, it's happening already, and she's receding. Though maybe it's *me* who's receding. Or retreating, or . . . succumbing . . .

Eventually, I drift back to sleep, a dreamless one, and when I open my eyes again a few hours later, it's time to get up and go to work.

It's a long day at Barcadero, and a stressful one, but towards the end of my shift, it happens again.

This time the woman isn't there—which punches a hole in my earlier theory. *He's* there, though, with two older guys. I didn't see them being seated, because I was in the walk-in at the time, but they're definitely there now, and having an animated conversation. My guy is sitting in the middle, turning one way, then the other, like a talk show host.

I go on working, glancing up every few seconds, but, unlike the last time, there's no panic or sense of urgency—I'm not self-conscious or worried about who can or can't see him. I just stare at this man who bears an uncanny resemblance to me—or, as he might see it, *I* bear an uncanny resemblance to. And who knows, maybe up close we're different, maybe there are discernible variations in the size and spacing of our features, in our bone structure, in our complexion. But so what. For the moment, I'm happy to go along with whatever this is, to treat it as some weird . . . *thing*.

After work, though, the weirdness lingers, like a mood I can't seem to shake, and maybe one I don't even want to shake, because it has a dreamy, vaguely narcotic quality to it, an intensity that carries me along—through the streets and the subway tunnels, into my building and up the stairs, into the apartment, and all with only the slightest, gentlest ripple of anxiety.

Unsurprisingly, by the following day, the feeling has dissipated somewhat. I can't quite summon it, but I know it's there, in the background, submerged.

I wonder if it'll ever resurface.

It takes three days. I'm coming back inside after a break, walking along the narrow hallway towards the kitchen. A bit farther on is where the restrooms are situated. As I'm turning towards the kitchen, one of the dishwasher guys is on his way out, lugging a heavy black sack, and I stand aside to let him pass. Just then the door to the ladies' opens and someone comes out.

It's the woman from that first night.

She's tall, with dark hair in a pageboy cut, and red lipstick. She's in a short, checkered dress. It's hard not to stare at her legs, and I do stare at them, but when I stop and look up, I see that she's staring intently at me. She seems mesmerized for a few seconds—but then figures it out I guess, realizes why she's staring at me.

I break away first. I head into the kitchen and make straight for my work station. It's a while before I dare to, but I eventually look out, and there they are, huddled at the table together, talking and laughing. Dinner is mustard-glazed hamachi, fattoush, branzino, blood sausage, cider mousse, verbena ganache, and I wonder if at any point during it she tells him. "The strangest thing, sweetheart: on the way back from the bathroom, I saw this *guy* . . ."

As they're getting up to leave, I contrive a reason to slip out of the kitchen. I rush along the hallway, yanking off my white jacket as I go. I make my way out to the street by a side exit, move a couple of doors down from the restaurant, and stop as though something in a window display has caught my attention. I glance to my right. This part of the street is quiet. A few people pass, walking slowly in either direction. Over by the curb, there's a young guy, no more than a kid, leaning against a parked low-slung sports car. He's busy with his phone.

I look back at the entrance to Barcadero, and after a moment they emerge, gliding onto the sidewalk. The sports car, of course—I should have guessed—is theirs, or *his*. The kid looks up as they approach and quickly pockets his phone. There is an exchange of keys and what I assume is a fat tip.

The man holds open the passenger door of the car to let the woman get in. As he walks around to the driver's side, I'm struck by how similar in height and build we are.

A moment later, the car hums to life. It's sleek and curvy, shiny, a sort of ultramarine blue. As it pulls away, the woman turns her head slightly in my direction, and for the second time this evening, even if only for the briefest moment, our eyes meet.

I live off this for the next few days, the whole thing—her, *him*, the likeness, the otherness of it, the feeling it gives me. It's not rational, and, if I were to talk about it, or look it up, I know things would go from mysterious to banal in seconds flat.

Hey, I have a cousin looks just like that Seth Rogen.

"BuzzFeed's 21 People Who Met Themselves."

So I keep quiet about it. I certainly don't mention it to Kate. What I do, in fact, is just wait for it to happen again. I even work on my day off in case I miss an opportunity to see them. Or to see *him*, really. She's something else, no question about that, with the legs and the lipstick and all, but what am I, fourteen? No, he's the source of interest here—whoever *he* actually is. And I try to find out. I make overtures to Stanley about maybe gaining access to bookings info, but he looks at me like I'm an axe murderer. I even try to chat up one of the girls who sometimes works front of the house, but that doesn't go too well either.

After another few days, I begin to lose heart. Because something occurs to me. What if he's been in the restaurant every single night for dinner *but sitting at a different table*? I've just been assuming that he always sits at the corner table, that it maybe has some significance for him. But what if I'm wrong?

A few more days pass, I keep a careful eye out, and he still doesn't show. Then one morning I'm heading into work on the subway. Sitting directly opposite me is a large man in a crumpled suit who has a briefcase lodged tightly between his knees. He's flicking through a copy of *Businessweek* and chewing gum. I figure he's a rep of some kind, or maybe an ad exec on the prowl for new accounts. Whatever. After a moment, I glance down at the cover of the magazine. The layout is a grid of nine photos, each one a headshot, each one a face. I squint for a second, trying to bring the whole thing into focus. And then my heart stops.

Because one of the photos, the last one . . . bottom row, on the right . . .

It's of *him,* of the guy . . . of *me.*

Fuck.

I'm about to lean forward to get a closer look when a lady with shopping bags shuffles along the car and blocks my view. The train is about to pull in at my stop anyway, and, as I stand up to get off, I peer over the woman's shoulder to try and get another glimpse of the cover, but it's all too fast, and I miss it. The next moment, I'm out on a crowded platform walking towards the exit, the train pulling away to my left.

Once I hit the street, I look around for the nearest newsstand. Ten minutes later I'm in Bryant Park with a triple espresso macchiato in one hand and a copy of *Businessweek* in the other. I find a bench and sit down.

It's definitely him.

The title of the article is "The Unusual Suspects: Nine Innovators with the Future in their Crosshairs." I take a few sips of coffee, glance around at the bright, trafficky Midtown swirl, and then start riffling through the magazine, looking for the article. When I get past all the glossy ads for SUVs, watches, vodka, data storage, and banks, I find it—and it is what it says on the cover, a survey of cool young business guys running cool, innovative companies. There is a two-page introductory spread, and then a page apiece for each of the so-called unusual suspects. I quickly flip to the one I'm looking for.

The first thing is the shock of the photo—this weird, dream version of me, posing, in a studio, in a suit . . . me looking handsome, confident, wealthy. And those differences I'd anticipated? Those subtle but significant variations in facial features? Not there, not visible, not that I can detect, not at all.

This really could be me.

In some fucked-up parallel universe.

I glance around me again, to make sure I'm still in *this* universe, and then I look back at the article. Scanning the text, I find it hard to concentrate, to process or retain what I'm reading, but two things stick.

His name is Teddy Trager.

And the company he runs is called Paradime Capital.

5

I look at the article again several times during the day, pulling the torn-out page from my back pocket and consulting it like it's the fucking oracle at Delphi. I'd say I divide my time fifty-fifty between staring at the photograph and poring over the piece.

The photograph itself is wild because I look so much like Teddy Trager in it that every time I just *see* the image it's as if memory cells start sprouting in my brain and I get a vague sense of having been at the photoshoot, of recalling it, of *feeling* it—the make-up retouches, the hair adjustments, the silky texture of the suit, the intensity of the lights, the constant click and whirr of the camera. *A little to the left, Teddy, chin down . . . eyes, eyes, that's great . . .*

But I wasn't there, and I've never worn a silk suit, and my name isn't Teddy. So is this how false memories form? And stick?

I don't know.

When I reread the article there is no equivalent sense of familiarity or recognition. It's all new to me, and alien. I mean . . . running a venture capital company? Betting on technology start-ups? Making billion-dollar investment deals? Having significant shareholdings in Twitter, Tumblr, Paloma, Zynga, Etsy? Dating an impossibly

73

attractive woman who runs her own tech company? I don't think so. (The girlfriend's name, by the way, is Nina Schlossmeier. She designs and develops mobile apps. Or her company does. Or something.) The weird thing is, the phrase "billion dollar" appears three or four times in the course of the article, in connection with Teddy Trager, and yet I've never heard of the guy before, or his company. Can you be worth that kind of money and remain anonymous? I look him up on my phone and there's a ton of information about him, and about Nina Schlossmeier too—but only, I suppose, if you go looking for it. The way you might go looking for information on Civil War memorabilia and find that there's a thriving community of people out there passionate about Civil War memorabilia. Also, he's lumped in with eight other people in this magazine piece, and I don't know any of them either, not a single one.

I expect to see Teddy Trager in the restaurant that day. It seems like that would be fitting, that it *should* happen, but it doesn't. And the later it gets, the less inclined I feel to look at the now crumpled-up magazine page in my back pocket, to take a hit from it.

At home, I'm tempted to pull my laptop out from under the bed (something I haven't done since I got back from Afghanistan) and conduct an in-depth search on Paradime Capital (and its founder, and his girlfriend), but I hold off. I don't know what this resistance is, if it's a creeping resentment towards Teddy Trager, or just self-consciousness on my part, or embarrassment even, but the more I resist the easier it gets. In fact, before I go to bed, I tear the folded-up page into little pieces and throw it in the garbage.

On waking the next morning, however, my first thought is . . . where's the photograph? I want to see it again. I *need* to see it again. Of course, I could conjure it up on my phone in a matter of seconds. I could print a large version out and stick it on the fridge with a magnet. I could show it to Kate and say, "Get a load of *this* guy." But I don't do any of that. Instead, on my way to work, I stop at a newsstand and buy a replacement copy. By the end of the week I've bought and disposed of three more.

It's on my next day off that I give in and pull my laptop out from under the bed. Kate is deep into her coding MOOC now—maybe using it to shut me out, maybe not, I don't know—but I decide to give her a little space anyway. I take my laptop to a café on Third Avenue and get settled in with a sixteen-ounce latte. I put in earbuds and get started.

So.

Teddy Trager.

Right off the bat, I OD on Google Images. I scroll through dozens and dozens of pictures of someone who could be me, but isn't, and in settings—conference rooms, symposium panels, art galleries, yachts—that are too numerous and too diverse, too weird and too glamorous, for there to be any chance that my brain might trick itself into thinking I even *vaguely* remember them. Trager also looks great in most of the photos—he's in good shape and is handsome (something I wouldn't ever think in relation to myself). In a few of them, he's with Nina, and they exude, I don't know . . . *something*.

I click back to the search results and look for information, basic stuff—how old he is, for instance, his date of birth. And as soon as that thought occurs to me, so does the obvious follow-up: maybe we were born on the same day. We weren't, as it turns out. But we are the same year. I'm April, he's September.

Which makes me older. Technically.

Anyway, personal info on Trager is sketchy. He seems to have first appeared on the radar about ten years ago when he and a partner co-founded a tech start-up called Janus. Then they hooked up with an investor, private-equity "maven" Doug Shaw, and two years later sold the company for $1.9 billion. Trager's original partner dropped out, and together Trager and Shaw went on to form Paradime Capital, which has since invested in countless start-ups, including some of the biggest names out there.

As I read through this stuff—articles, profiles, interviews—I find it hard to get a handle on where Trager is positioned, which side of the divide he's on. Is he a money guy or an ideas guy? At a glance, it would seem clear-cut—Shaw is money, Trager is ideas—but I don't think it's ever that simple, because surely it's a false dichotomy to begin with, surely the two sides are bound up with each other in ways that are inextricable and maybe even mysterious. But listen to Warren Buffett here, right? Because what the fuck do *I* know?

Nothing.

And what's the best thing to do when you know nothing?

Watch some YouTube clips.

And there's a ton of them. I'm wary at first, because with a photograph, if you see a likeness, okay, it's there, it's in front of you, but it's frozen, it's two-dimensional, you don't really have to believe your eyes. With video—I'm assuming—it's a different story.

Anyway, the first thing I watch is a two-year-old clip from *Real Time with Bill Maher*. Trager is on the panel alongside Nancy Pelosi and Ezra Klein, and it's definitely him, but it's a wide-angle shot at first. They're talking about the economy. Maher says something I don't catch, Pelosi laughs, and then Trager says, "But look, let's not get started on these giant food companies, okay, the biotechs, and the way they've got everyone hooked on their trans fats and high-fructose corn syrup . . ."

After a moment or two, they cut to a close-up, and the effect—on *me* at any rate—is electrifying. I'm sort of used to the look by now, the strange familiarity of it, but there's a density to this, a complexity, with physical movement, with his voice, that I hadn't anticipated. If there are subtle but significant differences between us, they're not in his appearance, they're in his gestures, in how he sounds. When he's talking, he does things with his hands that I would never do, little movements that make him look confident and assured. Same thing with how he uses certain words. And we have different accents too. Mine has traces of where I'm from, smoothed over but still detectable; his is Rich Person Neutral. It's weird, but in all the things that I've read about Trager I've never once seen it mentioned where he is from, but my guess is that it's not anywhere near Asheville, North Carolina.

". . . and then, of course," he's now saying, "there's what my dad's generation used to innocently call 'the phone company,' the same people who are currently carving up any semblance of what we all once considered our private lives."

Bill Maher smirks, throwing his hands up in mock resignation.

The clip ends, and the screen does that YouTube thing of showing the six or eight or ten relevant ones you'd maybe want to watch next, my reflection now visible against a grid of small and varied Teddy Tragers.

I hover over a couple of likely clips and pick one of Trager and his partner, Doug Shaw. They're on the sidelines at some investment conference being interviewed by Bulletpoint.com journalist Ray Richards.

Shaw is older, midforties. I think I recognize him from that second time I saw Trager at Barcadero. The discussion is lively, but it's technical, with lots of financial lingo, the kind of terms and acronyms I've heard a lot over the past few years but still don't really understand. As I watch, I wonder if there isn't a hint of tension between the business partners. Ray Richards certainly picks up on this and tries to stoke it, but Shaw sees what's going on and quickly shuts it down.

In another clip, some money-honey type on MSNBC is quizzing Trager about his "passions." He gives her what sounds like a standard spiel about how hard he works, and about wishing there were more hours in the day, but then he tells her what he's into anyway—and what he apparently does have time for: collecting art, learning to play the cello, and white-water kayaking. "Another interest I have," he adds a little tentatively, "is space exploration."

"As in tourism?" the interviewer asks.

"Well, yeah, that too, but also from a business point of view . . . you know, the possibility of taking a closer look at the asteroid belt, for example. There are abundant resources out there and sooner or later we're going to have to find a way to access them."

I look up for a moment and glance around the coffee shop.

I'm transfixed now, and don't want it to stop. In fact, I'm not sure I'll ever be able to get enough of this shit.

I glug down some of my latte and return to the screen.

Over the next few days, I find that I really can't stop watching and re-watching these and other clips I come across. It gets to be addictive, a compulsion, and whether consciously or not—I don't know—I start to mimic Teddy Trager's gestures and way of speaking.

It's not hard either. Even the accent thing isn't an issue. If you've lived in different places, if you've been in the military, if you're circumspect by nature, then your accent is up for negotiation all the time. Put me in a room with my cousins or people I worked with back in Asheville and it's only a matter of time before I'm dropping *y'alls* to beat the band. But on an FOB or in the kitchen of a fancy New York restaurant you wouldn't know where the hell I was from. Trager's cadence I can get pretty much with a little tinkering, and as for the gestures—there's a hand roll, a head tilt, he's big on eye contact—I just have to remember to include these, to space them out, and to not overdo it.

But it's not as if there'd be consequences if I were to fuck it up. I'm alone here. I'm in a tiny bathroom. I'm looking in a mirror. No one's watching. No one can hear me. In fact, there's probably a clinical element to this, but who cares? As pathologies go, you'd have to consider it fairly benign. And it's definitely making things a little easier with Kate. Maybe focusing so much now on Trager, on this strange likeness, this alignment, has quieted something in me, my anxiety, calmed the outward ripples of it. We're not talking yet, not the way we should be—the elephant is still in the room, but he's slouched in the corner and seems a little sedated. Kate and I are both busy, okay, we're both working hard, and there's a rhythm to that, sometimes a lulling one. But I'm also less tense, and therefore probably less *intense* to deal with.

Anyway, time passes, and, inevitably, something starts to bother me, to gnaw away at my equanimity. Why is it that Teddy Trager and Nina Schlossmeier don't show up at the restaurant anymore? I can't understand it. I take every opportunity that arises to scan the whole dining room and I even finally get to have a quick look at the bookings database. This happens one morning when I'm in the office. Stanley is outside, pacing the corridor, arguing with a supplier on his cell phone. I'm near his desk and see what's on the screen, so I very discreetly scroll back through a few weeks of bookings. It's only a matter of a minute or two, but I'm pretty sure I see Trager's name all of three times, which is precisely the number of times I've seen him from my prep station in the kitchen—twice with Nina Schlossmeier and once with that pair of paunchy, middle-aged fucks, one of whom might have been Doug Shaw.

In one way I'm relieved to find this out. It means I haven't missed anything, but it also means that Trager isn't exactly a regular. Maybe he won't be back for months. Maybe he'll never eat at Barcadero again. Then something so blindingly obvious occurs to me that I have a hard time understanding why I'm only thinking of it now.

Teddy Trager—I'm assuming—exists independently of Barcadero. He goes to other restaurants. He has an office. He walks around. He interacts with people. He lives somewhere. So if I want to see him again, why does it have to be through the pick-up window of the kitchen where I work?

And, of course, it doesn't.

With this in mind, I go back over all the web searches I've done on Trager, but this time with a slightly adjusted focus.

According to one web site, Paradime Capital is a stalwart of New York's Silicon Alley, which apparently isn't a geographical location anymore but a state of mind. Anyway, they're based in Midtown, in an office building on Sixth Avenue somewhere in the low fifties. I track down the exact address with a quick search. Not surprisingly, Trager's personal address is a different matter. There are references to his several "homes," but nothing specific, no giveaways.

And what do I do with this information?

To begin with, nothing. I delay and vacillate, but it doesn't take me more than a couple of days to reach the conclusion that either I forget about the whole thing and move on or I take some kind of action.

So the day after that I leave early for work and get an F train to 57th Street. The morning is sunny, and traffic is flowing along at an unhurried pace. I walk south for a few blocks and pass some of the vast corporate monoliths that line this part of Sixth. At the foot of one of these, in the middle of a small plaza, a tourist is leaning backwards, trying to comprehend—it would seem—the scale of the massive object before him. This is the Tyler Building, home to Paradime Capital. The next building along has a similar plaza in front of it with a fountain at its center. I keep walking, and, as I get closer to the fountain, the sound of its gushing water gradually emerges from the blanket roar of the traffic.

I sit on the edge of the fountain and remain there for about an hour, watching people enter and exit the Tyler Building, way too many to track. But it's not as if I really expect to see Teddy Trager in person. Chances are, in any case, that even if he comes here, spends any time here at all, he enters through the underground parking lot. But I want to get a feel for the place, to see the kinds of people who frequent it. And most of them, of course, are what you'd expect, just ordinary people who work in a big, impersonal office building.

Eventually, I stand up, check the time, and head off to work myself.

I do this again the next day, and again the day after that. On the fourth day, I'm sitting at the fountain, crouched over, doing something with my phone, not really paying attention, and when I look up, there he is, standing at the curb doing something with *his* phone. He's next to a parked limo, which it looks like he just got out of. After a moment, he puts his phone away and walks towards the entrance to the building.

I stand up now and watch him as he moves across the plaza. I check the time on my phone.

Through all of this, I remain calm, but as I'm walking to work afterwards I realize something. I'm excited. I'm energized. And as the day progresses, I can think of little else.

The next morning, Trager arrives at the same time, in the same way, and I feel as if I have cracked some sort of code. But it's all very quick and fleeting, so the day after that I decide to try and get a closer look at him. I position myself, wait for the limo to appear, and then move slowly along the sidewalk, passing by just as the driver is opening the door to let Trager out. I catch a glimpse of the car's interior, a flash of mahogany and leather, a glint of crystal maybe. A few quick steps on, I stop and take my phone out. I pretend to be answering a call, and casually turn around. Trager is doing the same thing, talking on his phone, just standing there . . . the two of us just standing there, eight, ten feet apart, people passing in either direction.

"Look, that's not my concern," Trager is saying, a sudden boom to his voice. "Just *arrange* it."

There almost seems to be an aura around him. I know it's probably my imagination, or the position of the sun or something, but everything has a shimmer to it, an intensity—his suit, his shirt collar, his leather shoes. And I can practically smell his cologne. In a sort of trance, I watch as he puts his phone away and moves off the sidewalk and onto the plaza.

After a few seconds, I turn and look the other way. The limo driver is still there. He's at his door, on the street side, ready to get back in the car. He glances over the roof in my direction. Our eyes meet

for a moment, and I register something, the merest flicker of . . .
recognition, puzzlement, I'm not sure.

And then he's gone.

Later, at work, I tell Stanley I need a few days off. It's out of the blue
and I don't frame it as a request, which clearly rankles, but just as he's
about to read me the riot act, something stops him. I don't know what
it is, a sudden realization that he can use this to get rid of me? Maybe.
In any case, he shrugs, and says, "Okay."

I tell him thanks, that I appreciate it.

"Whatever," he says, and adds, fuck-you style, "there's plenty of
cover available out there, you know."

"I'm well aware of that, Stanley," I say dismissively, in my best Teddy
Trager voice.

This confuses him, but he lets it go.

As for my few days off, I certainly don't need them, and I don't tell
Kate I'm taking them. What I figure is that I can explore this thing a
little further, push it to some reasonable limit, then maybe exhaust it,
get it out of my system. Because that's what this feels like—something
in my system, a virus.

But if that's what it *is*, the next day things ramp up to fever pitch.
I'm waiting at my usual spot, at the usual time, and at first nothing
happens: there's no limo, it doesn't appear—not that it arrives at exactly the same time every day or anything. But after about twenty minutes, twenty-five, a half hour, I start to get impatient. I start to resent
the position I'm in. I start to resent Teddy Trager—whoever the fuck
Teddy Trager might actually *be*, this guy with all the homes and the
suits and the visionary ideas for a better future. And I have to wonder, you know, what if he had spotted *me* somewhere? Would he have
started delving into *my* life? Would he have lasted five minutes? Would
he have even looked twice?

Before I can get anywhere with this, I glance across the street and see a yellow cab pulling up. After a moment, Nina Schlossmeier emerges from it, followed by Trager. Walking slowly, and with Nina doing most of the talking, they move along the block to the lights. They wait, cross, and make their way onto the plaza in front of the Tyler.

As I watch them now, I feel a sense of panic. In a few seconds they'll be inside the building, and that'll be it, done, today over. I could wait until one or other of them comes out again, but there's so much activity around here I'd probably miss them. All it would take is a tiny distraction, and I wouldn't even know. So what do I do? I can't go to work. I can't go home. My throat is dry, and the prospect of the empty hours ahead is unbearable. I'm actually about to freak out, but then something happens. Teddy and Nina stop, maybe ten yards from the entrance to the building, and turn to face each other. Are they saying good-bye? If so, what then?

If she takes off, I could follow *her*.

The sudden, unexpected creepiness of this thought causes my stomach to churn. But then it becomes clear that they're *not* on the verge of a good-bye smooch. In fact, they seem to be locked into a more serious sort of conversation, with Teddy now doing most of the talking. After a moment, they start moving again, but this time they veer left and make their way back onto the sidewalk. They go south, and I follow at a discreet distance—the creepiness somehow mitigated by, I don't know, numbers, gender balance . . .

I'm clearly out of my depth here.

Nevertheless, as we move, I study them closely. As usual, Teddy looks like he's wandered off the set of a magazine shoot, and, although Nina is just in jeans and a T-shirt, she looks amazing.

We're half a block apart now.

I wonder where they're headed, and what's next, and what would happen if one of them looked over their shoulder and saw me. I wonder who all these other people on the street are.

I need to keep focused.

Two blocks later, Teddy and Nina go into a coffee shop, a pricy boutique place that does locally roasted organic brews and gluten-free pastries. I cross the street and wander around for a bit, waiting, giving them some space. But I'm excited, and I guess I lose track of time. When I next check, it's been over ten minutes and I'm on Seventh Avenue.

How do I know they weren't getting their shit to go?

Fuck.

Stretched out like some optical illusion, the block between Seventh and Sixth seems longer than I remember, longer than it can possibly *be,* and when I eventually get to the end of it I'm out of breath and ready to throw up. I look over at the coffee shop and suspect I've blown it. I wait another five minutes, and then cross the street. I approach the entrance, look inside, and realize I was right. They're gone.

I hang around for a while but eventually give up and go home. I tell Kate I had to leave work early because I felt sick. She's concerned and wants to help, but I insist that I just need to go lie down. Staring up at the bedroom ceiling, I replay the events of the morning in my head. Pretty quickly, however, it all comes to seem a little unhinged to me, a little crazy. It's just that . . . I don't really feel that way. I don't feel unhinged, or like I'm stalking this guy. In a way it feels like he's stalking me. Because I didn't ask for this, or go looking for it, and I certainly don't understand it. But I can't ignore it either.

In fact, I don't really see an alternative.

So the next day I'm up and at it again. Trager arrives at his usual time and enters the building. An hour or so later, he reappears with Doug Shaw, and I follow them to a place on Madison, where they have coffee. But afterwards, on the way back, it all starts to feel a little weird again. It's as if what I'm doing is utterly pointless . . .

So do I stop? Do I turn away?

Maybe this is an attempt to force the issue, but what I do instead is get closer to them—so close that as they slow down at the entrance to the building, backed up in a short line of people waiting to file through the revolving doors, I end up directly behind them. I'm so close that I could reach out and touch the back of Trager's head, or stroke the fabric of his suit, or whisper his name and get him to turn around.

But then what?

At the last moment, I step to the left, out of the line, and watch the two men go inside. Through the copper-tinted glass I follow them as they stroll across the lobby. At one point, Trager stops and pulls out his phone. Shaw makes a gesture at him with his hand and keeps going, walking over to what I assume are the elevators.

I then stand there, staring through the window, and it takes me a while to see it, for it to click—my own reflection in the glass is superimposed on Trager. He's facing in my direction but is busy with his phone and doesn't appear to see me. For my part, I switch focus from one image to the other, from mine to his, and back again, until I get confused . . . Trager scruffy and unshaven one second, me groomed and in a suit the next . . .

6

I *think* I bought a suit when I was younger, or it may have been a rental, I don't remember, but this feels like the first time. I'm not in a hurry, so I start with a tour of a few menswear departments—Blooming-dale's, Saks, Barneys—just to get some ideas. Then I sit with my phone for a while in a coffee shop and scroll through the web sites of various magazines—*GQ, Esquire, Details*—looking for advice, tips, the basic vocabulary I'll need if I'm going to do this.

Within minutes I'm all over it—cuffs, vents, lapels, gorges, folds, quarters. I also search around to see if I can find out what—or who—Teddy Trager wears. He seems to go for a classic look, two-button, slim fit, charcoal grey or navy. No brand names are mentioned, but he has to be a Tom Ford or Brioni type of guy. I'm assuming. Anyway, by midafternoon I'm ready. I decide to take my chances with a small menswear place on 53rd Street that I come across on Yelp. It does off-the-rack and bespoke and gets a lot of five-star reviews. I go in and don't pretend I know more than I do. There are two assistants, one older, probably in his sixties, but he's on the phone, so I get the younger guy, which is fine. It's stupid, but I feel intimidated by the atmosphere. I catch sight of myself in a couple of different full-length mirrors and realize how scruffy I look. But then . . . what does that matter? For all these guys know I could be a billionaire.

The young guy is attentive and knowledgeable. He takes my measurements, gets me to try on a few things, and then calls out a tailor from the back room, who adjusts, tugs, smooths, and before I know it I'm actually buying a *suit*. There are a few minor alterations needed, with the hems, which will take about two days. I'm impatient about this, but I want the damn thing to look right.

Oh, it will, the tailor reassures me, standing back, nodding his head, making all the right noises.

I have no doubt that whatever exorbitant amount of money I'm about to shell out here (money I don't have), it's only a fraction of what someone like Teddy Trager would be prepared to spend on a suit.

And of course that's not all.

As I'm taking out my credit card (the only one I have left that works, thanks to Phil Coover), I hear myself asking about shirts, ties, and accessories.

When I'm outside again, on the sidewalk, I take another look at the credit card receipt, and as I walk to the nearest subway stop, the number keeps turning over in my mind, continuously, as though on a loop . . . three thousand two hundred seventy-nine dollars, three thousand two hundred seventy-nine dollars, three thousand two hundred seventy-nine dollars.

Holy shit.

And that—it suddenly occurs to me—is without a proper pair of shoes.

A couple of days later, after I pick up the suit (plus two shirts, a tie, and a pair of cufflinks), I go to a place on Fifth for shoes (another four hundred bucks) and then take the whole lot home in a cab. Kate is in Brooklyn at some coding study group, a new thing she's taken to doing. I hide the stuff under the bed, stand there like an idiot, and almost immediately take it all out again. I put on the suit, with one of the shirts and the tie. I go into the bathroom and stand in front of the mirror. The suit looks fabulous, but I feel very self-conscious in it. Maybe I need to shave and do something about my hair.

I usually only shave every three or four days. It's a look, I suppose, and one that in my case is probably due more to laziness than anything else. I do a proper job of it now, though, and it definitely works better with the suit. But still, my *hair* . . .

I carefully fold and bag everything and put it under the bed. Then I head out to a barbershop I sometimes go to on Avenue A. When I'm in the chair, I'm not sure what to say, what instructions to give . . . a bit shorter, tidier, part on the right? Again, I'll bet Trager pays a fortune for a haircut, and that he probably flies to Paris or Milan to get it done. Nevertheless, I come away with at least some approximation of his look. But only as I'm walking back up the stairs to the apartment does it occur to me that I'll have to have a conversation about it with Kate.

She notices all right, but I wouldn't exactly call it a conversation. She makes a face, does a weird thing with her eyebrows, and mumbles something. *I'll talk about your haircut,* she seems to be saying, *I'll talk about anything, but you've got to talk to me first.*

Fair enough . . . but where would I begin? I end up saying nothing.

The next morning, I shave again, and really take my time over it. I'm not sure what Kate's exact plans are today, but when I come out of the bathroom I see that she's already gone, with her laptop and a folder of notes—I'm guessing to Brooklyn again. I feel like this can't go on, but I don't know what to do about it. The worst part is that we're caught in an economic rat trap. To put it at its baldest—and I'm not saying I want this to happen or anything, I don't—but if we were to split up, and I were to leave . . . Kate would no longer be able to afford the already modest rent on the apartment, and she'd have to leave too. Her outstanding student loans would stymie her at every turn, and she'd probably end up living back with her folks, getting turned down for cashier jobs at the local Walmart. And fuck knows where *I'd* end up. So, whatever we do or think or feel now is polluted by this knowledge. It's driving us apart and turning us both into liars. She can't call me a coward for not standing up to Gideon, in case that drives me away, and I can't tell her I'm now effectively dependent on Gideon, in case that drives *her* away.

It's fucked up.

And doubly so if you count the fact that I've just spent our rent money for the next couple of months on new clothes that I don't need. I mean, maybe *I* think I do, but I can't tell Kate that. It'd be easier to tell her I spent the money on blow and tequila or lost it playing online poker.

I'm in a bad mood now. I take out the suit, put it on, go into the bathroom and stand in front of the mirror for a few minutes, adjusting my hair, straightening the tie. I'm already frustrated, but when I try out the voice and do a couple of the gestures, I begin to feel really awkward.

Maybe I shouldn't be doing it here.

Leaving the apartment is hard. I feel incredibly self-conscious, like a kid dressed up for his grandmother's funeral, so the last thing I want is for someone I know to see me and start a conversation—anyone, the guy down the hall, the mailman, that lady from the nail salon next door who spends half her life taking cigarette breaks. But I keep going, and by the time I get to Union Square, and down onto the platform, I'm invisible, just a guy in a suit on his way to work.

I get out at 51st and Lex and wander for a bit. I steer clear of the general area around the Tyler Building at first—the risk of exposure, I decide, is too great. Of course, I wouldn't know anyone there, but the potentially terrifying thing is that someone there might know—or think they know—*me.*

After a few minutes, I relax and start to enjoy it. There's an undeniable thrill involved in this, an adrenaline kick from pretending to be someone else—or maybe it's just from being dressed differently, I don't know. But isn't that a thing? You see it in the army. Put a uniform on a guy, and he changes, he puffs up, gets a little cocky. With this suit on, I find it's like that, I'm walking with my chest out, not quite strutting, but . . . I catch my reflection in a store window and can imagine being that guy—a venture capitalist, a fund manager, a Teddy Trager.

But for how long? At what point do I either give up or decide that this simply isn't enough? I'm not sure, but when I look around me now and realize how close I'm getting to the Tyler Building—circling the area, stealthily, like a predator—I have to concede that I probably have no intention of giving up at all. At the same time, the closer I get to Trager, to being in a position where I might bump into him on the street, the less confident I feel—the intense thrill of earlier giving way to a confused flush of anxiety.

The closest I get is to the fountain in front of the building next to the Tyler, the spot where I based myself on that first day. I sit on the edge of the fountain, phone in hand, and just . . . wait.

Thirty, thirty-five minutes pass, and nothing happens. I suspect that a part of me is almost relieved, but then I glance over and see Doug Shaw emerging from the revolving doors of the Tyler. My heart starts to race. I track him as he walks across the plaza. At one point he turns and looks in my direction. I could swear that our eyes meet, but at this distance it's hard to tell. In any case, I have a nano-sized panic attack and look down at the ground. When I look up again, he's gone.

Fuck.

But what would I have done? Gone over and spoken to him? The impossibility of this, the ridiculousness of it, strikes me now with considerable force. What do I think I'm doing? Not just here and now, but generally? My behavior, the stalking, the suit, my attitude at work, the way I've been treating Kate? All along, as this has developed, I've had a growing sense that something in me is unhinged, or broken, and that feeling now surges through my body, stirring up concomitant feelings of shame and inadequacy.

I stand up from the edge of the fountain and move away. I cross Sixth and go south. The pace I'm walking at now is different, slower, more self-conscious. I'm reluctant to go home, but at the same time I can't wait to change out of this suit.

Twenty minutes later, I'm on First Avenue, approaching 10th Street, for the most part staring down at the sidewalk in front of me. But then I look up. On the next block, coming in the opposite direction, coming towards me, is Kate, carrying her laptop case. After a second, she too looks up, and I'm pretty sure we make eye contact, but she doesn't seem to recognize me. She doesn't react at all. What she *seems* to do is stare right through me, as though I'm not even there. At the corner, she turns left onto Tenth. I turn right, and cross over. When I'm a few feet behind her, I call out her name.

Tensing immediately, she spins around. It takes her a second to focus, her face registering confusion, recognition, then shock. I'm aware, obviously, that I look different, but it's only now that I realize just *how* different, and how weird this must be for her.

"Danny . . . ?"

"Hi."

We're standing there, facing each other, half a block from our building, from our *bedroom,* and it feels as if we're total strangers.

"Jesus—"

"I had a job interview," I say quickly, "and I . . ." This is horrible. "I didn't tell you about it because I didn't want to get your hopes up."

"But—"

She doesn't know what to say, torn between obvious incredulity and even more obvious irritation.

I stumble through some improvised details, saying it's a front-of-house thing, sort of a . . . managerial position, in one of Barcadero's sister restaurants, a new one opening soon . . . downtown. I can't believe I'm saying this stuff, because it doesn't add up, and Kate has to know that. I'm a kitchen guy, not FOH, I work prep, I work the line, I work with *knives*.

But she's barely listening anyway.

It's the suit. With her free hand, she takes the lapel of my jacket between her fingers and feels the material.

"Holy shit," she says, "this is . . . what is it, cashmere?"

"Yeah." I swallow. "And wool. Merino. It's a mix. A guy at work lent it to me."

She looks into my eyes, holds my gaze. I can tell that her mind is racing, that she might even be a little afraid and is no doubt asking herself . . . what kind of fucking PTSD is *this*?

"Come on, Kate," I say, "let's go. I want to get this damn thing off me."

As we walk the half block to our building, go inside, collect the mail and make our way up to the fourth floor, the tension between us is palpable. The obvious thing would be for Kate to ask me how this supposed job interview went, but she can't bring herself to do it.

I get the suit off, have a shower and change into normal clothes. As Kate chops up some fruit to put in the juicer, I sit at the table and open the mail. Most of it's junk. One piece is a reminder from the debt collection agency—another in the regular series that Kate has been receiving for over a year now.

I slide it across the table, so she'll see it when she turns around. Which she does almost immediately. She picks the letter up, glances at it, then steps on the pedal of the trash can beside her, and drops the letter in.

Without saying a word, she goes back to her chopping.

I sigh. It's deep, and audible, probably louder than I intended. It's not directed at Kate in particular. I'm tired. I'm confused. It's a *sigh*.

Clearly not how it sounds, though.

"*What?*" she says, turning around, knife up.

"Nothing, I—"

Seeing me notice the knife, she rolls her eyes and puts it down.

"Look," she says, "*you've* got a job now, this Barcadero thing. *I* can get something too, I'm trying, I'm out there."

"I didn't mean—"

"In fact, just today, I heard of a possible thing, part-time to start with, but maybe more, it depends."

"Kate—"

"I met with Harold Brunker again, and he was saying he could put in a word with some people he knows, movement people. There's a web site they run, and there could be an opening. It wouldn't be much at first, but we could use the money." She pauses. "I mean, *obviously* we could. Right?"

Put in a word? What has she been saying to this guy?

"Well, Danny, couldn't we?"

I shift in the chair. Squirm, really. "Yeah, we could, sure, of course . . . but come on, Kate, a fucking *web site*? Jesus Christ, what about your dreams? What about law school?"

"I don't know, Danny, what about it? I'm twenty-five years old and already drowning in debt. And why?" She throws her arms up. "Because I took out a student loan in order to get a worthless degree from some shitty college no one's ever heard of. *That's* why. It's a debt I can't repay and that will always show up in credit checks. It's a debt that ironically means I'll probably never be able to get a decent job, certainly not one as a fucking lawyer, that's for sure. So, I don't know, working for people who want to change things, and make a difference? That actually sounds pretty okay to me. But working for people who want to make companies like Gideon Logistics accountable? To expose their hypocrisy? To make them bleed?" She pauses. "I'm all *over* that, Danny. Bring it fucking *on*."

I shift in the chair again. "But—"

She waits to hear whatever it is I'm going to say. The only problem is I'm waiting too.

After a while, I just shake my head.

Kate turns around, picks the knife up, and starts chopping again.

I'm due back at work the next morning, but I can't bring myself to go in. I don't even call in sick. I just don't show up. And when my phone starts vibrating, I ignore it. Also, with no help from me, Kate eventually works out that I don't appear to be going anywhere, so she gathers up her stuff—laptop, notes, phone—and heads out herself.

I stand in the emptiness of the apartment, but only for about ten minutes. As fast as I can, I put on the suit. I go down to the street and hail the first cab I see.

Fifty-seventh and Sixth.

The city passes in a quickening blur, its sounds merging into white noise.

I pay the driver, get out of the cab, and there, right in front of me, pulling into sudden and sharp focus, is the Tyler Building, this vast, refractive slab of crystal and gold. I step onto the plaza and walk across it. I hold my head up and make eye contact with anyone who cares to look my way.

And, as I'm approaching the entrance to the building, I hear a voice behind me.

"Teddy?"

I don't react.

"Teddy?"

I can't quite believe I'm hearing this.

I slow down and come to a complete stop. Then I turn around, ready for whatever weirdness is about to unfold.

Before me are two guys, one burly, one slim, both about forty. They're both in suits which aren't unlike mine but not quite as nice either. The burly guy has red hair and a pasty complexion.

"Hey, Teddy," he says, "that was *so* great yesterday. I just wanted to say."

I swallow and nod at the same time.

"I mean, man, you really crushed it with those guys." He laughs. "And I think you may have crushed their spirits too."

"Well, that's possible," I say, acutely conscious of my voice now, but more worried about how I sound than what I might say. "It was never my intention, though."

"Oh, for sure. Of course. And listen, *I* can't hear that stuff too many times, either, you know."

The slim guy nods along, as if he's agreeing, but then says, "Hear what?"

"I *told* you," the burly guy says, trying to stifle his irritation. "That pitch meeting yesterday."

"Oh yeah, you said . . . don't . . . what was it again, don't . . ."

The burly guy looks at me now—half embarrassed by his friend, I think, and half fishing for permission to continue.

I shrug my assent, though it's barely perceptible. We're moving now, in any case, towards the revolving doors. One by one, we spin through them and into the lobby.

". . . it's the baseline for any start-up," the burly guy is explaining. "Don't go *looking* for a problem to tackle, because that way you're already compromising the solution . . ."

"Oh, that's awesome," the slim guy says. He looks at me. "That's awesome, Mr. Trager."

Just then, an older man passes us on his way out. He's clearly in a hurry, but, as he goes by, he pats me lightly on the arm. "*Teddy,*" he says, delivering the word softly, half in a whisper. Almost like an invocation.

I watch him slip out through the doors.

When I look back at the two guys, I become aware, for the first time, of where we are—inside a vast multi-story atrium, a marble and brushed-steel echo chamber teeming with corporate execs. "You know what fellas," I say, suddenly feeling queasy, "you head on up . . . I've . . . I've just remembered something."

I mumble this last part as I turn around. I go back through the revolving doors and straight out onto the plaza. Before I get to the sidewalk, I glance over my shoulder at the building. It's not that I'm escaping or running away or anything.

I love this. I fucking *love* it.

The whole thing.

But I'm not an idiot. I know that if I want to pull this off properly, I need to be prepared.

I need to have some coherent shit to say.

I need to do more homework.

7

I open my eyes and stare up at the ceiling. After a second or two, sounds crowd in—morning traffic, a thumping bass beat, voices from the apartment next door, voices from the street below. I roll sideways off the bed and get up.

I look around. Where's Kate?

I find her in the living room. She's about to go out and is all dressed up. I stand there in my boxers and T-shirt, looking at her. She always dresses well, but in a casual way. This is a notch or two above that, not quite on a par with my insane upgrade, but still, I'm taken aback.

"What's going on?"

"Nothing."

I see a flicker of irritation in her expression. She was obviously hoping to get out the door before I woke up.

"Where are you going?"

"I have that thing," she says.

I stare at her, not so much confused by what she's referring to, or by her reluctance to engage with me, as entranced by the unfamiliar hint of color around her eyes.

"What thing?"

"I told you, that interview. It's today."

"*Oh.*" I nod. "Of course. The web site thing, yeah. Sorry."

She hesitates, with her hand on the door, as though she's waiting to be released.

Does she hate me now? I wouldn't blame her.

I move forward a little. She tenses.

"Good luck with it," I say.

"Yeah."

I give her a peck on the cheek. "You know, *they'll* be lucky to get *you.*"

She half smiles. I think that's what it is. Though it could be something else—a look of pity, of incomprehension, of disgust even. I'm not sure.

And then she's gone.

I go into the kitchen and put on some coffee.

It's been five days since that little encounter at the Tyler Building. And two since I quit my job at Barcadero. Not showing up was bad enough, but not calling in? Not getting back to them? Holy shit, for a kitchen guy, even a lowly one, that was unconscionable. They would have fired me anyway, so I just figured I'd save them the trouble.

I don't know what Kate thinks about this—though I suppose I might have a better chance of finding out if I actually told her. I'm just sort of assuming that she's figured it out because, well, I'm *here* most of the time now. For her part, she's taken to leaving the apartment every day, and I'm never sure where she goes, so I suppose—in some twisted, fucked-up, non-sustainable way—we're even.

What I've been doing with my time is a lot of online research— background reading, interviews, profiles, financial reports. I've been immersed in it, day and night, but the frustrating thing is that whatever I've learned is all on the surface. I've absorbed terms and vocabulary, names, dates, references, memes, factoids, but do I really understand any of it, do I have the ability to pull it all together, to gestalt it up into a convincing Teddy Trager? I doubt it. I might have thirty seconds of material, a minute maybe. After that, I suspect I'd run dry. But I guess there's only one way to find out.

I shower and shave, then suit up. Twenty minutes later I'm on the subway, and then, like a scene change in a dream, I'm back. As usual, what I do is walk, block after block, Sixth Avenue, Fifth, Madison, the high forties, the low fifties. I almost fall into a mindful state, what you might even call a trance, and if every now and again I end up near the Tyler Building, so be it. I'm open to anything, to any encounter . . .

At one point, my phone goes off. It's just before midday. I stop at a corner and look around. I'm on 53rd and Sixth.

I reach into my pocket.

"Yeah?"

"Danny, I *got* it."

I have to think for a second. She got it. Got what? Oh, the interview, the *job*. That's actually great. I need to say it. "Kate, wow . . . I'm—"

But I stop there, my heart starting to race, because I'm also looking straight ahead along the sidewalk.

"*Teddy?*"

And holy shit if that isn't Doug Shaw coming towards me.

"Danny!" This is in my ear. "Are you there?"

"Yeah," I whisper, "I'm here."

I respond to Shaw with a nod.

Getting closer, he says, "Come on, Teddy, we need to talk."

"Did you hear me, Danny? I said I *got* it. They were really nice, and it's actually going to pay a bit better than I thought, but I'll probably have to—"

"Wait . . ." *Shit*. "I've got to go, Kate. Sorry."

I slide the phone away from my ear, ending the call and flicking it to silent.

"Teddy," Shaw says, right in front of me now, practically in my face. "Teddy, Teddy, Teddy."

"Yeah?" I say, nervously, close enough to peer into his eyeballs.

"It's a bit early, but what do you say we get some lunch?"

Next thing I know he's got an arm out, and seconds later a yellow cab is pulling up at the curb. As we're getting in, Shaw says, "I've been craving some of that blood-sausage thing Jacques does."

My heart stops racing at this, nearly stops altogether.

Before he even utters a word to the driver, I know what's coming. "Forty-fourth Street."

The short cab ride to Barcadero passes in a flash. I'm sitting beside my supposed business partner, impersonating *his* business partner, and all I can think about is what awaits me at my former place of employment. Shaw does all of the talking, but I don't actually listen. All I catch is the word "sign." He says it more than once, his voice low and gravelly. He's also wearing a distinctive cologne. That's what I get. That's the sum total of what I'm able to process.

And I don't open my mouth once.

Shaw pays. Then we're on the sidewalk outside Barcadero. We head for the entrance, and, depending on who's doing front-of-house today, this might all come crashing down within the next thirty seconds. We go inside, and, while the place isn't busy, it isn't empty either. Croatian, sapphire-eyed Karina, one of the daytime hostesses, glides over to us, smiling.

"Mr. Shaw, Mr. Trager, how nice to see you today."

I look at her directly. There's nothing. But then, why would there be? Have we ever even spoken? Why would Karina pay any attention to some surly jerk like me who works in the kitchen? No, I think, the real trouble here will be with the server, or maybe the wine guy. I know most of them, and they know me.

Without checking her list, Karina just leads us into the main room and—I hadn't even thought of this—over to the corner table. Before I know it, I'm sitting there, settling in, afraid to look up, afraid to look at anything—at the pick-up window, at the menu, and, most of all, at

Doug Shaw, who has just put his reading glasses on and is doing something with his phone, sending a text or checking his e-mail.

I close my eyes for a second. What the fuck am I doing here? I need to be outside, on the street, walking, moving.

"Gentlemen, how are we today?"

Oh God. This is Brian, an intense, wiry guy from Boston. I've had several conversations with him, even had a drink with him once. He's a physics major and intimidatingly smart. I may as well just give up right now.

"This is a quickie," Shaw is saying, as he removes his glasses. "I want that blood-sausage thing. I want the kale with apple and pecorino salad. And water's fine."

I look up. Brian is staring at me. But, again, there's nothing. He's just waiting for me to tell him what I want to eat. I don't understand what this is. Some kind of psychological syndrome? Perception based on predetermined expectations? A form of confirmation bias? Danny Lynch doesn't wear a suit, he doesn't come to Barcadero with Doug Shaw, therefore people here aren't even going to *see* him?

"Sir?"

Or is it that I look *that* different?

"Teddy, we haven't got all day."

Shit.

I glance down at the menu. I could make it easy and say I'll have what Shaw is having, but that might be weird. Besides, I *know* this menu.

And so does Teddy Trager.

"Let me have the . . . hamachi and artichoke. Water as well. Thanks."

Then he's gone. And I realize something. *Now* is the hard part. So what if people here recognized me. That would have been awkward, humiliating even, and, let's face it, exposure would have been the end of the road. *This* thing, on the other hand—whatever it turns out to be—is still in play. I look Shaw directly in the eye now, maybe for the first time since he walked up to me on the street all of, what was it, fifteen, twenty minutes ago? He holds my gaze, and with an intensity that I find really unsettling.

But I decide to dive in. "You said we needed to talk, Doug. So let's talk."

Then it occurs to me that maybe he already said whatever he wanted to say in the cab, when I wasn't listening, when I was so over-wrought with nerves that I couldn't even *hear* him. I also wonder why he had to approach me on the street like that, when it's my under-standing, from stuff I've read online, that he and I—he and *Teddy*—both have offices on the seventieth floor.

"I don't know if I *can* talk to you, Teddy, not anymore. That's the problem. You're going off on these batshit crazy tangents all the time now, and . . . frankly, you have me worried."

Shaw is unprepossessing in appearance, but up close like this there's something compelling about him—a nervous energy, a sort of magne-tism.

"I don't know what to tell you, Doug."

"Look," Shaw says, "you know I get it, right? The great Teddy Trager? He doesn't just think outside the box; he eats, sleeps, and shits out there too. He's a visionary, has all these grandiose ideas, and, fine, some of them fly, some of them don't, whatever, so believe me, I *do* get it, you need space, and time, a bit of latitude . . . but Jesus Christ, you're losing sight of what got us to where we are, Teddy. I mean, what's happening with this PromTech deal? We're just going to let *that* one slide too?"

As Shaw speaks, I avoid his eyes, stealing glances instead at his shirt collar, at his watch, at his soft, manicured hands, at the texture of his suit, but at the same time my mind is racing, I'm *thinking*, and so rap-idly that it can't be conscious. What I must be doing, I guess, is trawl-ing through some mental database of stuff I've read, searching for a match, a loose thread to pick up and spin an answer out of. Shaw is watching me closely now, and I have to say *something*. Because grunting or nodding along won't cut it for much longer.

"Come on, Doug," I say, tugging at my own jacket lapel, "I wear a suit to the office every day, what more do you want? I'm supposed to worry about volatility in the markets now as well? About earnings, and price ratios? You want me to get excited about some new start-up? Why? So we can take their game-changer of an idea and suck the life out of it, reduce it to an efficient revenue stream? Well, I can't do it. My heart's not in it anymore."

I'm aware that Trager and Shaw have their differences, and, while I'm vague on the details, this seems to be at the core of it. It's an argument I've seen rehearsed again and again in interviews and magazine profiles.

"Fuck your heart, Teddy, where's your brain? Where are your *balls*? Our business runs on confidence. You don't need me to tell you that. So for the two of us to be seen squabbling publicly about this—or, by the way, about *anything*—is . . . is . . . it's like we're dysfunctional, like the company is, I mean, Paradime. That's how we're being perceived. And it can't go on or it'll destroy us."

I have a pretty good idea of what Trager's counterargument might be, but the very fact that I do strikes me as odd. Because if *I*, as an ordinary member of the public, know what it is—if it has filtered *that* far out into the ether—how come Trager and Shaw are still having this conversation? Is it that the matter remains unresolved? That they're going around in circles on it? That there really *is* an element of dysfunction here?

"What will *destroy* us, Doug," I say, barely able to believe the exasperated tone I'm adopting, "is this insane notion of infinite economic growth. I mean, what's our big game plan? Make more money? Seriously? Is that all we're ever going to use our energy and creativity for? We talk about leadership and innovation and fostering fresh ideas, but the only thing that companies like Paradime *really* want to do is fatten these new ones up for IPOs so we can strip them to the bone after-wards."

Shaw sits back and stares at me. "Wow."

I wait a second. "What?"

He gives his head a quick shake. "Nothing, it's just . . . the blood sausage. I can smell it from here."

At which point Brian arrives from behind me with our orders. There's a moment or two of business with plates and cutlery and napkins, during which I try to gauge Shaw's reaction to what I just said, or even if it counted as a reaction at all. Needless to say, I'm not hungry, and the artfully arranged food in front of me looks deeply unappetizing, almost like something from a Surrealist painting. It also occurs to me that I might have gotten a detail wrong—maybe you strip companies to the bone *before* an IPO?

"So, Teddy," Shaw says, after his first couple of bites, "that was a nice little speech and all, but you didn't answer my question."

Which was?

Holding my fork over the plate, eyebrows furrowed, I try to remember, the delay now as much about avoiding the food as working out how to respond to Shaw.

"PromTech?" he says, nudging me along.

"Yes." I put the fork down. "You want . . . you want me to *sign.*"

"Of course. But what I really *want* is harmony. What I really *want* is for Paradime to show a united front. Is that so much to ask?"

I have no idea what to say, because, let's face it . . . harmony, a united front, it sounds reasonable, but is that what Trager would think? I have to admit I'm lost here and skating on very thin ice. I don't know PromTech either, or what their deal is. Actually, I can't even believe I'm having a conversation with Doug Shaw. The thing is, I find all of this thrilling, but part of the thrill is knowing I'm only ever a few seconds away from everything imploding. Because what if Teddy Trager were to call Shaw up right now on his cell phone, or to walk in the door of the restaurant? Or how about *this?* What are the odds—if I actually make it through lunch here—that when Shaw goes back to the office, the first person he meets, wearing a different suit and talking about *going for lunch*, is Teddy Trager? Pretty high, I'd imagine, so in a way does it really matter what I say? Where I take this?

"Well, you see," I say, picking up my fork again, "that's exactly what I'm talking about, Doug. PromTech. We need to wean ourselves off this kind of thing, I don't know, these . . . sugar-rush start-ups, these . . ."

Shaw laughs for a second, then shakes his head. "Are you *drunk*? These start-ups are our bread and butter for Christ's sake."

"Yeah, but . . . it's . . ." I'm floundering now. "It's all short-term thinking, it's—"

"Okay, okay, okay." Shaw waves this away, dismisses it. Then he says, "Tell me. How's Nina?"

"*Nina?*"

"Yeah." He takes another bite. "Tall chick? Good-looking?" He smiles. "What's going on with you guys?"

I want to throw a counter jab here but realize I know nothing about Shaw, if he's married, gay, attached, whatever. I don't know anything about Nina either. But I do remember reading this one thing.

"We're good," I say. "She keeps telling me she wants a baby, though."

Shaw nods his head. "Yeah, I can see that. You should go for it. Nothing like a kid to give you a little perspective on things."

Lost for a response, I maneuver a small slice of the hamachi onto my fork and raise it to my mouth. I feel sick, but pop it in anyway. As I'm chewing the food, I look at Shaw, but he's already cleared his plate and seems distracted now. He keeps glancing around, checking his phone.

When it comes time to leave, I have a brief moment of panic. Brian arrives with the check, Shaw is texting, and it looks as if I might have to pull out my wallet, which is worn and faded and only contains a photo of Kate, two maxed-out credit cards, a MetroCard, and twenty dollars in cash.

But without looking up from his phone Shaw reaches out and grabs the check.

A few minutes later, standing on the sidewalk in front of Barcadero, I still feel a little sick and know instinctively that getting into the cab Shaw is hailing will end badly, so I tell him I have a "thing," an appointment, that it's nearby, a couple of blocks east, and that I'll be around . . . maybe later, maybe tomorrow.

As the cab pulls up, Shaw says, "Just remember who you are, Teddy. Remember *what* you are." He opens the door, and holds it for a moment, gazing along the street. Then he turns to me. "And let's keep our eyes on the *real* prize, okay?"

He gets in, and I stand there, watching, as the cab pulls away again and disappears in traffic.

I go straight home and, without changing out of the suit, grab my laptop, sit at the kitchen table and start researching PromTech. It turns out they're just what you'd expect from the name, a tech start-up . . . robotics, drones, quadrotors, nano solutions, all that stuff. They operate out of a lab in New Jersey, probably some windowless, stinky, estrogen-free geek pit, but the guys there must be cooking *something* up because it seems that Paradime—or Doug Shaw, at least—really wants to fund them. After that, I look up Shaw, and the first thing I find is a Bulletpoint.com profile by Ray Richards with the header "The Other Side of Paradime." It describes Shaw's legendary deal-making skills and goes into detail about his activities prior to, during, and after the late-nineties dot-com bubble. It also transpires that he's married and has a very young daughter, with a second one, from a previous marriage, in high school. He does a lot of charity stuff and likes Broadway musicals. None of this does anything to quell the sick feeling in my stomach. I found Shaw weird and his attitude opaque.

But towards the end of the piece, he is referred to as "probably the one man who knows Teddy Trager better than Teddy Trager knows himself," and it concludes with the observation that Shaw's only real rival in Tragerworld is Nina Schlossmeier.

So I switch my focus to her.

I hit Google Images first, predictably, but man, there's plenty to look at—glamorous Nina wearing Tom Ford, casual Nina in a Windbreaker on the side of some mountain, Nina at a web summit, Nina on the red carpet. She's a native New Yorker, brought up in Tribeca, but her parents, both artists, are German. She speaks the language, it appears, along with Russian, Italian, and Japanese. A couple of years ago she founded Pincer, a search-engine app, and built the proprietary algorithm herself. Although she has led the start-up to profitability, the company is apparently still small, and Trager has had no direct involvement in it.

I look her up on Twitter and scroll through her feed for a while. Then I search around for some video and find a YouTube clip from an interview she did for a TV profile of Trager. In it, she talks quite frankly about her relationship with him.

"It's not easy, that's the first thing, because a guy like Teddy can't be tied down, you know, his head won't let him, it's taking him in too many directions at once. But I understand that, and I support him. I mean, what am I going to do?" She laughs here, leaning towards the interviewer, her laugh full and generous. "Rein him in? *You* try it. Good luck with that. Listen, every day with Teddy is a challenge, every day is an adventure . . ."

I pause the clip and linger over the still of Nina on the screen. How long would I last talking to her? Lunch with Doug Shaw was a strain, but would I even get through five minutes with Nina? Someone who expects me to make every day of her life an adventure? It's preposterous. And it's not just that she's out of my league in the crass sense of her being too good-looking for me. What did that profile say? She built the proprietary algorithm herself? She speaks fucking *Japanese*?

Yeah.

Still, I can't look away and am sort of mesmerized by her now—the expression in her eyes, her intelligence, her overall quality of "high-ness." Whatever that means. High cheekbones? High German? (High Anxiety?) I eventually take a screen grab of the frame and print it out. It's on plain paper and the quality isn't very good, but I lay it down on the table next to the laptop and glance at it every now and again as I continue reading and following links, burrowing down into a rabbit hole I have no idea how I got into or how I'm going to get out of.

At some point (I've lost track of time, but it must be late afternoon), I hear a key in the latch and look up to see Kate coming in. She sort of slopes through the door, flicks it closed, and leans back against it. She's still dressed up, which is when I realize that I am too (and inexplicably, it must seem to her). Then I remember how I ended our phone conversation earlier.

Mid-sentence.

In the street.

Mid *her* sentence.

Bad enough doing it so abruptly, but not calling her back? There's no excuse that'll undo that, and I'm not going to try. Besides, I have a sudden feeling that what happened earlier might not even be on her agenda anymore.

"What are . . ." She's still leaning against the door and has a quiz-zical look on her face. "What . . . no, *why* aren't you at work?"

I hesitate, but then just say it. "I quit."

"Oh." She furrows her brow. "You *quit*?"

"Yes." I don't know what I can add to that.

"Well, that's nice. I guess. For *you*."

She stands there staring at me, looking a little confused, as though I'm out of focus or something, and then I get it—I *am* out of focus, because she's shit-faced, or approaching it.

"Why are you wearing that God-awful suit again, Danny? Did you have another interview?"

"No," I say, shaking my head (and shock-absorbing the "God-awful"), "I didn't."

Pushing back at the door, she launches herself gingerly across the room. When she gets to the table, she reaches over, and before I can stop her, before I realize what she's doing, she picks up the printed screengrab of Nina Schlossmeier. After studying it for a couple of seconds, she says, "So, who's your girlfriend?"

"It's no one."

"Oh, come on, Danny." She's swaying slightly on her feet now. "I'm sure the nice lady wouldn't like to hear you say that. She's *very* cute."

I find the sudden collision here between reverie and reality unnerving, which maybe explains how I'm able to say what I say next. "Kate, have you been drinking?"

Her response is a grunt mixed with a laugh. "Oh, I think you could say that." Staring at me, she holds up the sheet of paper again. "So. Who *is* this?"

"It's *no one*." I roll my eyes. "Jesus."

Then, within seconds, we're arguing, full-on, about the picture, about the phone call, but eventually about everything . . . money, commitment, the apartment, our future together, when (or if) we're ever going to have a kid. It's no surprise that we end up *there,* since the question is something we've discussed so many times before.

"I DON'T KNOW, KATE."

But when I say this, when I shout it, I simultaneously bang my fist on the table, causing Kate to recoil, as though from an explosion, and something in the room changes, there's a dynamic shift—in temperature, or mood, or even at some molecular level—because right in front of me Kate recovers, she regains her equilibrium and almost visibly sobers up. She sits down at the table, looks into my eyes and starts trying to engage with me, rationally, to connect. Fighting back tears, she describes a recent conversation she had with Harold Brunker about the complex nature of PTSD and how it can present in a whole variety of ways.

". . . so maybe, I don't know, *maybe* it could help explain—"

I swallow. "Explain *what*?"

She shakes her head in what looks like disbelief. "*You,* Danny . . . explain *you,* and what's been going on. You haven't been yourself lately, you need *help,* you—"

I bang my fist on the table again and stand up. "What, so this is the support I get?"

"*Danny.*"

"You go sneaking off to Harold fucking Brunker and talk about me behind my back? You *diagnose* me? What's next? More medication? A straightjacket?"

Kate deflates, seeming tired all of a sudden, and maybe halfway back to being drunk—but not empowered drunk this time, not smart-ass drunk. More the drained, addled kind.

"No, Danny, of course not." She looks up at me. "But you . . . you're not alone, you know . . . listen, they say at least ten or twelve percent of returning—"

"Oh *please,* Kate, you have no idea about any of this, no idea what you're talking about at all."

I take the sheet of paper from the table, the picture of Nina. I crumple it up into a ball and fling it across the room. My anger is real, but there is an element of misdirection to it, of calculation. Because I don't want to talk about this stuff, I can't, I'm too far gone in the other direction—and while I might not know where that direction leads, it's more real to me now than anything happening here in this room.

Which is why I have to leave it.

I close my laptop, pick up my phone, and head for the door. As I'm going out, I look back. Kate is still sitting at the table, slumped forward now, her head in her hands.

I go to a bar on Second Avenue, thinking that if she can drink in the afternoon, then so can I . . . except that now it's late afternoon, early evening really, and the place I've come to is filling up with a noisy after-work crowd.

Besides, I don't really want a drink.

I order a club soda and sit at the bar with my phone. Within a minute I'm scrolling through Nina Schlossmeier's Twitter feed again. Most of it is incomprehensible to me: references to tech stuff, Pincer updates, links to articles, as well as the occasional jokey or personal tweet. I go back to the top. This is her most recent one, from three hours ago: *Totally stoked for @pollylabelle's opening at the Carmine tonight. Be there or be polyhedral.* I google the Carmine. It's a gallery in Tribeca, off Hudson, about fifteen blocks from here, give or take.

I nurse my club soda for another twenty minutes or so and then leave. I walk across town, moving slowly, block after block, a warm tinge of dusk seeping into everything. When I get to the Carmine, the place seems fairly quiet and dark. It's barely recognizable as a gallery, and, apart from its big windows, looks more like a warehouse or an abandoned factory.

I stand in a doorway across the street, watching, waiting. But soon, and as though I'm somehow conjuring it up, lights come on inside the gallery, then town cars and limousines start arriving, and people appear from everywhere—hipsters, arty types, collectors, critics, photographers—so that within minutes, literally, the joint is jumping, and Polly Labelle's opening is in full swing.

Nina Schlossmeier's entrance is unmistakable. She emerges from the back of a black SUV, alone, and glides inside. I watch from my post across the street as the energy of the event, the heat of the room, seems to coalesce around her. I realize I'm in the grip of some kind of fever now and that nothing will satisfy me except one thing.

To be there, in the room, standing next to her.

I keep glancing around, checking my phone, delaying, expecting Teddy Trager to appear, but as each minute passes, I become more firmly convinced that he isn't going to.

So on an impulse I propel myself forward, cross the street and walk straight into the gallery. I continue moving, like a targeted drone strike, until I'm in Nina's direct line of vision.

"Teddy," she says, as I close in. "Oh my God, I thought . . ." Then she smiles and holds up her glass.

I'm unsure how to read this, but I think it's okay. And in what feels to me like only a few seconds, a glimmer, the next twenty or thirty minutes disappear down some weird sinkhole, part dream, part hallucination. Nina parades me around, introducing me to one bizarre group of people after the next, then introducing me to Polly Labelle herself and getting me to pledge what will easily be the biggest sale of the night, and the centerpiece of Polly's exhibition, *The Circle of Willis*. I nod along, saying, "sure, sure," my throat so dry I feel I'm on the point of asphyxiation. Then, slightly panicked, I pat my jacket up and down to imply that I've left my wallet at home, but this just cracks Nina and Polly up.

After that, I find myself being led by the hand and taken through a maze of hallways and corridors to a cramped, dimly lit back office, where Nina shuts the door, locks it, and turns to face me. Leaning forward, she takes a firm hold of my belt and, before undoing the clasp, whispers in my ear, electrifyingly, *"Teddy, I'm so glad you made it tonight . . ."*

In another glimmer, I find myself rolling off a hastily cleared mahogany desk, and, as Nina reassembles herself in the corner—muffled, distant music thumping in the background—I notice for the first time that the walls of this little room are eerily adorned with dozens of framed black-and-white photos of the city's high-society gallerati, most of whom I don't recognize, though out of the corner of my eye I do spot De Niro, and there's Mario Batali, and there, in front of me now, wielding a champagne flute, looking directly out—looking, in fact, it seems, directly *at me*—is Teddy Trager.

I feel a rush of guilt here, but also, as I glance over my shoulder at Nina, of dread, because in the afterglow of such intimacy how will it be possible, I wonder, for us to talk to each other, to even look at each other, without the truth becoming immediately apparent. But a combination of Nina's phone going off, a burst of raucous laughter out in the hallway, and a strange forward momentum sweeps us back into the main exhibition space.

At a certain point, Nina is whisked away for photos with Polly, and I slip outside. It's ostensibly to get some fresh air, but once I start moving, I can't stop, driven forward by a dynamo of thoughts spinning inside my head, a flickering blooper reel of the past half hour, the past few *weeks*. Was that me trying to negotiate a garter belt? Was that me cheating on my girlfriend? Was that Danny Lynch stalking some billionaire tech guy he bears a resemblance to—stalking the man like an overexcited web rat who's ventured out of his mom's basement? *Jesus.* At the end of the block, on the corner of Hudson, I look back towards the gallery and feel dizzy. I keep walking, but it doesn't take me long to realize that I'm heading back the way I came, that I'm heading east . . . that I'm . . .

What? Going home? Back to the apartment? To Kate?

After what just happened?

On West Houston, I hail a cab and tell the driver to go uptown. I get him to stop at 57th and Sixth, and for a while I circle the area. I'm still operating on nervous energy, but I eventually slow down and come to rest on a stretch of the sidewalk directly opposite the Tyler Building. I give it a few minutes, then cross over, step onto the plaza, and head straight for the entrance. The security guy lets me in, no questions asked, and within seconds I'm in the elevator and surging up towards the fabled seventieth floor. I wonder who'll be up here. Maybe Teddy Trager? Who knows? If he is, though, wouldn't the security guy have been puzzled just now? Whatever. I don't really care anymore, and perhaps there's even a part of me that hopes Trager *is* up here, that we'll get to look each other in the eye, and even talk.

When I emerge from the elevator, the first thing that hits me is the coruscating Manhattan nightscape. I walk—almost stumble—across reception, and apart from the Paradime logo, which is everywhere, I can't really focus on anything.

"Mr. Trager?"

I turn, and a young man is standing next to me with a bottle of chilled water on a small silver tray. I look at him for a moment and then take the bottle. It's actually quite welcome. I hold it against my cheek, close my eyes and exhale. Then I open my eyes again and look around. The place isn't deserted, as you might expect, but it's not busy either. Most of the offices are visible through lightly frosted panels or walls of glass. I can see Doug Shaw, for example, in his huge corner office, slumped behind a desk. He's on the phone, facing away from reception.

The young man is still standing next to me, and I turn back to him. This is going to be a weird question, but I ask it anyway.

"Which office is mine?"

A barely perceptible twitch is all he reveals of his surprise. "Of course, Mr. Trager. Please, follow me."

As he leads the way, I open the bottle of water and take a long slug from it. Trager's office is similar to Shaw's. It's on the opposite corner of the seventieth floor and is bigger than everything around it. The young man holds the door open for me.

"I'm sorry, sir," he says, "but Mr. Shaw asked me—*again*—to leave those papers for you to sign. They're on your desk."

I mumble something, dismissing him with a nod. I head straight for the desk, settle into the swivel chair behind it and just . . . *swivel*, slowly, rhythmically. Because this is it, this is the seat of power. This is the heart of Paradime's corporate empire.

But what happens next? Where do I take this?

And how long before someone calls security?

I glance around the office and, after a moment, catch sight of my reflection in a large window opposite where I'm sitting. Disconcerted, I lean forward in the chair and gaze at the image. Is that who I've become? *That* guy? A venture capitalist, a speculator with a portfolio in the billions?

I lean back in the chair and swivel some more.

Though how hard can it be, right? As work, I mean. You sit around all day making phone calls, reading quarterly reports, trying to pick winners, signing shit? The truth is, I'm not sure you'd get a cigarette paper between one of these VC guys and your average degenerate gambler studying racing forms at Belmont or Saratoga.

Just then my eye falls on a neat stack of papers in front of me on the desk. I stare at it for a while. I pick a few pages up and flick through them. It's no surprise that the name PromTech jumps out at me, though nothing else I see here makes much sense. It's financial jargon, legalese. It's a contract.

But now it's my *job*, as well. At least in theory.

So—I find myself wondering—is PromTech a winner? Does it have form? I look around for something to write with. I scan the desktop, then rummage through a few drawers. I soon find a very elegant silver fountain pen.

But how does this guy sign his name?

I go through a bunch of other stuff in the drawers and eventually find something with Trager's signature on it. I copy it out several times on a separate sheet of paper and end up doing it quite well. Then I identify where in the documents I have to sign. There are twelve places, but spread out over three separate copies of the contract. In each place, Doug Shaw has signed, as have two others, people from PromTech, presumably.

I hold the pen suspended over the first page.

Fuck it. Here goes.

I sign twelve times, getting faster as I go, and when I've finished, I toss the pen back onto the desk.

There. Action.

Or forgery, more like. Malicious personation, fraud. Whatever it is, it should get me a decent slice of jail time.

I lean back in the chair now and close my eyes.

Fuck.

Is this what I wanted? Power? Wealth? Respect? When all that could possibly be on offer was just the fleeting illusion of these things? The shiny surface of them? What a jerk I've been—indulging this fantasy, going on this inverted and insane tour of duty, behaving recklessly.

Stupidly.

And *meanly.*

I open my eyes and take out my cell phone. Swiveling again, I call Kate and, after a tense initial exchange, ask her to just *listen* to me. Then I tell her—solemnly, almost whispering—that I'm really sorry, that my head is a mess, that I've done some fucked-up things, and that, yes, maybe I do need some kind of help, treatment, therapy, whatever, but that more than anything else in the world I don't want to lose *her,* I don't want to lose the future we have together . . . *that I love her* . . .

"Well, then," Kate says, audibly stifling tears, "get off the phone and come *home,* you moron."

This is a huge relief to me, and after I put the phone down I sit for a while in the stillness of this empty office, taking it in, processing it. But when I'm ready to leave, to get out from behind the desk, I look up and see, through a layer of frosted glass, the blurry but unmistakable figure of Doug Shaw approaching from the far side of reception.

I flop into the chair again and sigh. Are we at the end of the line here? Are the security guys on their way over too?

Shaw soon appears in the doorway. He stands there for a moment, looking in.

"You okay, Teddy?"

"Yeah."

But I'm not, and this is weird. I let the mask slip there by making that call to Kate, and I feel as if Shaw should somehow know this and be using my real name.

Calling me Danny.

He enters the room and walks over to the desk, almost sidles up to it. He eyes the documents. I glance at them myself, having more or less forgotten about them. He picks a wad of pages up, simultaneously slipping on his glasses, and flicks through them. He cracks a thin smile.

"You signed them?"

I nod again, but don't say anything.

"Well, *that's* an interesting development."

But he seems a lot more than interested. He seems excited, and maybe a little agitated, or even confused. He picks up the rest of the pages and shuffles them all together. Holding them against his chest now, he moves away from the desk and across the room. When he's at the door, he turns and looks back.

"I'm glad you did this, Teddy." He pauses. "And stick around, yeah? I'm going to make a couple of calls. Then I think we need to have a proper talk. And maybe a drink? To celebrate?"

"Sure."

After Shaw leaves, I stand up. What the fuck did I just do? Green-light the PromTech deal? Okay, on one level, *cool* . . . but on another, does it matter, and do I really care? No. Teddy Trager would have signed in the end, he would have succumbed, that seems inevitable to me, because after a certain point with these people money isn't about what it can get you anymore, it's all just numbers, and the acquisition of it becomes its own motivating force . . . a little money, a lot, an obscene amount, what's the difference? It's a joke. Whereas *I* don't even have enough of the stuff (it's just occurring to me now) to get a cab ride home, having blown most of my last twenty bucks coming up here.

But at least I have a MetroCard.

I go to the door, and hover in front of it. I'm nervous. I don't want to be seen, but reception is pretty much deserted now, so I head straight for the elevators. As I'm waiting for a car to arrive, I look back over at Shaw's office. It's hard to tell, but there seems to be something going on, a flurry of activity. Shaw himself is on the phone again, pacing up and down, staring at the floor as he talks. The young man who greeted me with the water earlier is standing near the door, consulting a tablet. And a young woman is leaning over the front of Shaw's desk. She appears to be rearranging some papers.

An elevator car pings open, and I slip inside.

I have no idea what just happened up here, what's real anymore, what isn't, but as I descend to ground level and make my way out of the building and along the street to the nearest subway stop, and as I sit on the train, and then walk the last few blocks to my building, I know I've had enough, that I'm done here, that it's over. But an inevitable consequence of this realization is that my sense of desperation reboots. Because making up with Kate on the phone like that? The rush of emotion? The flood of honesty? The declaration of love even? None of that is going to pay the rent or clear the bills. None of that is going to ward off a future of shitty, soul-sapping jobs . . . a future in which people like me and Kate are disposable, in which we're little more than monetizable data points in some algorithmic sequence. And is that what I *want*? For her? For me? For the kid we've so often nearly conjured up in conversation? A life of attrition? A future that is circumscribed, constricted, already bankrupt?

Is there any choice?

When I'm about half a block from my building, I slow down, almost to a crawl, not because I'm changing my mind or having second thoughts . . . it's because up ahead I see something that obliterates any possibility of thought. Parked along the curb there is a distinctive-looking, ultramarine-blue sports car, and leaning against it is a man who's about my height and build.

I stop, and he turns to look at me.

8

Teddy Trager steps forward from the car. Within seconds we're in front of each other—three feet apart, right there on the sidewalk. At first, all I can do is stare at him. I'm aware of traffic sounds, of people passing by in either direction, of the suit he's got on, but mostly I'm aware of his face, its familiarity, its growing strangeness, its sudden unreadability.

"So, tell me," he says, breaking the silence. "What's your next move?"

I don't know what to say here. I don't *have* a next move. All along, this has been an extended trance, a fever dream. I shake my head slightly but don't say anything.

"Well?"

A part of me wants to reach out and touch his face, check if it's real—to check if *he's* real.

"There is no move," I say eventually.

"Come on." His voice is soft and measured. "You must have something in mind." He makes a gesture with his hand. "I mean . . . all of *this*?"

What does he mean? Is he referring to *my* suit? I'm not getting into that with him. I'm self-conscious enough as it is. Besides, I have more immediate concerns. Like how he knows who I am and where I live. Like what *his* next move is. But my mind is tripping over itself now, and the question I manage to ask, in a whisper, is as basic as it gets.

"What is this? *What's going on?*"

Trager shrugs. "Nothing really. It's just that . . . I know a lot of people, as I'm sure you're aware, and I thought . . ."

"Yeah?"

"I thought I might be able to help you in some way."

"*Help me?* Look, Mr. Trager, where did you—"

He holds a hand up to stop me, and then nods at his car. "Come on, let's go for a drive, cruise around for a bit, talk." He pauses. "And by the way, it's Teddy."

I feel sick. Is this *happening?*

Leaning back slightly, I look to the left and up at our building. I look at our fourth-floor window. Where Kate is waiting for me, right now.

I'm assuming.

I turn back and look at Trager, barely able to focus. What if I'd come home, I wonder, walked up the stairs, opened the door, and peered in to see *him* there, with Kate reassembling herself in the corner . . . a muffled bass thumping through from the next apartment and the kitchen table swept clear, everything strewn on the floor . . .

"How about it, Danny?"

"Okay," I say.

I'm nervous, but as I follow him over to the car, I feel an unexpected rush of excitement. I've read about how he likes to drive around at night, how that's when he does his best thinking, so there's no reason why this shouldn't at least be interesting. I settle into the passenger seat and Trager starts the car. It hums softly to life, takes off, and soon we're on First Avenue, heading uptown.

Trager does most of the talking and seems to know a lot about me. When he mentions Gideon and Afghanistan I must act surprised, because he picks up on it.

"Don't you realize," he says, "how easy it is to accumulate data about someone, once you get a line on them?"

"But how did you get a line on *me*?"

"A simple tail at first, a bit of surveillance, a background check. You didn't exactly make it hard."

I swallow.

They're watching you like you're a video game, Danny.

I look at Trager. "Yeah, but when did you—"

"Does it matter?"

"Was it your driver? That day outside the Tyler?"

"Yes. But *I* could have spotted you just as easily."

And he's right, I suppose. I was there a lot. "So, what did . . ." I'm not sure how to frame the question.

"What did I *think*?"

"Yes."

"Well, I . . ."

But then he goes silent for a while, seems to be giving the question serious consideration. We pass 23rd Street and get a run on the lights. Then, after he turns west onto 34th, he starts talking again, riffing on the idea of doubles, the doppelgänger. "So what exactly is it, a ghostly replica? An evil twin? A foreshadow of something awful? A foreshadow of *death*?" He shakes his head. "No, that's all bullshit, because you know what, Danny? It's a coincidence, pure and simple, I'm your look-alike, you're mine, and there's no mystery to it. We weren't separated at birth. We're not clones. Okay, we're pretty much identical, but the one thing we *don't* have in common is the same genes." He pauses. "Now what are the odds of that?"

I don't think he's expecting an actual answer.

"Well, let me tell you. Given the component parts of the human face, and the possible variations in their structure and arrangement— distance between the eyes, for example, width of the nose, shape of the cheekbones, skin texture—given all of that, the figure, apparently, is one in a billion, or a little under."

I want to say *holy shit,* but I just nod.

"They've made huge advances in this recently," he goes on, "in face-recognition technology, retinal scanning, biometrics. I think Paradime even owns a company that does this, but the point is, with *seven* billion people walking round the planet, what do you know?" He waves a hand back and forth between us. "It's like we have a winning lottery ticket here . . ." He seems excited, energized, as if this is a game or a puzzle to be solved. He keeps talking, getting into the science of it, the math, probability theory, even briefly sketching a couple of what I assume are supposed to be equations in the air directly in front of him. Then he gets into psychology, the nature of identity, of repression and alienation, he mentions Freud and Lacan, he talks about virtual avatars and the influence of video-game technology. I get fairly engrossed in what he's saying, and when I sort of snap out of it for a second to look around, I'm alarmed to see that we're on the Hudson Parkway, moving north, and moving pretty fast too.

I want to ask him where we're going, but I don't want to interrupt his flow either. He's the same charismatic Teddy Trager I've seen in multiple YouTube clips, but up close like this the experience is different. It's more immediate, and a lot more compelling.

"So that's what we have here, Danny, it's just one of those things in nature, a weird anomaly—and don't get me wrong, I think it's truly amazing—but it *can* be explained. It doesn't have to be magic, or a metaphor for something else. I mean, we have science. We understand now that a clap of thunder isn't the roar of an angry god. We don't worship the sun anymore." He pauses. "We're rational beings, right?"

Weirdly, I think he *is* expecting an answer to this one.

"Yeah, sure. Of course."

After another silence, he says, "I researched all of this, after you popped up on my radar. I got curious. But I guess what I'm wondering now is, how do *you* feel about it? Because it seems to me like you're maybe a little confused, or . . . thrown off balance by what's happening."

I look at him. "What do you mean?"

"That suit you're wearing, for instance. Quitting your job. The fact that you've been more or less stalking me." He clears his throat. "My guess is that—"

"Sounds like *you've* been stalking *me*."

"No, no," Trager says, shaking his head, "that was in reaction to what *you* were doing. Look, my guess here is that you've been under a tremendous amount of pressure lately, still are, in fact, and that this . . . this thing, whatever it is, has sent you—and understandably— into something of a tailspin."

"What? That's . . . ridiculous."

"Oh, you're *not* under pressure? Is that what you're telling me?"

"No . . . I mean, okay, I *am*, but . . ."

"Afghanistan, right?" He turns to me for a second, then looks back at the road. "There was a situation at the base, people got killed, there's legal fallout, Gideon are screwing with you, the banks won't leave you alone, you've got debts, you can't find work, whatever . . . look, I get it."

Am I hearing this right? He *gets* it?

"Okay, Danny, that probably sounds a bit rich coming from some-one like me . . . but I mean it. And when I said I might be able to help? I meant that too."

I consider this for a moment. "Help how?"

"There are various ways." He taps his fingers on the steering wheel. "And believe me, Danny, I know how to do it. I run a couple of foun-dations. I gave away four hundred million dollars last year."

I've read about his charity work all right, but none of it really sank in. It didn't seem that interesting at the time.

"Why would you help *me*?"

He shrugs. "Isn't it obvious? *Look* at us. The thing is . . . I feel . . ."

"What?"

He waves a hand in front of him, as though trying to summon an answer from thin air. "Well, I feel a sense of responsibility. Is that in-sane? And despite what I said earlier about being rational . . . I have to confess something." He laughs. "I'm finding this incredibly weird. Aren't you? Not only do I *feel* like I'm talking to myself, I look at you and realize that I actually *am*." He laughs again. "And *you* are too, right? I mean, like it or not, we have something here, we're connected in some way. So of course I'm going to try and help."

I'm confused. My initial resistance to Trager is quickly breaking down. He's charismatic and forceful, there's no denying that, but he seems sincere too. Is that possible? Or is it just that he mentioned money a moment ago and I *want* to believe he's sincere? I look around again. We've left the city well behind us now and the Hudson has become the Saw Mill. Where are we going? Someplace upstate?

Trager shakes his head, and shrugs. "Sorry to talk about money like that, by the way. You must have thought I was trying to impress you or something. I wasn't."

"I know." Now I actually am warming to him. "I've read about your foundations," I say. "I've read quite a bit about you, in fact." I pause. "I'm a good stalker. Attentive."

"I wouldn't expect anything less."

We let this little icebreaker work its thing for a while. Trager focuses on the road, and I focus on the car's interior, on the rich, creamy leather upholstery and the polished mahogany trim.

Then he says, "You know, the thing is, I more or less made my money by accident. It was all about timing, all about being one of those special-ed übergeeks who comes along with a really cool idea at *just* the right moment. In my case, I'm talking ten, twelve years ago . . . I was young, I was naive, the markets had a hard-on for anything tech-related, investors were circling. What could go wrong?"

"But you did well."

"Yeah, I did well, by *any* standard, but man, when that spigot opens up and starts gushing out money, there's no way of stopping it, and it changes everything."

"How so?"

"You end up playing the game, whether you want to or not. You end up sitting across boardroom tables from people who spend every day of their professional lives behaving like cornered rats." He turns to look at me for a second. "What, you think if you put on an expensive suit it'll all be nice and civilized? Like that's some form of protection? This is a war zone. Forget Afghanistan. Forget Iraq. Forget *Vietnam*. You want the real *Apocalypse Now*, watch Bloomberg News, read the *Wall Street Journal*." He exhales loudly in exasperation. "I gave this talk at a university once, a few years ago, you can see it on YouTube, it was meant to be a kind of mission statement where I tried to lay out an alternative vision for all of this stuff. But you know what? No one took any notice, because the ironic thing is, the richer you get, the less people actually listen to your words, all they can hear is the sweet fucking ka-*ching* of your money . . ."

"But isn't that what you do? Invest in companies? Aren't you a money *guy*?"

"Yeah, I am *now*, but that's because I have so fucking much of the stuff. It becomes its own self-replicating system. It takes you over. It's a trap." He makes a snorting sound and bangs his hand on the steering wheel. "I know, I know, you should have *my* problems, right? *Jesus*. Tell me to shut up."

"No, no, I'm . . . I'm . . ." enthralled, is what. But I'm not going to say *that*. "It's okay, go on."

And he does. "So lately I'm doing some work with this company called Prometheus Technologies, right? PromTech. And it's incredibly exciting, the ideas that are spinning around that place, you'd love it, it's like DARPA on steroids, or CERN, big data, adaptive systems, the singularity, AI, longevity, biometrics, remote DNA tracking— *that's* a revolution right there—but you know, take your pick, it's all long-view stuff. I mean, these guys are essentially redrawing the map, or it's like they come from the future or something. But you know what their problem is? They haven't got enough money. It's insane, almost hilarious. And they want *us* to fund them, and officially we, as in me and my partner, want to fund *them*, but you know what? I'm not going to fucking allow it, because we'll just end up infecting them with our own special brand of toxic shit."

Staring at the road ahead, I feel as if my heart is being slowly dipped in liquid nitrogen.

"You see, here's the thing," Trager goes on, "one of the products they have in the pipeline is a new type of VR game console, they're calling it the LudeX, and it's pretty amazing, but still, it's just a fucking game console, it's a toy." He waves a dismissive hand in the air. "With money behind it, though, it'll burn through the hype cycle and dominate the market, I know it will. I also know from experience that that kind of success will destroy PromTech, it'll sideline all their other ideas and distract them from the bigger picture."

"Your partner," I say, almost in a whisper, "that's . . . Doug Shaw?"

"Correct. Now, he's really anxious to get his hands on the LudeX, because he sees the potential in it. He had the contracts drawn up weeks ago and has been bugging me to sign them, but I'm not going to do it. I'm *not*. I made that mistake once before in my life, and it's not going to happen again. I don't care. I mean, how rich can you be? It's absurd."

"But . . ." I close my eyes. "Won't someone *else* just give them the money?"

"Sure, probably, I can't stop that from happening. It won't have been *me*, though. That's the point. That's what matters."

I open my eyes. "What about Shaw?"

"What about him? Everyone knows we have our issues, I've talked about it, so has he, in interviews, it's common knowledge, but really, the stuff that's going on now, it feels like a line in the sand for me . . ."

It's the weirdest thing. This is the Teddy Trager I know from what I've been reading (and whose positions, as a result, I was able to parrot earlier to Doug Shaw), but this is the first time I've actually listened to him, this is the first time that what he's saying seems real to me. In fact, the only thing that doesn't seem real to me at all—or true—is what *I* did about an hour ago up in Trager's office.

In the silence that follows, I look around me. Wherever we are, the roads seem quieter, less busy. I don't remember us leaving the Saw Mill, but we're on a back road now for sure, trees and hedgerows on either side, the moon ahead of us periodically visible through a busy rush of passing clouds. I run various scenarios through my head, but it doesn't take me long to conclude that those documents I signed will have no legal standing whatsoever. And of course once Trager realizes what I've done, any talk of being rational will almost certainly evaporate. As it probably *should* . . . because if there are now going to be two Teddy Tragers in this world, in whatever form, *I'll* be the one who signed the contracts, *I'll* be the version that sold out, *I'll* be the one who crossed that line in the sand . . .

That's what's in my head when Trager suddenly starts talking again, when he asks me about Kate and whether or not we want to have kids. I'm taken aback, but I say, "Yeah, sure, some day. I mean, we've talked about it."

"Man, do you know how lucky you are? Even to have the possibility of a child, of a family? There's no form of wealth that can compare to that."

I'm not sure what's going on here. The obvious thing would be to turn the question back on him. What about you and Nina? Didn't I read somewhere that . . . ?

But I can't bring myself to do it.

"Yeah," I say, "you're probably right."

"No, Danny, really. I envy you."

Envy? It sounds as if he means it, but at the same time, under the circumstances, isn't that a little over the top?

"So let me get this straight. You'd step into *my* shoes, is that it?" I just blurt it out.

"No, Danny, *no*, that's not what I meant. It's just that . . ." He pauses. "My girlfriend and I have been trying, and, you know, when it doesn't work out . . . it's not easy."

I stare straight ahead and say nothing.

"There are other options, sure, but . . . it's a big adjustment to make."

There is silence for a while. Then he says, "Do you know her? My girlfriend? Nina?"

"Uh, no, I don't think so."

"Nina *Schlossmeier*? If you've read about me, you've definitely read about *her*."

I swallow. So it *is* a game. Trager knows. He *has* to know. He's had me under surveillance, hasn't he? That's what he more or less said.

We're on a fairly quiet road now.

Holy fuck.

This is *his* move.

I nod my head. "Well, yeah, I . . . I've come across the name."

"Sure you have."

It's obvious what Trager is up to here, leading me on, being my friend, offering up confidential information. He's playing a game of cat and mouse. But who'd blame him after the shit I've pulled?

And especially tonight.

I'm too tired for this. I lean back in the seat and groan. "Okay, okay."

"What?"

"I swear, Teddy, I didn't mean for it to happen."

"Didn't mean for what to happen?"

My heart is thumping so hard I can actually hear it. "You have to believe me—"

"Didn't mean for *what* to happen?"

"Tonight, me and Nina, we just—"

"What are you saying? *We*? I don't . . . *what*?"

Trager swerves the car and turns sharply onto an even quieter side road. There's an open field to our right, trees to our left.

"Teddy, please—"

"You and Nina? *Where*?"

What have I done?

"At the . . . gallery, at . . ."

"At the Carmine? At Polly Labelle's thing? You can't be fucking *serious*."

He's driving really fast now.

"I'm sorry."

He bangs his hands on the steering wheel. "You're *sorry*? This is unbelievable."

"I didn't set out—"

"Don't."

"I mean, look, she was—"

"Don't say another fucking word."

I take in—and hold—a very deep breath.

"Let's be honest," Trager says after a moment, "you're the one who wants *my* life. You want all the shit *I* have, the money, the status. And you know what? Fine. You think I care? But Jesus Christ, my *girlfriend*?"

I'm torn here between the horror of remorse and a nagging confusion. "But you saw everything happen, Teddy, you were watching, why didn't you stop—"

"I saw it happen? What are you, insane? *How* did I see it happen?"

"You said it yourself, surveillance—"

"Surveillance? Not twenty-four-seven. Jesus, don't flatter yourself. That was just to get some background on you . . ." He bangs the steering wheel again. "I came to *you*, Danny, because I wanted to see if I could help. I mean . . . *look at us* . . ."

I turn and see that he's got tears in his eyes.

"We've been given this incredible opportunity, this once-in-a-*billion* chance to . . . no . . . oh shit—"

"What?"

"I can't . . . Jesus . . . *I can't* . . ."

I look straight ahead, at the dark, open countryside plunging towards us.

What the fuck?

Trager is pounding the steering wheel now, going crazy, dancing on the pedals, it seems like—then—"Get out, Danny! Get out of the car! Get out of the car *now!*"

"WHAT?"

In one rapid movement, he reaches across me, clicks my seatbelt loose and flicks the door open.

"Get out! *Now!*"

Then he's pushing me out. It's like he's gone completely insane. But at some point my reflexes kick in and I simultaneously reach up and grab onto the sun visor with one hand and lash back at Trager with the other, striking him hard across the side of the face, drawing a spurt of blood. There's a renewed effort on his part, and soon he's edging me off the leather seat. My hand has slipped from the visor, and I'm hanging out of the car, precariously lodged between the side skirt and the open door. I pull my knees up to my chest and just let go. I roll on impact, hitting the ground with my bunched forearm and then with my shoulder. I keep rolling and end up on a grass bank by the side of the road.

The car speeds on.

A moment later I'm dimly aware of a second car speeding past, and then I hear a sound—it's quick, loud, very intense.

With great effort, I manage to stand up. I move off the verge and back onto the road. I'm able to walk along the side of it for a few yards, fuelled by adrenaline—but I'm limping, and groaning, various pains announcing themselves as I move. My jacket and pants are torn, and I can taste blood in my mouth.

It's sort of dark, but there's a reddish glow in the sky, reflected light from a nearby town probably, and the moon, when it appears, is extremely bright. Up ahead, there's a slight curve in the road, and, when I reach it, I see something in the dimness a little farther on. I have a fair idea of what it is, what it *must* be. I keep going and eventually get to Trager's car, which is rammed up against a tree, the front of it crushed like a beer can.

No sign of the second car.

But . . .

There *was* a second car, wasn't there? I glance around. It's very quiet. It's late. I'm not sure of anything anymore.

I move closer to the car and look inside it. Trager is slumped in the driver's seat, his neck twisted, a streak of blood on the side of his face.

He's clearly dead.

Holy fuck.

Teddy Trager is *dead*.

A single, clear question forms in my head. What just happened? What just happened? *What just happened?* Trager was really angry—and, okay, with justification, I can't argue with that—but he pushes me out of *a speeding car?* That's the kind of shit you get to pull when you're a billionaire? I switch my gaze from Trager's face to my own clenched fist, to the corresponding streak of blood on it, and I almost throw up. I was acting in self-defense, that's obvious—that's *obvious*—but did my punch to his face make him dizzy, cause him to lose control and crash the car?

Fuck.

Then something occurs to me. There's no airbag. Why is there no airbag?

I look around and try to focus. I do a quick, panicky rundown of my options. One, get the hell out of here right now, run and keep running until I'm far away. Two, wait for the cops to arrive, come clean, explain everything—it'll sound weird, sure . . . but it was just an accident, this last part, the crash part, Trager was out of his mind, out of *control* . . .

"But sir, if that's the case, why do you have traces of Mr. Trager's blood on your fist?"

Fuck, fuck, *fuck*.

A cell phone goes off, fracturing the stillness, and I freeze. It has to be Trager's. Because it isn't mine. I let it ring out, but once silence is restored, I stand there paralyzed. Almost immediately the phone starts to ring again.

I reach into the car through the open door and extract the phone from Trager's jacket pocket. The small screen swims before my eyes. It's a blur. But I can just make out the name on it: Doug Shaw. Again, I let it ring to the end. Then I put the phone away—this time into my own pocket.

As I stand there, pain throbbing faintly beneath icy sheets of adrenalin, a third option forms in my mind. But without allowing it any time to unravel or choke on its own absurdity, I dive right in. I lean forward and start going through Trager's other pockets, taking out his wallet and keys. I then go around to the other side of the car. The door is buckled and I have to force it open, which is difficult, because as my adrenaline ebbs it's becoming increasingly evident to me that I have sustained serious injuries. Nevertheless, drawing on some sort of override mechanism, I proceed to pull Trager's body out of the car. When I have him on the grass, I look behind me.

There are more trees, lots of them, and I think I can hear the sound of a river or a stream somewhere in the background. I lean down, take a hold of the body and drag it—wheezing, grunting, struggling, swearing—until I get it maybe twenty yards off the road. There's a steep incline here that ends at the edge of what is indeed a small river. I roll the body part of the way down, as far as it'll go, and then do my best in the near darkness to cover it up with loose branches and leaves.

At one point, as I'm standing there, out of breath, there's a break in the clouds, and moonlight briefly illuminates the misshapen heap in front of me. It looks like something else at first, I don't know what, I'm confused, and then it looks like what it *is* . . . a partially covered dead body. And in the fraction of a second it takes me to turn away, I catch a glimpse of my own face, a greyish, bluish version of it, streaked with something darker, blood or mud, probably both, its eyes open and staring vacantly back up at me . . .

Feeling dizzy, I move a few steps away. Then, as I limp up the little hill again, I take out my phone. It's on silent, but there are four missed calls from Kate, as well as a single, all-caps text from her that says, "WHAT'S HAPPENING?" Seeing this message on the tiny display is like a severe punch in the gut. It yanks me back to the reality of what *is* happening, and of what I've just done. I want to hit Reply, but I can't bring myself to do it, because how do I explain this? And apart from anything else, this body here behind me will be pretty much *visible* in daylight, it's not as if I've buried it or anything, nor is there any prospect, in these circumstances, of me being able to . . . so once tomorrow morning comes, what are we looking at? What's the window? How long before someone takes a walk by this river?

I'd say a few hours, at best.

And then what? All hell breaks loose? The initial, queasy confusion pulls into the tight focus of an OMG news story? I'm hunted down, arrested, end up in prison or the psych ward?

But . . .

Backing up a little here, what did I think was going to happen? That I'd finally become Teddy Trager? That I'd take his place? That I'd get to live his life? That I'd get to spend his money? That if there weren't going to be two Teddy Tragers in the world, couldn't there at least be *one*? Even if only for a short while? The level of this delusion is breathtaking and certainly not anything I can subject Kate to—not anymore, she's already put up with enough shit from me as it is. But at the same time, there's really no reversing this. It's not as if I can decide to go for option two instead and drag the body back up to the car. I wouldn't be able to. I'm in too much pain. And, let's face it, I wouldn't *want* to. I've set this little exchange program in motion, so whatever the fallout from that turns out to be—and however fast and relentlessly that rains down on me—I'm going to have to take responsibility . . . for everything.

Which I guess means I'm on my own.

After a moment, I turn around and toss the phone—*my* phone—back in the direction of Trager's partially covered body. I do the same with my wallet and my keys. It's a vain gesture, I know, an impotent protest, little more than a cheap piece of misdirection that won't fool anyone for very long.

But I don't care. I limp back towards the mangled car. I take a deep breath and climb in—this time into the driver's seat. I look at my face in the rearview mirror, at the smears of blood and the bruising. I lean back in the seat and exhale, trembling—first a bit, then a lot, then shuddering. Soon this will be uncontrollable, and as the pain intensifies, as the general trauma overwhelms my stress response, pummels it and then smothers it, I may go all the way and lose consciousness. In fact, I can already feel this beginning to happen, but before it does, I reach into my jacket pocket and take out Trager's cell phone.

I fumble with it for a few seconds, then lift it to my ear. I wait, but not for long.

"Nine-one-one, what is your emergency?"

9

Before I open my eyes, I know I'm in a hospital room. There are tell-tale sounds—beeping monitors, ventilators, pagers, carts. At first, these seem abstract to me, more like faint rumbles and pulses, signals from somewhere deep in my unconscious, but they soon coalesce into the comprehensible and the familiar. I also feel an uptick in pain awareness. This is nothing alarming, a fact that I'm sure can be explained by the woolly blanket of medication—morphine, probably—that I seem to be wrapped in.

Although it's easier not to, I do eventually open my eyes, and what strikes me at once is that no healthcare plan *I've* ever been on would provide a hospital room even remotely as luxurious as this one. It's an entire suite, with a comfortable seating area, a coffee table, and what from here looks like . . . *a wet bar*? That's not right. I squint and do my best to stay focused, but I can't make out what it is. Probably some kind of medical unit.

But that raises a more important question. What am I doing here in the first place? I clearly *need* to be in the hospital, because there's a ton of shit wrong with me that I'm only now becoming aware of—these tubes attached to my right arm, for instance, the bandages around my skull, the swelling I can feel in my face.

But what *happened*? And where's Kate?

Faint memories rise to the surface . . . a rotating blue light, the intermittent crackle of a dispatcher's radio, urgent voices all talking at once—but after that, there's nothing.

Before it, though, if I concentrate . . .

Fuck.

Of course.

Everything comes back to me in a rush. Panicking, I look around the room again. What time is it? I can't see any windows. How long have I been here? Without thinking, I move forward suddenly in the bed, and feel a jolt of pain. It starts in my chest and extends across my right shoulder. I lean back on the pillow, and, as the pain recedes, I take a long, deep breath and release it very slowly.

So . . .

Hospital, yes, okay, but why *this* one? I don't even *have* a health-care plan.

There's only one explanation.

My cheap piece of misdirection is still working. Is that possible?

I look around the room again, this time for clues. There's a bed-side table to my left with nothing on it apart from a reading lamp and a glass of water—but it does have a drawer, which is partially open. With great care, I ease the drawer all the way out. There's something inside it, I'm not sure what, but it looks like a see-through evidence bag. I fish it out and hold it up. Inside it, there's a cell phone, a set of keys, and a wallet.

The wallet isn't mine—it's too big, too thick with credit cards. They're not my keys, either. And it's not my phone. These items are Teddy Trager's, but taken from the pockets of the suit *I* was wearing.

How long can this go on? Is it now a race between someone finding the body by the river and a doctor realizing that my lab results don't square up with Trager's medical records? It has to be one or the other.

I look over at the door and get the feeling that someone is about to walk through it. I replace the bag in the drawer and gently close it. A couple of seconds later, a young nurse breezes in, consulting a chart as she moves. When she looks up and sees me, she stops. "Oh, Mr. Trager, you're awake . . ."

The next few hours see a steady stream of nurses, doctors, consultants, and therapists into the room, a level of attention you'd imagine maybe the president getting, after a heart attack or an assassination attempt. I have multiple opportunities to call a halt to it, to look some highly qualified trauma specialist in the eye and tell him to stop, that I'm a fraud. But why would I? He's a trauma specialist, and someone just pushed me out of a speeding car. It also seems to me that if I'm headed for prison, which has to be a real possibility now, I need to be in better shape than I'm in. Apparently, I have a couple of broken ribs, some other minor fractures, severe facial bruising, a concussion, and possible abdominal injuries, so . . . what, I'm going to *refuse* this treatment?

Anyway, it's easy enough to take. I don't have to say much, apart from answering simple questions about whether a specific part of me hurts or not—which is something I can answer without having to pretend I'm someone else. Also, the pain medication provides me with a cloak of passivity, of anonymity almost, as does—I find, to my shock, when I get to look in a mirror—the extensive bruising on my face. Apart from the medical staff, no one else comes into the room (at least not as far as I'm aware), but at a certain point during the course of the day I do notice that in the hallway outside there appears to be some kind of a security presence. Is this more of the executive-branch standard of treatment I'm getting here or should I be worried?

I go with worried.

There are too many reasons not to. A guard outside my door? No visitors? The high probability that Trager's body has been discovered by now? Plus, there's the fact that to any trained specialist worth their salt my injuries would surely be inconsistent with the physics of the accident I'm *supposed* to have had. Because wouldn't a collision like that—at high speed, with no airbag deployed—have killed me outright? As it actually *did* kill Teddy Trager? And wouldn't some of these specific injuries I do have, in their assumed context, make no medical sense whatsoever?

If I'm right about this stuff, I don't get any indication of the fact from a single doctor or nurse.

What I do get, early in the afternoon, is a visitor.

Doug Shaw comes into the room followed by one of the consulting physicians, a lean guy in his sixties with a salt-and-pepper beard, and the two of them stand by the door for a few minutes talking. I don't hear what they're saying. The doctor leaves, and then Shaw walks over to the foot of the bed. He doesn't speak. He just looks at me, examining my injuries, tilting his head this way, then that, as though *he* were a doctor.

I'm awake, and my eyes are open, but I sort of play up how spaced out I am by staring at a fixed point on the wall behind where Shaw is standing.

"How are you, Teddy?" he says eventually.

I don't react, don't even look at him.

"A lot of people are asking about you."

After a moment, Shaw sighs loudly, then gets his glasses and cell phone out and starts texting. He paces the room as he does this, stopping every couple of seconds to check what he's just keyed in. When he's finished, he looks over at me again.

"Who?" I say.

"Who what, Teddy?"

"Who's asking about me?"

"*Everybody.* Holy shit." He whips his glasses off and comes over to the side of the bed. "I mean, yeah . . . and look, the story got out, I tried to keep a lid on it, but you know how it is." He seems kind of agitated, like he's coked up, or just had a drink and needs to know where the next one is coming from. "Anyway, Jesus. So how *are* you?"

"I could be better."

I then stare at him, in silence, and for maybe ten seconds straight. Does he *know*?

I'm sure he must, and I'm on the point of being reckless, of telling him to cut the bullshit, to drop the act, when something gives me pause, some instinct for self-preservation. Because what if it isn't an act? What would that mean? And more to the point maybe, what if it *is*?

"So tell me," I say instead, drawing in a deep and obviously painful breath. "What about Nina? Is *she* asking about me?"

"Of course. Yeah. She was in here all last night. She sat there." Shaw points at a comfortable-looking but empty chair next to my BP monitor. "But she had to leave early this morning for some *thing*, some event, in . . . where is it, Phoenix?"

I nod, implying that I know what he's talking about.

But really—I think—Phoenix? The other side of the country? I have to ask myself what Nina saw or maybe heard last night, sitting in that chair, looking at me.

"And your sister called from Paris," Shaw says, "a couple of times, but we've reassured her—*I've* reassured her—that you're going to be fine."

I nod again.

I have a sister? How did I not know that? Trager, of course, is what I mean. How did I not know that *Trager* has a sister.

Had a sister.

"Anyone else?" I ask, after a moment.

"Yeah, there have been a lot of calls, messages, people wanting to drop by, but . . . you know, let's give it a little time. You're not ready yet." He pauses. "That's what the doctors are saying."

I look at him for a moment.

Sure they are.

Then I close my eyes.

And they're right, of course. I'm not. They just don't know how right.

Over the next few hours, whenever I open my eyes, Shaw is there in the room, or just outside it in the hallway. He spends a lot of this time on the phone, and every now and again his PA shows up with some document to be looked at or a paper to be signed. I want to tell him that he doesn't need to stick around like this, that I'm fine (that I'd actually prefer him to leave), but I never feel quite up to it. I'm still on a morphine drip for the pain, so my response times are slow, and whenever an opportunity arises I either miss it or deliberately let it slide.

But this is also, in part, because I'm confused about what's going on. Why hasn't Trager's body been found yet? Why haven't the cops shown up? It's been more than eighteen hours. And if Shaw doesn't know what's really going on here—and let's just say for argument's sake that he doesn't—why is *he* the one in charge? Where are Trager's people? *His* PA? *His* staffers?

The screw on my paranoia tightens when I tell Shaw that I want my laptop brought in—or at least access to a device, an iPad, something, so I can catch up.

"Uh-uh," he says, shaking his head, "not such a good idea."

"Excuse me?"

"That doctor? The one I talked to earlier? He said screens are out of the question, it's not safe apparently, not even TV . . . at least until they've done an EEG or an MRI or whatever it is they have to do. I guess it's the concussion, something to do with brain-wave activity?"

I look around. There's a TV on the wall, turned off, but no remote anywhere. I don't buy this brain wave activity shit for one second, but I'm not going to argue with Shaw about it. When he's out of the room for a few minutes I open the drawer of the bedside table and take Trager's phone out of the evidence bag. I try to activate it, but nothing happens. It's dead. The battery must have run down, and, of course, there's no charger.

Later on, after Shaw has left for the night, I go through Trager's wallet. There's five hundred dollars in cash in it and about fifteen different pieces of plastic—credit and charge, as well as various security and membership cards.

Maybe I should just slip out of the hospital with it and take my chances.

But then . . .

Using any of these cards would be asking for trouble, and how long would a lousy five hundred bucks last? There's also the matter of this guy out in the hallway, my security detail. I don't know what his instructions are exactly, but in my current condition—two broken ribs and high as a fucking kite on painkillers—do I really want to risk finding out? Besides, given the level of medical attention I'm getting, and which I actually need, it'd be pretty stupid of me to go anywhere right now.

What I do instead is ask one of the nurses on the night shift if she can hook me up with a laptop or an iPad . . . ten, twenty minutes is all I need, a little session, I tell her, with Dr. Google. When she hesitates, I spot her one of the fifties from Trager's wallet, and that does the trick. A while later she returns with a colleague's iPad, and I launch into a quick trawl through the past twenty-four hours . . .

No body by the river, that's the first thing—the *NYT*, the *Post*, the *Daily News*, a couple of smaller local papers, a site that tracks police reports even—nothing. How could that be? Then there are these: "VC Maven in Single-Car Collision" and "Wall Street Car Crash." In the financial sections, it's a little less lurid: "Paradime Partner in Auto Accident" and "Teddy Trager Injured." But that's it—short reports, light on detail, no photos . . . Trager's car hit a tree on a quiet road, he's in the hospital, his injuries aren't life-threatening.

Nothing to see here . . .

I check Nina's Twitter feed. Her last tweet was that one about the event at the gallery. I also check a few blogs and come across several brief references to the accident, but it soon dawns on me that these, along with the newspaper reports, can all be traced back to what must have been a press statement released early yesterday by Paradime's head office, a statement that was probably drafted—or at least approved—right here in this very room.

After I give the iPad back to the nurse, I fall asleep and have a dream about the other night—I'm in Trager's car, but with Doug Shaw . . . one minute *he's* driving, then *I* am, then we're in a Humvee . . . or is it a . . .

Whatever.

It's a fucking dream, it doesn't have to make sense.

But when I wake the next morning, it seems clear to me that I've been in thrall to the dream aspect of this whole thing for far too long. Yesterday, for example, I was asking myself if Shaw knows. Today that seems like a ridiculous question. Of course he knows. He *must* know. Trager knew, and, as he said in the car, *I* made it pretty easy for him. So either Trager shared his discovery with Shaw or Shaw found out for himself. It would go some way towards explaining how weird he seemed over lunch at Barcadero that time and then later on up in Trager's office. But why is he acting like he *doesn't* know? What is he up to? Other questions naturally flow from this—like, for instance . . . does it have anything to do with PromTech? Why did Nina feel compelled to put over two thousand miles between herself and this hospital room? *And what happened to Trager's body?* But a wave of exhaustion hits me and my mind fogs over. Soon, it's as much as I can do to submit to having my dressings changed.

A bit later, Shaw reappears and announces that I'm going to have a few visitors this morning—it'll be quick, five minutes each, no more, and all I have to do is attempt a brave smile, nod wearily, and listen. This is one of those weird moments when I feel like Shaw isn't even pretending. He's just *telling* me what to do. But how would that go down if I were the real Teddy Trager? Not too well, is my guess, and I'm on the point of calling Shaw out on this—because I *am* weary—when his cell phone goes off. He answers it, listens for a moment, then looks at me. "Okay," he says, "we're up."

We?

He turns to face the door, and waits.

Both of us now waiting.

But for what? The Homicide Division? The Fraud Squad? A couple of psychiatric orderlies, one with a hypodermic syringe in his hand and the other with a straightjacket?

The man who walks through the door is familiar-looking, but it takes my brain more than a beat to pull up his name—which is a little worrying, given how famous he is.

George Clooney greets Shaw with a quick handshake and then approaches the bed. When he sees my facial bruising up close, he puts on a pained expression. "Oh man, that's rough."

I look at him. This is a tanned, suave Hollywood A-lister standing in front of me. If it weren't for the morphine, I'd probably be a little flustered right now. "Well," I say, "you should see the tree."

Clooney laughs.

I shoot a glance at Shaw, who's over in the corner, smiling nervously.

"So. Are they treating you okay?"

"Take a look," I say, making a sweeping gesture with my arm, indicating the room, how nice it is, how spacious, but the sudden movement hurts, and I wince.

"Whoa . . ." Clooney winces too, in sympathy. "Take it easy there, Teddy."

I roll my hooded, morphine eyes at him. "It . . .'s fine."

Me and George.

I have to wonder . . . are we buds? Have I been to his place on Lake Como? Am I involved in some campaign of his? I don't remember reading about this, but I may well have. It wouldn't have seemed real to me at the time, so I wouldn't have paid that much attention to it. Weird thing is, *this* doesn't feel real either. So what have I got to lose?

"When they're making the biopic," I say, pointing at my bruises, "will your vanity be able to handle these?"

"Oh, what, *The Teddy Trager Story*? Yeah, right." He does that thing, makes that face. "I'm a bit old to play *you*, Teddy, don't you think? Even Matt's too old for *that* role. Besides—" He pauses here, weighing up his words. "Somehow, I don't see . . . I don't see a script getting out of the development process *alive,* frankly." He clears his throat. "Not if there's any contractual obligation to, you know . . . take any of *your* notes seriously."

"Oh, fuck you, George."

I'm not looking at him, but I can tell that Shaw's face has probably drained of all color by this stage.

Clooney reaches over and gives my arm a gentle squeeze. "I'm going to let you get some rest, Teddy."

I wink at him and then watch as he turns and walks out of the room. I observe his shape and posture. Out in the hallway, there is something of a commotion, and I can feel it, reverb from the huddle of heat-seeking attention he must attract wherever he goes.

Fifteen minutes later, the next visitor comes in, and I don't recognize him at all. He seems to be some kind of investment guy and is obviously someone I should know. I exaggerate my grogginess and let him do most of the talking.

Shaw seems surprised afterwards. "You didn't know who that was?"

It's a bold question and could easily open up an awkward conversation here, but I just shake my head.

"That was Ray Dalio, Teddy." He pauses. "Bridgewater Investments?"

Trager would obviously know this name, he probably goes fucking *skiing* with Ray Dalio, but with me any name is a crapshoot—I might or might not have come across it in an article or on a web site. What this brings home to me again is that being Teddy Trager is a tricky business, fine in small doses, when I can walk away and take off the suit, but pretty much a minefield in any kind of extended situation.

And I'm certainly in one of those now.

I look at Shaw. If he isn't going to blink, though, neither am I.

"Sure, Doug. Bridgewater. Ray Dalio. I knew that. I'm just having a little . . . brain-wave trouble is all."

"Well, you won't have that problem with your next visitor." He glances at his watch. "I can guarantee you that."

My twenty minutes with Bill Clinton has a dreamlike quality to it. He pulls a chair up beside the bed, leans in, locks eyes with me, and just talks—quietly, flowingly, nonstop. I barely listen, but I think he's filling me in on some initiative we've been working on. The conversation, such as it is—the monologue, more like—is conspiratorial, dense with detail, and exhausting.

When he's gone, though, I miss it, and while I have no idea what Shaw's grand plan here is, it's becoming increasingly clear to me that *my* cooperation, *my* continuing compliance, is an essential part of it. And unless I'm imagining things, there's now a sort of unspoken agreement between us: so long as I go on looking and sounding like Teddy Trager, Shaw will see to it that everyone else treats me as if I *am* Teddy Trager.

And I think it remains unspoken for a reason.

If Shaw acknowledges that I'm Danny Lynch, a line cook from North Carolina—or if *I* acknowledge it—that will break the spell. It will undermine his plan.

Which gives me a certain degree of leverage.

Because while I don't know what's in this for Shaw, it has to be a lot, and if I play my cards right, there might well be something in it for me too.

Later on, I slip the night nurse a second fifty from Trager's wallet for a little more iPad time. That's when I come to realize just how high

149

the stakes are. Because it's not the real Teddy Trager who's out of the picture now, it's the real *me*.

A full forty-eight hours after I left Trager's body by a river in Westchester, there is no mention of the fact anywhere on the web. What there *is* mention of, however, and as reported in yesterday's *Post,* is a corpse floating in the Hudson River off of West 42nd Street in Hell's Kitchen. The NYPD responded after a witness called it in, and soon afterward the body was pulled to shore at Pier 81. The victim, a man in his early thirties, was fully clothed—in a suit, apparently—and had ID on him. There were some signs of trauma, but the police are still waiting for the Medical Examiner's Office to determine an exact cause of death. They're also not releasing the victim's name until his family has been notified.

I stare at the screen. That could be anyone, though, right? The Harbor Unit probably have to do this a couple of times a week.

But if it *is* just anyone, why does it feel so wrong? Why does it feel like I've been sucker-punched here?

I go to Metro and scroll down through the stories for today. And there it is: "Man Found in River Named."

My eyes burn as I try to focus and make sense of the words on the screen:

The identity of a man who cops fished out of the Hudson River early yesterday morning has now been officially confirmed by his girlfriend. A distraught Kate Rozman named the thirty-three-year-old Iraq veteran from North Carolina as Daniel Lynch. Previously employed as a line cook in a Manhattan restaurant, Lynch was heavily in debt and was said to have been struggling with unaddressed mental health issues. No foul play is suspected, and police are not looking for anyone else in connection with their inquiry. Funeral arrangements have yet to be made.

Holy shit.

I read the piece again.

Holy shit.

If you ever need to get things in perspective, you know what'll do the trick? Seeing a reference to your own fucking *funeral arrangements*. But that's not the hardest part about this. For me, what's even harder is reading about Kate and how distraught she was. Because it was never my intention to hurt her. Obviously. Much less to put her through anything like this.

But could I have anticipated it? Anticipated that someone—people, Shaw, I don't know, *whoever*—would exert the influence required to have a dead body moved from one location to another and then have that body officially passed off as mine?

As *me*?

It's insane.

One thing it does tell me, though, is that whoever's behind this is deadly serious. And that what they're serious *about*—I can only conclude—is me.

The next morning I have to undergo another round of tests and some physio, and by the end of it I'm exhausted. However, one of the doctors tells me that I'm in pretty good shape—no internal damage, nothing showing up in the PET scan, and that going forward, as the various fractures heal, it'll just be a question of pain management.

Not bad, I'm tempted to point out, *for a dead guy*. But I resist, and instead put a simple question to him. "Okay, if that's the case, when can I check out of here?"

The doctor hesitates, squinting at his chart, clearly unwilling to commit to an answer. It's as if he thinks he's said too much already. But I let this go, because the answer is pretty obvious. All things being equal, I could probably walk out of here right now.

When Doug Shaw appears a while later, I put this to him.

"*What?*" he says, phone in one hand, takeout coffee in the other. "You crashed your car into a fucking oak tree, Teddy. I don't think you're ready to hit the streets *just* yet."

Maybe it was unconscious on my part, but this is exactly what I was hoping he'd come out with. "Well," I say, "that's not what happened, Doug. Not to me anyway. And I think we both know that."

Shaw stops, and his shoulders seem to slump in resignation. After a moment, he puts the coffee down, then glances in my direction, but without saying a word or even making eye contact. For some reason, he doesn't look well this morning. He's pale, tired-seeming, as though he's sick, or hungover maybe.

"Doug?"

He holds his free hand up. "Just give me a minute, will you?"

Then he looks down at his phone, keys something in, and brings it up to his ear.

"Yeah, Karl, please."

As he says this, he's already walking out of the room.

I watch him go.

Why is he acting so weird? And who is this Karl person he suddenly needs to talk to?

I wait ten minutes, then fifteen, then twenty, during which time my resolve evaporates. It was stupid to show my hand like that. Shaw has huge resources at his disposal—influence, money, a private security apparatus. What do I have? My *face*? Shaw wants to "use" me, to take advantage of my uncanny likeness to his business partner, fine, but if I prove to be a liability in some way, slipping out of character at inopportune moments, how long will I last? How long will Shaw's patience last? How long before I end up following myself into the fucking Hudson River?

I pull the covers aside and am about to get out of the bed—about to try and make a break for it—when the door opens, and Shaw reappears.

Sighing, I close my eyes and slump back against the banked-up pillows. How far would I have managed to get? A few yards along the hallway? Down to reception? Even if I made it out of the hospital, where would I go in any case? The apartment? So I could give Kate a massive heart attack? Which, assuming she survived it, would swiftly be followed by all sorts of other trouble—financial, legal, emotional—every last bit of it my fault?

"Okay," Shaw says, "listen carefully."

I open my eyes. He's standing next to the bed and looks distracted, sweaty, anxious, like this *really* isn't how he imagined his day shaping up.

"We need to have that conversation," he goes on, "the one we've been putting off . . . but we're not going to have it here, we're not going to have it in the hospital." He takes a deep breath. "Anyway, I spoke to"—he waves a hand behind him—"some of the team, and, okay . . . yeah, we can . . . we can move."

"Move?"

"To your apartment."

"Oh." I have a quick, disconcerting vision of Shaw standing in the living room of our cramped walk-up on 10th Street. "I see . . ."

But that can't be what he has in mind.

"So, Doug," I say after a moment, and as discreetly as possible, almost in a whisper, "remind me, where do I live again?"

10

The Mercury is a condominium skyscraper on the northern edges of what everyone is now calling Hudson Yards, a zone that's shaping up to be Manhattan's biggest makeover of an entire neighborhood since Battery Park City. But the Mercury predates this development by a good fifteen years. It was meant to spearhead the project, but zoning issues got in the way, followed by the financial crisis, then by *more* squabbles between developers and city planners. "You know, the usual story . . ."

I *don't* actually, and why it's something Shaw feels compelled to share with me as we move across town in the back of a limo I'm not really sure. Maybe it's a form of displacement, a way of further delaying this conversation we're supposed to be having.

Anyway, the apartment itself—which is on both the eighty-second and eighty-third floors—turns out, in every respect, to be nothing less than eye-popping. I'm accompanied up by Shaw and two assistants, and we're then greeted in the vestibule by a small domestic staff. I move slowly, nodding at each person in turn.

Shaw tells me he has urgent business to attend to at the office, but that he'll be back later. As he glances around the apartment, and then at me again, he seems more anxious than ever. I try to let him know he has nothing to worry about, not on my account. He seems to accept this, but he also can't help leaving me with the impression that at no time will I actually be alone here. I take this to mean . . . what? I'm not sure. That I'll be under constant surveillance? That some of the domestic staff report to *him*? Even if neither of these things is true, of course, the mere suggestion of them is enough to make me behave as though they are.

Nevertheless, when I *am* alone, or as good as, I take the opportunity to have a look around. Flooded with natural light, the apartment is very spacious, and everything in it—being made of either marble, steel, or glass—seems to reflect this, and to amplify it. The whole place is oddly clinical and sort of forbidding, not unlike a spread in the *Architectural Digest*. It does have these amazing multi-angle views, though, and from pretty much every room. But while the apartment is so high up that no one except maybe a helicopter pilot would have any chance of invading your privacy—of catching you in the middle of a lewd act, say, or even just parading around in your boxers—the uncomfortable feeling of exposure this generates (and I'm getting it after only ten, fifteen minutes) is relentless and inescapable.

Essentially, the place doesn't have a lived-in feel to it, and there's nothing I'm seeing that gives me any indication of what Trager was like as a person. There are no traces of Nina Schlossmeier, for instance, no what you might even call feminine touches. The closet off the main bedroom is certainly impressive, with its incredible array of suits and shirts and shoes, as is the bathroom, which is about twice the size of any regular person's entire apartment. But I have to admit that it's the billiards room, the swimming pool, and the walk-in humidor that really sell me on the place. Because with all of that going on why would you ever need to leave? I mean, holy shit, you want a lived-in feel? Give me a week here, give me a few days, and I'll *show* you a lived-in feel.

An impediment to this little fantasy getting off the ground, however, is the domestic staff—I counted five of them earlier. Do they *live* here? The very idea of having servants, live-in or not, makes me uncomfortable, and that's without considering the possibility that these people might already be spying on me.

So what am I saying? I want out? I can't handle this? I don't know. Maybe. I'm still in a lot of pain, still on medication, and that can interfere with your judgement. Is it dampening my perception of the threat level, for example, or merely ramping up my paranoia? Who knows? But as I go from room to room now, walking slowly, careful to avoid any sudden movement, my mind has time to wander, and it occurs to me that there's plenty of what looks like valuable stuff here—ceramic bowls, glassware, pieces of sculpture, a series of small paintings that line the main hallway (one of which, I *think,* is an original Picasso)—my point being that with the proceeds from a single item, discreetly lifted from the apartment, I could probably clean up financially and avoid a lot of unnecessary trouble . . .

But while this is a tempting plan all right—and several notches up from the one I had at the hospital of just lifting Trager's *wallet*—really, on reflection, it'd be nowhere near as easy to execute as it sounds. And how do you go about disposing of stolen valuables anyway? Especially when you have no underworld connections? How do you say the word "Picasso" without setting off alarm bells? And, what's more, how do you operate in a world in which—officially, at least—you no longer even exist?

By the time Shaw returns, a few hours later, I'm at the point of wondering if staying in the hospital mightn't have been a better option. I'm resting on a leather couch in the main, ballpark-sized living room, gazing out over the river at the Palisades, when he is shown in by one of the domestic staff.

And he isn't alone. He's accompanied by another man in a suit— late fifties, medium height, wearing rimless glasses.

As they approach, I sit up, but don't stand.

Opposite the couch I'm on there is a corresponding one, and Shaw sits there, hunched forward. The guy with him remains standing at a discreet distance behind it. Shaw still looks tired and anxious, but he also seems a bit more focused.

"Okay, Danny, I'm going to lay it all out for you, straight up, no bullshit."

I flinch at this casual use of my real name, and, even though it finally confirms what I've suspected all along, it still comes as a shock.

"The bottom line here is that you look and sound like Teddy, okay, but you're nowhere near as batshit crazy as he was—for which you should be grateful, by the way—but that means it's never going to be easy to pull off any extended encounters. This is why I've been trying to keep you more or less isolated. You need a little fine-tuning, to say the least."

In his quiet, gravelly voice, Shaw then goes on to explain that it was actually Teddy who brought the whole business to his attention, Teddy who told him about seeing this guy at Barcadero one night. For Teddy, it was exciting, a game, something he wanted to explore, to understand the meaning of. Shaw took a different view. He immediately saw an opportunity, the potential for a practical application of the thing.

The strategic use of a double.

"Which is nothing new, to be honest; kings and presidents have used them down through the centuries—body doubles, decoys, whatever. FDR is supposed to have used one, and Churchill too. More recently, you have Saddam Hussein, Putin . . . and probably others we don't know about."

"Yeah," I say. "But this is a *little* different, isn't it? Because presumably when Putin is using one, he's actually calling the shots." I glance at the man standing behind the couch, and then back at Shaw. "This isn't a decoy. This is a *replacement*."

Shaw emits a dry laugh. "It is *now*."

"Well, what was it before?"

"To be honest, Danny, it was all a bit vague. When Teddy first told me about you, I was intrigued. I tracked you down and took a good, long look at you, but . . . I didn't think it'd work. Frankly, I thought you were too unstable, and, for what it's worth, I still do."

Ignoring this last part, I say, "You didn't think *what* would work exactly?"

"Oh, I don't know, Danny. It was a tantalizing *idea,* that's all. It opened up some possibilities." He pauses. "And I explored them."

"On your own?"

"If this is the route you want to go down . . . yeah, sure, on my own. Teddy was becoming a liability. I felt he needed to be controlled or even contained. And this seemed like a possible way to do it."

I can feel my insides churning. "How?"

"I didn't think it through, Danny. There was no big plan." Shaw looks over his shoulder at the man behind him for a moment, then turns to face me again. "As I said before, I didn't think you were really suitable, so I had this biometrics company we own run data on it, to see if we couldn't find another match, maybe someone . . . easier to handle, let's say . . . but no one came anywhere *near* your numbers. So . . ."

"Yeah?"

"So we kept an eye on you."

Kept an eye on me? Jesus Christ. I exhale loudly. Is there anyone who *isn't* keeping an eye on me?

Shaw ignores my reaction. "How it would all proceed from there," he goes on, "was anyone's guess. There was no real strategy, and we were more or less improvising. Anyway, you pretty much took over the reins, Danny. Once you saw Teddy for yourself, you did all the heavy lifting, up to and including—and we couldn't have foreseen *this*—signing those papers." He makes a whistling sound. "But why did you run off like that? Why did you sneak out? Why didn't you stick around the way I told you to?"

I look at him and shrug.

"Of course we should have factored in how unhinged Teddy himself was, that he'd inevitably want to track you down again, and stroke you like a pet monkey." He pauses. "Right, Karl?"

The man standing behind him nods slightly, but doesn't speak. After a moment, Shaw waves a hand vaguely to his side. "By the way, Danny, this is Dr. Karl Lessing."

Now it's my turn to nod and not speak.

"Anyway, the point is," Shaw continues, "*we* may have been a bit behind the curve in all of this, but *you* went ahead and made your decision regardless, am I right? You moved Teddy's body. You got in behind the wheel of his car. You knew what you were doing. So let's be honest with one another here . . . you totally want this."

My stomach is still churning. I have about a dozen very specific questions I could ask right now, knotty procedural points in the main—timing, sequence of events, when people got to the scene, stuff that isn't clear to me or that doesn't quite add up—but it seems like there's really only one direction this conversation is going in.

"Want *what,* Doug?"

"I think you know what, Danny. But just so we're on the same page." He clears his throat again. "You get to *be* Teddy Trager. You get to wear his clothes and drink his liquor. You get to bang his girl-friend, drive his car, spend his money, whatever. You get to live *here*—I mean, look at this place—and, in return, you close the book on your old life, no contact, no crossover. You keep a low profile and let *me* take care of company business. And every now and again, as the necessity arises, you make a public appearance and endorse . . . whatever needs to be endorsed, whatever's going on with the com-pany at the time."

"And if I refuse?"

Shaw laughs. "Why would you do that? This is your ticket out of the shit, Danny."

"But if I did? For argument's sake?"

He exhales loudly. "I don't know. We'd think of something. We've got deep pockets. You've got nothing. Besides, you're into some murky stuff here already. Forgery, personation. None of that would play too well in court."

He's right. But I still need to understand something.

"If it's about control of the company," I say, "what do you need *me* for? Why didn't you kill Teddy off long ago, when he became a liability? Wouldn't that have been easier and less complicated?"

"Jesus Christ, Danny. *Kill Teddy?* What kind of people do you think we *are*? Teddy was my friend. He died in an accident."

I hold his gaze, and a long, tense silence follows. I don't play poker, but I imagine it's something like this. "*I'm* not your friend," I say eventually. "Why not get rid of *me*?"

Shaw leans back a little on the couch. "You're a trip, you know that?" He half turns around to look at Lessing. "I *told* you, Karl. This guy is fucking nuts."

Lessing takes a couple of steps forward and puts his hands on the edge of the couch. "No," he says quietly, "I don't think so."

There's definitely an accent here, German maybe.

Squinting slightly, Lessing studies me for a few seconds, then says, "He's puzzled, that's all. He's trying to understand why we would be doing this. He's goading you."

Not German, though maybe South African?

Shaw nods impatiently. "Okay, okay, I get it." He turns to face me again. "Look . . . like I said, there was no big plan here, no big design. Teddy dies in a car crash, it's tragic, but now we have this . . . *opportunity*. With you. Because the way I see it, Paradime as a brand, without the oxygen of Teddy Trager, even the illusion of it, is seriously diminished. Now, Teddy had his issues, stuff you don't need to know about, believe me, but at the same time he was unique, he had charisma, he had his very own, what do they call it"—he clicks his fingers—"reality distortion field. And here's the thing: the man brought a loyalty to the Paradime brand that *no* amount of money could buy. But now he's gone." He leans forward, lowering his voice to a whisper. "Except that he *isn't,* is he?"

I swallow, totally out of my depth now.

"Or at least he doesn't have to be," Shaw goes on, "because we have someone who can step into his shoes. We have *you*. Which means we have a shot at keeping this thing alive, this confidence that Paradime inspires, that keeps investors and fund managers coming back for more. Call it the Teddy Trager effect."

This is moving too fast. I shake my head. "But . . ."

Shaw tenses. "Yeah?"

"You said it yourself. You think I'm too . . . what was it you called me? Unstable?"

"Yeah . . ." He smiles. "But come on, what do *I* know? My esteemed colleague, the doctor here, took a good, long look at you as well, then drew up a detailed psychological profile, and he assures me that you have a steely resilience and a,"—he looks around briefly—"what was it, Karl, a rare capacity for adaptability? In fact, it was Dr. Lessing's idea to wait before having this conversation. He wanted to see how long you'd hold out before the pressure got to you. I *think* he was impressed."

I glance up at Lessing. We make eye contact this time, but his face remains impassive.

"So, Danny," Shaw says, leaning forward, "what's it going to be?"

I wonder what else is in this psychological profile they have of me. My attitude to Kate, for example. Do they expect me to just forget about her? I'm hesitant to say her name, to bring her into it, but surely a red flag will go up if I *don't* mention her? Equally, they might perceive it as an area of potential weakness if I do. So I'm left with *how* I mention her.

"Okay, Doug," I say, hands held up in mock surrender, "I guess I'll have to go for it."

"Great." Shaw starts moving off the couch. "So let's—"

"But—"

He stops, and looks over at me. "*But?*"

In spite of how unstable he thinks I might be, Shaw clearly feels

I'm locked into this on two fronts already—the first being fear (of the law) and the second, desire (for Trager's lifestyle).

But I'm about to give him a third.

There is resistance at first, mainly from Shaw, and then there's a bit of horse-trading. Whoever this Dr. Karl Lessing is, he has serious clout because Shaw defers to him on almost every point. Not openly—he does his best to conceal it—but the body language is clear.

What I tell them is that I am more than willing to go along with this, but, as chaotic as my life may well have been, even up to a few days ago, I can't just walk away from it . . . and specifically I can't—and don't *want* to—abandon my girlfriend to all the fallout. So I tell them to arrange it somehow for Kate's student loans, including all accumulated interest and fines, to be paid off.

Expunged, erased, whatever.

"And then I'm *yours*."

Locked in, triple down.

I know I'm running the risk here of confirming Shaw's worst fears about me, but it's the only move I've got. When they agree to it, I have to work hard not to seem too relieved.

"We'll figure out a way to do it," Shaw says. "It can't be that hard. Then we'll run the details by you. Okay?"

"Okay."

The quid pro quo comes pretty fast.

Shaw says there's a thing in the next couple of weeks he needs me to do, a TV interview—the two of us, only five, ten minutes, but it's important.

"PromTech?"

"Yeah. Teddy had a couple of the guys over there pretty spooked about this deal, so we need to shore that up, we need to show a united front."

"Doug, I may have signed those papers, but I have *no* idea—"

"Don't worry about that. We'll coach you through it. Right, Karl?"

"Of course," Dr. Lessing says, with a thin smile. "A little fine-tuning."

Shaw then gets up from the couch. "Okay," he says, straightening his jacket, "we'll get started on this tomorrow." Then he turns to me. "So, Teddy, we good?"

"Yeah," I nod, and glance out across the river, "we're good."

Good, that is, apart from the idea of appearing on TV. After Shaw and Dr. Lessing have gone, this looms large in my mind because it seems insane—the real-life equivalent of that dream where you find your-self naked in public. Why would you actively choose to do it? And in this scenario the whole thing gets pushed a little further into the thickets of dream logic by the fact that I'd be appearing as someone else but would still very much look like *me*.

I also wonder what they meant by "a little fine-tuning," but that becomes fairly clear the next morning when Shaw arrives, not with Dr. Lessing but with a guy about my own age, maybe a bit older, who turns out to be a voice coach. Tall and good-looking, Matt Becker has a booming, actorly voice, and it later transpires that he *is* an actor, as well as an occasional stand-up comic.

Anyway, Shaw sets us up, and we get straight into it. I do my Teddy Trager voice for Matt, and he pretty quickly tears it to shreds. At first, he says it's *okay,* but then basically has a note for every third or fourth word I say. He uses recordings and YouTube clips of Trager, and it's not long before I realize how much there is to this—cadence, timbre, register, rhythm, a whole bunch of shit you wouldn't normally think about. We spend hours at it, doing drills and breathing exercises, and Matt is very professional, very circumspect, making no reference to the fact that with no effort whatsoever I already *look* so much like the person he's helping me to *sound* like.

I'm assuming, therefore, that he's being paid really well, and not just for his skills but also for his silence.

From the next day, he divides his time with a colleague, a movement coach named Arturo, who works with me on posture and coordination, on gestures and hand movements. It's an intense few days that also includes regular visits from a doctor, a nurse, and a physiotherapist. Shaw stays away, and I don't leave the apartment at all, confining myself to just a couple of rooms. I have no access to TV or the Internet, nor do I engage with the domestic staff on any issues other than those relating to either food or laundry. This makes the whole thing feel sort of bootcampish, as well as a bit claustrophobic, but I accept it all because I guess I'm looking at this as a sort of trial period.

Anyway, by the fifth day I'm pretty satisfied with my new, deluxe Trager 2.0, but I'm also mentally and physically exhausted, so I decide to go for a swim. The experience of floating alone in a blue pool high above the streets of Manhattan turns out to be weird and relaxing in about equal measure. On my way back to the main living room, one of the staff members, a severe Korean woman in her fifties, appears and informs me that I have a visitor. My immediate reaction is irritation. Who is it? Some friend of Trager's? Some person I'm going to get tangled up in knots with as we try to hold a conversation? I can just see it . . . they think they know *me*, I have no idea who *they* are. It'll be a nightmare.

I step into the vast living room with its wraparound floor-to-ceiling windows. There is a woman sitting over on one of the couches. She has her back to me and seems to be gazing out at the deepening, red-flecked evening sky. As I get nearer, I realize that she's not so much a woman, actually, as a girl. She turns and smiles at me. "Hi."

Who is she? Trager's niece or something, the daughter of a friend? She's probably about sixteen or seventeen, possibly younger. She's wearing a small black satin sheath dress. She has pixie-ish blond hair, pale skin, red lipstick, and really striking blue eyes—eyes that have locked onto mine now and show no signs of letting go. "I'm Sabrina," she says, her voice a little husky. She then leans back on the couch, simultaneously crossing her legs and biting her lower lip.

Something catches in my throat, and I have to look away. I hold up a hand. "Sabrina, just . . . just a moment."

I turn quickly and walk out of the room. At the far end of the corridor I see the Korean woman, the . . . what is she? The housekeeper? I don't even know her name and can't call out to her. But I do get her attention, and, when she approaches, I tell her that I'm going out for a while and that when I get back I expect the young lady in the main living room to be gone. "Is that understood?"

The woman nods, with a slight look of panic on her face. "You go out?"

"Yes," I say, "out . . . *outside*," as it hits me for the first time that this might not be as easy as I think. But then I resolve *not* to think, to just go, and that's what I do, head straight for the vestibule, press the elevator button, and wait—aware all the while of a slight commotion somewhere, movement, voices, maybe from the kitchen, the Korean woman explaining, then another voice responding . . .

The elevator opens, and I get in, but as I descend to the lobby, I find it hard to contain my anger. Because what was that meant to be back there, a honey trap? A little insurance policy Shaw set up for himself?

When I get down to the lobby, I make straight for the exit, ignoring what seems to be a ripple of activity over by the desk involving the concierge and maybe one of the security staff. Outside, I hit the sidewalk, and, with traffic roaring past, I get about three blocks south before calming down enough to realize I don't have anywhere to go. I don't have any ID on me, or any money. I can't even go for a fucking drink. So what do I do? Go to 10th Street? Walk all the way *there*? But again, that option seems closed off to me. I can turn around here on Twelfth Avenue all right and retrace my steps to the Mercury, but that's not the same thing. It's as though there are two realms in this city, parallel and coexisting, and if you pass from one to the other, as I appear to have done, then that's it, you're stuck, there's no route home.

I turn around now and look up at this glistening tower of luxury condos dominating the night sky in front of me, and I have to say I find it ironic, even faintly ridiculous, that I have no choice but to go back in there, that I literally have *nowhere* else to go.

When I re-enter the lobby a few minutes later, I can't help feeling that I'm being watched—and not just from inside the building, by the guys over at the desk, but from outside too, from across the street maybe, from the back of a van, or—who knows—from an orbiting satellite two hundred miles up in the sky.

Then I get to the eighty-second floor and step into the apartment again. The Korean housekeeper seems relieved to have me back. Whoever is in the kitchen (the cook, I'm guessing) is talking loudly on a phone but in a language I don't understand and can't even identify.

I go into the living room and look around. Sabrina is nowhere to be seen, but all of a sudden I regret sending her away—not because I could have had her but because I could have helped her. Surely, in the circumstances, it was within my power to do something—slip her a ceramic bowl or even send her off with the goddamn Picasso. Because what kind of world does a girl like that come from, a girl conjured up out of nothing with a credit card?

"You want dinner, Mister Teddy?"

I turn around. The housekeeper has trailed along in my wake.

"Yes," I say, weary now. Then I look at her. "Sorry, excuse me . . . what's your name?"

Turns out it's Mrs. Jeong. She's been in this country for over twenty-five years and has two grown-up kids who are doing really well. She likes ballroom dancing and collects antique perfume bottles. And she works really hard. Which I can see is true. All of a sudden. I can also see that she is very patient, and probably very kind, and I have to wonder what she makes of Mister Teddy and how he treats his guests.

Do I tell her I have a headache now, that I'd like her to fetch me some Excedrin?

No, but . . . a thought strikes me. I walk past her and go to the kitchen, a huge affair that could easily service a modest-sized restaurant. There's a guy on a stool behind the breakfast bar. He's on his phone and looks startled when he sees me. He puts his phone away and gets off the stool. "Sir, is there something—"

"No," I say, "you're fine."

His name, it turns out, is Pavel, and he maintains the smart HVAC system for the whole apartment.

He and Mrs. Jeong are both temps, agency people. A couple of weeks ago they were working somewhere else. *In* a couple of weeks, who knows?

Like Sabrina.

I go over to the refrigerator, a stainless-steel, touch-screen Paloma Rex 3000, open it and start scanning for potential ingredients. I see anchovies, olives, capers, red peppers. I feel a little rush of adrenaline, like I should already have a knife in my hand, like someone should be calling me shithead and telling me to hurry up with the fucking *soffritto*.

"Mr. Trager . . . *sir*?"

I turn around. Mrs. Jeong and Pavel are both just standing there, staring at me.

"Are you guys hungry?" I say. "Because *I'm* making dinner tonight. I was thinking something simple, pasta . . . a puttanesca maybe?"

11

Shaw drops by early the next morning. It's clear from the look on his face that he's been fully briefed, so before he gets a chance to open his mouth I launch a preemptive strike. Does he think I'm an idiot? Does he think he can just *entrap* me? Does he not realize that, apart from anything else, sneaky, sleazeball *shit* like that is counterproductive? As I throw these questions at him, I'm standing in the main hallway with a kale and blueberry smoothie in one hand and a copy of the *New York Times* in the other and doing it—more or less unconsciously, I think—in my Trager 2.0 persona.

This is something Shaw hasn't seen yet, and when I'm done, he laughs out loud. "Holy *fuck*."

I take a step forward. "*What?*"

"Oh my God, Teddy . . . Danny, that . . . that is *amazing*."

I stare at him for a moment, hesitating, part of me gratified (stupidly) and part of me wondering how I can parlay this into further leverage. "Well, Doug, if it's so amazing, don't *jeopardize* it."

"Okay, okay." He holds a hand up. "I made a mistake. I wasn't trying to entrap you. Jesus, I just thought . . . you might . . ." He shakes his head. "You know what? Let's just forget about it, let's move on." He pulls out a sheet of paper from his inside jacket pocket. "This is . . ." He hands it to me. "Well, see what you think."

I put the smoothie and the newspaper down on a nearby console table and then take the piece of paper from him. I study it for a moment. It looks like some kind of financial statement. It shows a sequence of cash transfers that appear to end up in the account of the debt collection agency that owns Kate's loans. It's in the exact amount of what she owes.

I look at him. This is his idea of moving on? Is he fucking *serious*?

"Okay," he says. "We've sent Kate a message, fully pretexted. It states that a private loan forgiveness program run by an anonymous philanthropy group has liquidated five million dollars' worth of debt across a range of educational institutions."

"*What?*"

"I know, I know." He shrugs. "But believe me, stuff like this goes on. We modeled it on a real case."

Still shocked by his tone-deafness, I exhale slowly. "Look, I don't know . . . Kate's not stupid. I mean—"

"What, you think she's going to *contest* this?"

"No . . . I guess not."

"Anyway, it's done."

I hand the sheet of paper back to him. "Okay."

There's a lot more I could say here, but really, what would be the point? I decide to just move on myself. "Listen, Doug . . . you're going to have to loosen things up a bit." I make a gesture with my hand. "*Here*, I mean. The apartment. You can't expect me to believe that Teddy wasn't on the grid. I need Internet access. I need to watch some TV. I feel like I'm in a prison. This is a long game. Potentially. You're going to have to put a little faith in me."

Shaw thinks about this. "Okay, you're right. But I'll tell you what, let's get the Bloomberg thing out of the way first. It's early next week.

Then we can talk. But in the meantime, maybe stay out of the kitchen as well, will you?"

"What? That was . . . I just needed to *cook* something."

"Danny, these people, they're hired help, and, to be honest, you were making them a little nervous. We can do without that."

"Fine. Whatever." As I turn to pick up my smoothie again, something occurs to me. "By the way, what was that you said there, the *Bloomberg* thing?"

"Yeah, *Bloomberg TV.* Cristina Stropovich. *The Up Take.*"

"Oh . . ."

"*What?*"

"A lot of people watch that, right?"

"I guess. I mean, it's not *The Tonight Show* or anything." He looks at me and sighs. "You'll be fine. It's a business channel, people are focused on information. And besides, Teddy wasn't *that* well known, not outside the whole . . . VC tech start-up echo chamber. Which is something we can use to our advantage, by the way." He pauses again. "Maybe I'll get Karl to fix you up with something, Xanax or—"

"No," I say, picking up the smoothie. "Don't worry, I'm fine."

The next two days see the third and final phase of my so-called fine-tuning. Shaw himself takes over, with the focus now on lingo and terminology, on how to talk about and *sell* something like the PromTech deal. Each day, I undergo eight straight hours of hardcore presidential-debate–style prep. Covering more topics than could possibly be touched on in a single ten-minute interview, Shaw anticipates questions, one after the other, and then coaches me through plausible and natural-sounding replies. Occasionally he encourages me to improvise but then can't help shutting me down as soon as I veer even slightly from a position he's trying to push.

The day before the interview is scheduled to take place, we drive out to a PromTech facility in New Jersey. This is a research lab where technicians test drive some of the company's more speculative projects, stuff that has made it past the shoot-for-the-moon phase and into actual development. I'm aware that on this visit Shaw is sort of test-driving *me* too, that he wants to walk me around and see me interacting with people.

At one point, in conversation with an intense young roboticist named Zabruzzi, I start to feel dangerously out of my depth. I can now talk convincingly and at length about the business end of this stuff, but when things get technical, I'm lost. The problem is that while Shaw is seen here as a business guy, I'm seen as a science guy, as essentially one of *them*—someone who should be comfortable talking about capacitors and quantum dots and flexible interface hi-res . . . whatever-the-fuck. Before the conversation gets too awkward, I remember something Trager mentioned in the car, and I decide to bring it up.

"So," I say to Zabruzzi, "how is that remote DNA tracker, *tracking* . . . thing coming along?"

His eyes light up, and he launches into an impromptu and very welcome demo of what turns out to be an amazing piece of technology: a compressed rectangular unit of "opto-electrochemical nano-sensors" fitted to a neat little drone bot that can, in theory, roam around at a height of three hundred feet and over a radius of two and a half miles, picking out DNA matches from the populace below. *Holy fuck* is what I want to say, but I'm supposed to know about this shit already, and even be bankrolling it, so I keep my response muted.

Afterwards, in the back of the car, and channeling what I imagine to be at least a trace of Teddy Trager's passion for this kind of stuff, I ask Shaw where he sees Paradime taking PromTech in the long term.

Concentrating on sending a text, Shaw says, "What do *you* care?"

"Teddy obviously cared."

Shaw looks up from his phone. "Oh please. *Teddy cared* . . . Give me a break. Teddy was a boy scout. Teddy thought these guys could be preserved in geek formaldehyde. Teddy thought I had corrupted his soul by making him into a billionaire." Shaking his head, he turns back to his phone. "Can you believe that?"

At Bloomberg the following day we are greeted in reception by a senior producer. We observe security protocols and are then led up to a frenetic, open-plan, glass-domed newsroom and studio space, where we go through make-up and a sound check. There's a lot of small talk, a lot of standing around, and the whole thing passes like a particularly vivid anxiety dream.

When the interview finally begins, Shaw and I—well-oiled PR machine that we now are—sell the shit out of the PromTech deal. The interviewer, Cristina Stropovich, is well briefed but fairly soft in her approach. The questions are predictable and the answers boring. Nonetheless, we get our point across, and, although I'm nervous at first, mainly because of the unfamiliar studio setting, I don't feel at any point that I'm going to blow it.

Then, towards the end of the interview, she injects a shot of human interest into the proceedings by bringing up the accident. How am I doing? How has the recovery process been? I tell her I'm not going to lie to her, that even though my injuries could have been *so* much worse, it's the brush with mortality that leaves the deepest impression on you, the exposure to vulnerability that sparks a recalibration of your priorities. Then, a little tentatively, and as though she'd been saving this one up, she asks me about my perceived early ambivalence vis-à-vis the deal and if my recent change of heart had anything to do with the crash. I try to shrug this off, but when she persists in her line of questioning, I ramp things up a notch.

"What, I'm not allowed to change my mind? Come *on*. This is complex stuff, Cristina, sands are shifting all the time, and you've got to be able to adapt. What was that thing Walt Whitman said? Do I contradict myself? Very well then, I contradict myself. I am large. I contain multitudes." As I say this stuff, my heart is pounding. I'm aware of Shaw beside me, tensing up, and of Cristina opposite, leaning forward slightly, a subtle shift in her level of attention. And I'm not done yet, either. "You see, Cristina, the essence of good leadership isn't such a mystery, none of it is, not when you've looked into the abyss and realized what's actually *in* there . . . because let me tell you, it's not darkness, it's not the void, it's a *clock,* a gigantic LED display that's counting down the seconds and minutes and days of your life, so either you let that define and diminish you or you let it *drive* you. How? By thinking big, by never compromising, by finding smart solutions that impact the lives of people all over the world. Now I'm not claiming this as an original thought or anything, but time is our most precious resource and to waste it being idle or unfocused or *timid*?" I shake my head. "It's just not an option."

"Wow!" Cristina says, turning to the camera. "And remember folks, you heard it here first!" Then she turns back, her face just a tiny bit flushed. "Well . . . gentlemen, Mr. Shaw, Mr. Trager, that was great, and thank you both so much for dropping by the studio to see us today."

Out on the floor of the main newsroom, she's all over me . . . I must come back and do an in-depth interview, a one-on-one, a special, anything. She loved my honesty, it was so refreshing, so inspiring, and she knows her viewers will love it too. I nod along, and say *sure,* half aware of the buzzing ecosystem behind her and half aware of Shaw ten feet away talking to one of the producers.

As we're leaving the building a few minutes later, I can tell that Shaw is not happy about something. He doesn't speak until we're in the back of the car. He turns to look at me. "You went a little off the reservation there, no?"

"What? That all came up naturally, Doug. You don't think it's the kind of stuff Teddy would have said?"

"Oh, I do, for sure, Walt fucking Whitman, it was pitch-perfect, but maybe that's the problem."

I'm about to argue the point when his cell phone rings. He answers with a grunt. The call seems to go on for ages, but during it he says very little, apart from the occasional *yeah, okay,* or *fine.*

As we cruise down Lexington, I stare out through tinted windows at the city floating past—people, storefronts, sidewalks I've pounded—and wonder how I ended up here, in the back of a limousine. It's insane . . .

Shaw puts his phone away, sighs wearily, and takes a deep breath. "Apparently, you did a good job. A *very* good job."

Apparently?

I wait for more, but that's it. He doesn't say anything else. I look at him. He's perspiring. His jaw is tense. I wonder who he was talking to on the phone just now. I wonder what he was *told.*

With the media appearance out of the way, I push Shaw to deliver on his promise of Wi-Fi and cable. However, after a couple of days of continuous screen time, I start to get bored. I mostly stick to neutral stuff—restaurant reviews, industry blogs, aggregated news sites, listicles, shit like that. I also listen to a bunch of podcasts, watch movies, and season-binge some cable shows. But it's not as if I watch that much TV anyway, and I'm not a big fan of social media, so I inevitably max out. I can slip down the digital sinkhole as easily as the next person, but it's not something I have to do every day.

The laptop Shaw gives me is a Mac. It's new and has nothing on it. I have access to Trager's various accounts, from Amazon to Netflix, and that's it, but what was I expecting? All of his personal stuff? His list of contacts, notes, e-mails, documents? Hardly, but without any of *that,* how do I become Teddy Trager, how do I maintain even a shadow version of his life?

And this highlights a question I have that needs to be addressed sooner or later. Where *is* everybody? If Nina is supposed to be my girlfriend, where's *she*? Why hasn't she shown up at the apartment, or called me? Where are Teddy's friends? His business associates? The people who work for him? Why hasn't his sister called again? How sustainable is all of this? In a way, I don't care, and I'd be relieved to end it now, today. At the same time, I'm aware that ending it might be complicated, that if I stop cooperating, then surely they would have to . . . what? I don't know, frankly. But leaving all that aside for a minute, even on a purely practical level, the question remains: if I'm Teddy Trager, where's my *life*?

I bring this up with Shaw the next time he sinks wearily into what I now regard as his couch. At first, he's reluctant to engage, but I push him on it, and eventually he tells me that there is an "apparatus" in place, a sort of buffer zone between the outside world and . . . and . . .

"And *me*, basically."

"Yeah." He nods. "All calls, all communications, requests, invitations, whatever, are screened, and we deal with them. We're using the narrative of your recovery from the accident, your need for rest, for isolation—"

"As a pretext."

"Yeah."

I get up and start pacing back and forth, trying to block out or deflect or trick the light that seems to flood in up here, enhanced-interrogation style, at all times of the day or night. "Okay, then," I say, "what about the interview we just did? It was on television, Doug. I was there, I was talking, I was lucid. I even referred to my recovery. How do you square that circle?"

Shaw visibly deflates at this. He seems to be on the point of throwing his hands up and saying *I don't fucking know.*

I stop directly in front of him. "You know, Doug, I get it, there's a lot at stake here, and it could easily go south, but you're worrying about the wrong thing. *I'm* not the problem. *I'm* on board." I pause to let that sink in. "I mean, you're the one who said I get to be Teddy Trager. So come on, take the leash off. I can do this."

Shaw looks up at me. "It's funny," he says, "that's what *they* want. I'm the one who's being cautious."

I swallow. *They?* I'm not about to ask him if he means Lessing or someone else. Because maybe he thinks I already know. Either that, or he's not being cautious anymore—he's being reckless.

"Well, whatever." I shrug. "So how about it?"

He hesitates, then gets to his feet. He pulls his phone out and holds it up. "Let me make a call," he says with a resigned air, and moves away. He walks towards a section of window directly ahead of him, and, as he gets closer to it—closer to this sheer glass wall beyond which lies a dreamlike, hazy blue expanse of morning sky—it seems to me as if Shaw could maybe keep going, and not stop . . . as if he could slide right off the edge and simply disappear from view.

That afternoon, a package is delivered to the apartment by courier. Inside it is a USB flash drive that contains nearly a terabyte of data, all of it relating to Teddy Trager. It's his list of contacts, his e-mails, notes, letters, memos, photos—hundreds of files, thousands of pages—everything you could possibly need for a good first draft of a biography. What *I* need it for, however, is a little more intimate, and a little more immediate. Because once I've had time—four or five days, say—to familiarize myself with what's on here . . . the leash comes off.

Apparently.

I have no idea what this is going to mean in practical terms (and it's clear that Shaw still has serious reservations about the entire thing), but I'm all over it, because the alternative is fast becoming unthinkable.

I start with the e-mails.

I only get through a small fraction of them, but ninety percent of what I do read is fairly tedious, either that or just incomprehensible. There's a lot of working shit out, a lot of math, a lot of jargon. The remaining ten percent is interesting enough and tends to be personal—his struggle with social anxiety, his fear of emotional commitment, an account of a bruising lawsuit he was involved in, and then there's this whole e-mail exchange with some guy at MIT about his vision for the future of humanity, about space exploration and, specifically, about the possibilities of asteroid mining.

I remember he mentioned this in one of the first clips of him I watched. I find a lot more on it now in these notes—detailed proposals, budgets, a file with potential company names (Orbit Resources, Terra Nova, Offworld Exploration) and a directory of companies already working (or, let's be realistic, hoping to work) in the sector. The projected costs mentioned seem so insane to me that I have to wonder if any of this can be taken seriously. At the same time, it puts a dent in the notion of me being able to pass myself off as Teddy Trager in front of people who know him—people who might expect to hold an actual conversation with him about this shit.

The next day, however, I get an unexpected visit from Dr. Karl Lessing. He shows up alone and asks me how I'm faring with the "material."

"It depends," I say. "There's quite a lot of it."

I invite him into the living room, where he takes Shaw's place on the couch. I ask Mrs. Jeong to bring us some coffee. I sit down opposite Lessing and study him for a moment.

It strikes me that I have no idea who this person is, or who he represents. Is he a psychiatrist? That's the impression I got from some of the things Shaw said, but why would a shrink have the kind of influence that this guy seems to have? I don't know. I've dealt with psychiatrists in the past, and they tend to be slippery motherfuckers. Karl here isn't doing anything to dispel that notion. He's annoyingly calm, with a blank expression on his face that occasionally breaks into a self-regarding smirk.

His accent doesn't help either.

But he's also pretty good, because after only five minutes of conversation I hear myself saying, "Well, I sometimes feel . . ."

If it weren't for Mrs. Jeong arriving in with the coffee, who knows

where *that* might have led. Anyway, when she leaves again, I decide
to ask Lessing straight out what the hell is going on, who *he* is, and
how come he gets to walk all over Doug Shaw.

"It's not really like that," he says, "but . . . let's just stick with you
for the moment, shall we?"

"Fine," I say, taking a sip of coffee. "Okay, here's my problem with
the material, as you call it. It intimidates the shit out of me. I can do
a good Trager now, I know that, I can chat with Cristina Stropovich
for ten minutes, I can shoot the breeze on TV, but how do I talk to
his friends, how do I talk about some of this other stuff . . . I mean,
Jesus Christ, *asteroid* mining?"

Lessing stirs some sugar into his coffee. "Danny, let me explain
something to you. Teddy didn't have any friends, not really, nobody
close anyway. He had people who were in awe of him, and people
who envied him, but that's it." Lowering his voice now, Lessing leans
forward. "You don't have to impress them. These people are going to
be bending over backwards to impress *you*." He nods his head. "In
fact, the less you say the better. Play it cool. *That's* what's going to be
intimidating."

I stare at him.

"Believe me, Danny, no matter how weirdly you behave, no matter
what bullshit you come out with, as far as anyone you encounter is
concerned, you *are* Teddy Trager."

"But surely . . ."

He raises his eyebrows. "Yes?"

"I thought this was about trying to protect the Paradime brand."

"Of course, it is." He adjusts his glasses. "You're not *necessarily*
going to come out with bullshit, Danny. What I'm saying is that even
if you do . . . it'll be trademarked Teddy Trager bullshit." He pauses.
"No one's going to get upset, or call you out on it."

"But Doug—"

"Leave Doug to me."

"Yeah, but—"

"Look, in my opinion, pulling you out of the hat for an occasional press conference or a photo op on the sidelines at an investors' summit just isn't going to cut it. Doug's being cautious, I understand that, it's his nature, but . . . you need to be involved, you need to be proactive, you need to be *out* there. Which is what you *want* anyway, am I right?"

I hesitate, then nod.

His accent is such a weird mix—South African with an overlay of regular American, as if he maybe moved here as a teenager.

"And Danny," he goes on, lifting up his coffee cup, "for what it's worth, I have every confidence in you. Besides, like I say, you're more or less bulletproof."

"Bulletproof? How so?"

He takes a sip from the cup and puts it down again. "With all that material? You can draw on stuff that only Teddy could possibly know . . . facts, dates, stories, memories. It means you can preempt and second-guess. It means you can cover your tracks, if necessary."

"Hhnn."

A long silence follows. I feel like I've been here before. There's stuff I could say to Lessing, questions I could put to him, arguments I could present, but maybe it would be counterproductive at this stage.

There's one question I have to ask though. "What about Nina?"

Lessing seems surprised. "What about her?"

"Has she called? Or asked about me?"

"No, not that I . . ." He adjusts his glasses again, a stalling mechanism he seems to favor. Then he shakes his head. "No."

"Isn't that a little strange? Aren't we meant to be a couple? I get in an accident, she comes to the hospital one time, and then nothing?"

Lessing considers this. "Maybe so, yeah . . . in fact, that's a good point. Let me make a note of it.'" He takes out his phone, locates whatever app he uses, and keys it in.

As he's doing this, I glance around the room and then out the window.

Wispy, roiling clouds drift by.

I turn back to face him. "Dr. Lessing?"

"Call me Karl," he says and looks up from his phone. "Yes?"

"What happens next . . . Karl?"

"Well, I'd suggest you keep reading those files, get through as many of them as you can and then just . . . show up at the office for work on Monday."

12

I arrive on the seventieth floor of the Tyler Building on Monday morning, and on each subsequent morning—going, as they say, forward—but in all honesty I'm not sure I can call what I end up doing there actual *work*.

It involves a lot of sitting across tables from people, and listening to pitches and reports, and Skype calls, and being buttonholed in hallways and in elevators. There's also a lot of anxious time in front of the mirror at home before heading out to the office in the first place, and time sitting alone in the back of a limo inching through traffic in order to just get there. For me, though, the hardest part of it all is learning how to be a blank canvas, how to just sit or stand there and not show my hand to anyone. But once I do learn this it becomes like a superpower. Because Karl Lessing is right: playing it cool and saying very little intimidates the shit out of people.

It helps, of course, if you're Teddy Trager.

Doug Shaw is nowhere to be seen—he's working on some deal in Florida, apparently—and Karl Lessing doesn't show up either, but I do have two executive assistants (recent hires, I'm told) who take good care of me. Twenty-eight-year-old Nicole from Austin maps out, timetables, and tracks my every move, and screens all incoming communications. And thirty-year-old Lester from Kansas—more of a chief of staff, really—briefs me on just about everything: meetings I'm about to attend, calls I have to take, presentations I need to sit through, and he has my back in the event of any unscheduled or on-the-spot encounters. When the lines become blurry, or I display worrying "tendencies," Nicole and Lester are there to steer me in the right direction.

I don't know if these guys are on the same occult payroll as Matt and Arturo, but I don't ask and can only assume—and hope, for their sakes—that they are. Other recent hires include a personal trainer, a yoga instructor, and a new driver, a guy called Ricardo.

Even though I'm very busy, I'm not making decisions or anything, I'm not coming up with new ideas (I'm not actually working, in other words), but I am *on* all the time, and that's tiring in itself. One positive thing I get to do is draw up a list of high-end restaurants I might like to check out (steering clear of Barcadero, naturally), and then I get Nicole to schedule me in for lunch appointments at each of them in turn. As business "meetings" go, these lunches are easier than boardroom sit-downs or conference calls, because they have a rhythm to them, a built-in series of pauses and breaks.

Most of the people I've been meeting up to now are anxious start-up hopefuls, but it turns out that I'm also on the boards of Facebook, Pinterest, Foursquare, Paloma, Oculus, Uber, and a bunch of other companies, so it's inevitable that sooner or later I'll come face to face with a Zuckerberg, an Andreessen, or a Kalanick. Meeting Clooney, Dalio, and Clinton in the hospital was relatively easy, because, one, Shaw sprang that on me out of the blue, and, two, I had bandages on and was woozy from the morphine. But sitting across a table from Ray Dalio at some board meeting now would be quite a different experience.

Weirdly, though—and I haven't worked out yet why this is—it's not an experience I'm seeking to avoid. After a month of running Paradime Capital, sort of, I'm pretty comfortable in what I've come to think of as my new skin. At the same time, I'm not completely deluded. I know that a concerted effort has been made to keep me out of trouble. I also know that the real business of the company may well be going on in ways I am simply unaware of.

As the weeks go by, I get restless and feel an increasing urge to be doing something, so—even if only to convince myself of who I'm supposed to be—I focus my attention on certain areas of interest that really seemed to matter to Trager. And over lunch one day at the Modern I run into the producer of that interview segment Shaw and I did on Bloomberg TV. Apparently, Cristina Stropovich is still talking about it—and about me in particular—and would love it if I came back on to do the show again. This leads to a couple of follow-up conversations and eventually a meeting, at which point some other people get involved. Then, before I know it, the original proposal has been upgraded and there's talk of an appearance on *Charlie Rose* instead. *Charlie* is PBS, but the show is put together and taped at the Bloomberg studios, so the surroundings would be familiar but obviously the interview itself would be longer and more in-depth.

There is initial resistance from Lester (and whoever he and Nicole are talking to), but Lester is just my assistant. He's an adviser. So I tell him his advice has been duly noted but that as far as I'm concerned the interview is going ahead.

And it does.

The following week.

I expect a last-minute intervention of some kind, but it never comes. It seems I'm on my own.

Charlie Rose says he's happy to have me at "this table" and then proceeds to question me about the PromTech deal and tech trends in general. I have no problem answering questions like these, not after Shaw's little boot camp a while back, but what I try to do then is steer the conversation in a direction *I* want it to go in. It takes me a while, but I get there.

"So," Charlie says eventually, "a subject we're hearing a lot about these days is *asteroid* mining. Now, as ideas go, this one is pretty high in gee-whiz factor, I think that's undeniable, but what I'd like to know is—and explain it to me if you would because your name has been linked to it many times—how *practical* is this whole thing?"

"Well, Charlie," I say, shifting in the chair, my heart starting to pound, my mouth dry, "it all depends on how you look at it. I mean, the exponential rate at which the human race is consuming the earth's resources right now . . . is *that* practical? Is it sustainable? No, it isn't. And if we continue tearing the planet apart looking for precious metals to extract so we can put them in our cell phones and games consoles, just to keep shareholders happy, how's *that* going to end? So it seems to me that it's eminently practical—putting it at its mildest—to start searching for an alternative. And once you *do*, once you look up, and out into space, and realize what's there—i.e. literally billions of mineable asteroids, some of which are gigantic rocks packed tight with platinum or nickel or gold or thanaxite, others of which contain copious amounts of what may well turn out to be *the* most valuable substance of all, water—once you realize that this effectively infinite supply of resources is out there and accessible, you have to wonder what the hell we're doing down here on earth squabbling over carbon emissions and fracking and water rights."

"Okay, but I think if—"

"So, yes, of *course*," I say, cutting across him—because if I don't keep talking I may just keel over and die—"there's practical and there's practical, there's *We have to do it* and there's *Can we do it?*, and without a doubt, Charlie, many obstacles lie in our path, not the least of which is cost. I mean, we're talking mammoth amounts of money, multi-tier, investment structures, but there'll also be technical difficulties and challenges at every phase, at exploration, at extraction, at processing, there's working in zero gravity, there's how do we *mount* the damn things, on top of *which*"—I clear my throat quickly here—"you have the questions of ownership, of patents, of property, and naming rights. It's not going to be easy, and no individual, no one person, is going to do it alone—not Teddy Trager, not Elon, not whoever."

"Okay," Charlie says, "but if I understand it correctly, this would still be an old-fashioned land grab, right? And the normal rules of commerce would apply. So if asteroid mining ever does happen . . . we may well be looking at the world's first trillionaire."

"Maybe so," I say, "maybe so"—ideas and phrases from Lessing's flash drive now seeping out of my brain—"but you know what, Charlie? After all this time, after all we've been through, the Industrial Revolution, the Gilded Age, the Jazz Age, the post-war boom, the . . . the . . ."—I want to say *the fucking*, but I hold back because we're on PBS—"the nineties, the dot-com thing, and then . . . *what?* We step out into actual space, ready for humanity's next big evolutionary phase, and it's still *that* guy? It's still Rich Uncle Pennybags? It's Mr. Trillionaire? *He's* the one leading the way and calling the shots?" I make a gesture of incredulity here, an exaggerated one, for the camera. "No, Charlie, I think we have to do better than that, I think we have to devise a new way of doing business."

"But is that even—"

"Back in 1967 we all signed up to an agreement—the Russians, the Chinese, us, everyone—it's called the Outer Space Treaty, and it's a foundational document that sets down how we should conduct ourselves in space, as a species. Now I think that's a start right there . . . but today, fifty years later, when we finally have a realistic shot at this, at going out into space, what's happening?"

"Tell me."

"There are bills coming before Congress and more at committee stage that want to tear up that agreement and make new rules—rules that will almost exclusively benefit *who?* The shareholders of private American mining corporations, that's who. I mean, Charlie . . . haven't we learned *anything?*"

"Well, I don't know about that, but . . . let me just ask you one final question, Teddy. Have you ever considered running for public office?"

After the recording, there's a definite buzz around the studio, and, as I chat to a couple of the producers, I notice that Lester is busy networking and tapping numbers into his phone. On the way down to the car, he remains silent, reminding me of how Shaw was after that first interview, but this time I think it's more that Lester is puzzled. It's as if he somehow never got the memo.

When the segment airs the following night, the reaction is similarly buzzy. It attracts a lot of attention and generates a surprising amount of comment. Because of the asteroid thing, some of this is dismissive, ridiculing the idea as a pipe dream, but others point out that advances in technology make it at least potentially feasible. However, it's my statement at the end of the interview—when I said I wouldn't rule out running for public office—that gains the most traction. Soon the hashtag #voteforteddy starts trending, and blogs everywhere pick up the story, some concentrating on my radical views in relation to corporate profiteering, others declaring what an attractive candidate I'd make. Shaw once pointed out to me that Teddy Trager was actually quite a private individual, well known inside the tech and VC bubble but with a low enough profile otherwise (I know I'd never heard of him), so, given all of that, it's entirely possible that this is the widest net of media attention he's ever been caught up in.

But the reality, of course, is that I'm now the one who's caught up in it. And maybe the irony here is that, as an equally private individual, I don't seem to mind at all and, in fact, am even quite enjoying it. I conduct a few short interviews by phone and e-mail, and Nicole tells me that she's getting requests every day for me to appear on other news channels, on talk shows, and on podcasts. Again, I'm waiting for some form of intervention from Karl Lessing or Doug Shaw, a slap on the wrist maybe, or just a quiet word in my ear telling me to shut up, to keep a low profile, but no direct contact is made.

So . . . how far could I go with this? *Could* I run for public office? Most of the coverage I've seen, on blogs and even in comment boxes, is positive, a lot of it actively encouraging me to speak out further.

But just as I begin to believe that this is real, and that I might have a genuine opportunity here, there's the inevitable backlash.

A few nights after the *Charlie Rose* broadcast, I'm sipping a glass of single-malt Scotch whisky and flipping around the channels when I come across a still shot of *me* on the *Rachel Maddow Show* on MSNBC. That's weird enough, but then they cut back to studio and an interview with Bulletpoint.com reporter Ray Richards. ". . . So seriously, Rachel," he's saying, "on the one hand you have this guy preaching about corporate profiteering like he's Ida Tarbell"—and here a mock-indignant Richards bangs his fist on the desk—"these mining companies can't be allowed to plunder the resources of space. And, on the other hand, this *same* guy buys Prometheus Technologies, a company he swore blind he wouldn't go near, and then proceeds to pretty much plunder *them*. It's outrageous."

"I know."

"Oh, and by the way"—ramping up the sarcasm now—"elect me to the Senate, would you, cos I'm only thirty-three, and that's a little young for the White House . . ."

I sit forward, glass in hand, and stare at the screen in shock. Being talked about publicly is strange at the best of times, but like this? Being turned on and attacked? It's *awful*.

". . . and I don't really understand it," Rachel Maddow is saying. "It's kind of a mystery, right?"

"*Right*," Richards goes on, "because, I mean, you've got to ask . . . whatever happened to the great Teddy Trager? Was it the auto accident he had recently? That must have been a traumatic experience, no question about it, but one thing is clear, *since* then, whenever it was, a couple of months ago . . . Teddy Trager simply hasn't been himself."

Oh Jesus . . .

I drain the glass.

"Look, although Trager and Doug Shaw built Paradime Capital together, everyone knows there've been problems. Call it a clash of ideologies, call it what you like, but what we know today, in light of this awful PromTech deal, is that Doug Shaw has emerged the clear victor. He gets to play with his new LudeX. What we also know, however, in light of Trager's hypocritical posturing on *Charlie Rose* the other night is that *he* has ditched his principles—"

"He's crossed to the Dark Side."

"Exactly . . . so I suppose, here's my real question, Rachel: just who the hell *is* Teddy Trager?"

I raise my hand, stretch it back, and fling the empty glass at the screen.

Within about a minute, Mrs. Jeong appears in the room carrying a dustpan and brush, but I wave her away. I flick the TV off and walk over towards the window.

Who the hell is Teddy Trager?

What a question. And the irony, of course, is that I don't know. How would I? I only met the guy once. I know him from watching You-Tube clips, tons of them.

Then I remember there's one clip I haven't seen. Trager made a reference to it in the car. He said it was a speech he delivered at some university a few years ago, that it was like a mission statement.

It doesn't take me long to find it on my laptop.

And . . .

There he is, on a stage, pacing back and forth, headset mic attached, PowerPoint display behind him. ". . . because make no mistake," he's saying, "human nature is on a collision course with disaster unless we can do something very radical and very soon about re-engineering our fundamental 'greed gene.' But since the only thing any of us ever really seems to be greedy for anymore is *money,* let's just do away with the damn stuff, metal, paper, fiat, whatever, let's find another way to organize our affairs. Because take the monetary system out of the equation, take *profit* out of the equation, and there's no problem on this planet we couldn't all solve together in six months flat . . ."

I stare at the familiar image of Trager on the screen—familiar from the other clips, familiar from the hour we spent together in his car.

Isn't *that* who he really was?

Seems like it to me.

Wealthy, influential, maybe a little eccentric, maybe a little fucked up in the head, sure . . . but also bold, radical, maverick, idealistic, sincere . . .

Definitely not a hypocrite.

So what the fuck was Ray Richards talking about?

Then it hits me. It's not *what,* it's *who* . . .

Who signed the contracts? Who sold out? Who is the real hypocrite?

Although he didn't realize it, Ray Richards wasn't talking about Teddy Trager at all. He was talking about me.

13

I need to get out of the apartment. On my way down in the elevator I feel a bit sick, and the prospect of fresh air is welcome, but then, as I cross the lobby and get closer to the exit, I'm put off by the noise from outside, by the bustle and speed of the traffic on Twelfth.

Is Ricardo around? I'm still not sure how this works. He's always waiting for me in the morning, and he's there whenever I need him during the day. But now? What time is it? Nearly 10 p.m.? I call him on my cell phone. He says he'll be outside in fifteen minutes.

I stand waiting at the foot of the Mercury and stare out over the darkness of the Hudson.

When Ricardo shows up, I tell him to cruise around for a while. He goes north for a bit, then gets onto 57th Street, which isn't too busy at this hour. He turns right at Lexington and drifts downtown. From the quiet interior of the limousine, I gaze out at the city, at the passing figures on sidewalks and street corners. Through tinted glass, it all seems spectral, like the carefully textured background graphics in a gritty urban video game. But then—the farther down Lex we get—a weird feeling creeps up on me. As we approach 23rd Street, Gramercy

Park directly ahead, I tell Ricardo to take a left, to get onto Second Avenue, and to keep heading downtown.

I haven't been down here, in this neighborhood, around 14th Street—below it, now—since that night . . .

I look out the window, alternating my gaze, right, left. What I'm hoping for, all I'm hoping for—and it's taken me a while to admit this—is maybe to catch a glimpse of Kate. She could easily be going to the store, or walking home from something . . . 12th Street . . . 11th . . .

As we pass it, I glance down 10th and feel a rush of emotion. It's bad enough that I miss my old life, but this sense of having been completely erased from it is so much worse. Though, to be honest, now that I'm down here, I know what the worst feeling of all is.

It's missing Kate.

When we get to East Houston, I tell Ricardo to loop around and go back up First.

Okay, I missed her when I was in Afghanistan, and in a way I missed her even more when I got back . . . when I was lying next to her in our bed or sitting across the kitchen table from her, when I was looking *right at her.*

But somehow that was all negotiable. Now I miss her in a way that feels irreversible, that feels like grief—except that she's not the one who's dead.

I am.

Is that how she misses me?

I get Ricardo to pull over on the right, between 4th and 5th, and we sit there. I lean back and stare out as people float by in either direction. The thing is, I'm tired and confused, and I'm not really expecting anything to happen, I'm not even hoping at this stage. But after only a minute, and it's like an electrical jolt to my system, there she is, on the sidewalk. I see her from behind. It's through tinted glass, and there's a glare of storefront neon, but there's no question in my mind that it's her. I recognize . . . *everything*: how she's dressed, how she moves. It then takes me a couple of seconds to realize that she's not alone. Walking beside her—not just parallel to her, definitely with her—is some guy. He's young-looking, hipsterish. He has a beard and is wearing a jacket and T-shirt.

They get to the corner of 5th and keep going.

I immediately reach for the door, mumbling something to Ricardo as I open it. Within seconds, I'm out of the car and following Kate on foot—focusing on her, ignoring the guy. This is reckless, I know, and irresponsible, but I really don't care. I get close to her, then closer, and then I'm only a few feet behind her—head pounding—as she comes to a stop at the next corner and waits to cross.

In this moment, though, what's my plan? What am I about to do? Tap Kate on the shoulder? Whisper her name? Give her that long-delayed heart attack? End this whole thing in a sudden, sickly swirl of anger and insecurity and weakness and *jealousy*? I don't know, but it feels like a real possibility to me. Then I feel something else, a light tap on my own shoulder. I turn around. It's Ricardo. In a low, firm voice, he says, "Mr. Trager, please . . . we need to go now."

I look at him, and hesitate. I'm confused. I turn back to look at Kate.

The light changes.

Then I just stand there, paralyzed, and watch as she and the guy she's with cross the street, recede into the crowd, and eventually disappear.

When we're settled in the car again, me in the back, Ricardo up front, I want to press the intercom and say something to him.

I want to interrogate him.

But I also want to close my eyes, to rewind, to grieve. Something else I think I might like is a drink. Which is when I realize that the little mahogany unit directly in front of me here is probably stocked full of booze. If I want it.

Which I suddenly now don't.

I glance around at the leather upholstery and the walnut trim and the side panels and the monitors. I always sit in the interior cabin of this thing as though I can't wait to get out of it, as though it's an MRI machine or something.

"Sir? Where to?"

I look up, but don't say anything.

I'm curious about something. Who was that hipster guy? With his beard. And his new *friend*.

"*Sir?*"

"Okay, okay." I think for a second, then press the intercom. "Upper West Side, 68th Street."

Ricardo pulls out and joins the flow of traffic.

I wonder if he knows where we're going. I wonder if he knows that 68th Street is where Nina Schlossmeier lives.

It's another one of these preposterously luxurious condos with a huge lobby area that has a reflecting pool *and* a waterfall. I'm pretty sure the guy at the desk recognizes me, or thinks he does. I ask for Nina. He calls up, but she's not there.

"Would sir like to leave a message?"

"No, but . . ." I point at a seating area. "I'm going to wait over there for a bit, see if she gets back any time soon."

The guy nods, but seems a little puzzled.

I find a spot and sit with my back to the desk.

What am I doing here? Some talking head on TV effectively calls me an asshole, and *this* is where I end up? What am I looking for? Comfort? Consolation? No, it's that I need to talk to someone who's *real*. Not just someone else on the occult payroll, not just someone whose job it is to talk to me. Maybe Nina's on the payroll too, I don't know . . . but the way she walked out of Trager's life like that, when he was in the hospital? It never felt right to me. She must have realized at the time that I was a replacement. But then . . . where did she think Trager was? Where does she think he's been all along?

Does she know he's dead?

And if she doesn't, am I going to tell her?

These are questions I should have considered in the back of the limo down on First.

But it's too late for that now.

I look over and see Nina entering the lobby. She glides in, as though onto a catwalk. She's wearing some kind of a print dress under a pale pink coat. I stand up at once, and this sudden motion catches her attention. She turns and sees me.

I don't know what kind of a reaction I'm expecting, but it's not the one I get. She sort of flinches, a look of shock on her face. She turns away and heads straight for the elevators. I move swiftly in her direction and, out of the corner of my eye, sense the desk guy starting to move as well.

Shit.

"Nina!"

"Sir! *Sir!*"

By the time I get to within a few feet of her, she has already pressed the button. She turns around, looking composed now and, with two simple gestures, takes control of the situation. The first is a barely raised forefinger that stops *me* in my tracks. The second is an eyebrow maneuver directed over my shoulder that calls off the desk guy.

Then *our* eyes meet.

"What?" She delivers the word quietly, and it has the force of an ultimatum: you have until this elevator door behind me opens.

"Nina," I say, leaning hard on the second syllable, as if that'll somehow make a difference.

Ping.

She shakes her head.

"Nina . . ." Then a spurt of desperation. "I need to talk to you, *please,* come on, just five minutes."

How do we calculate these things? *Five* minutes? What, I have it all worked out? Four specific points to make, each one requiring seventy-five seconds?

Nina stares at me, clearly making a rapid calculation of her own. What is she seeing? On reflection, the shock I saw on *her* face just now might have been closer to fear. Does she recognize the same thing in me?

As the door behind her starts closing, she flicks an arm back to hold it open.

Her apartment is on the twenty-fifth floor. Naturally it's pretty big. The decor is an artful mix of modern and rustic, but the place itself is warm and feels really lived in—unlike Trager's place.

We didn't speak in the elevator, and now Nina directs me to a sofa and says she'll be back in a minute.

I sit down and stare at the pine floorboards.

Maybe she'll offer me a drink. That might help.

Or not.

Every day with Teddy is a challenge . . .

It's really quite disconcerting how beautiful she is. When she re-appears, she has changed into jeans and a loose-fitting powder-blue cashmere sweater. She sits opposite me.

She doesn't offer me a drink.

"Okay," she starts. "I have to say, this is pretty fucking weird for me, so . . . just who *are* you?"

I stare at her. "I'm Teddy Trager."

What am I doing?

"No, you're not."

"I *am.*"

Nina shakes her head. "Please."

"How . . . how do you know I'm not?"

"Because of everything. Because of how you're behaving. Because

Teddy would never wait for me in the lobby. And because . . ." She pauses. "And because I'm pregnant."

Almost in spite of herself, she smiles. And it's a wide, disarmingly radiant smile—which is what I react to first, because it obliterates everything in its path. Then the words sink in.

"You're . . . *pregnant?*"

She nods emphatically. "I knew almost immediately. I felt it. And then I had it confirmed within . . . ten days?"

I don't know what to say to this.

She leans forward slightly, holding my gaze, and whispers, "It's *yours.*"

My head starts throbbing. "But . . . I'm not your boyfriend, I'm *not* Teddy Trager . . ."

"No."

"But if I'm not Teddy, then . . . who do you think I am?"

She shrugs. "You're the guy who came to the gallery that night. You're the guy from the restaurant. I don't know who you are, and, to be honest? I don't care."

She looks down at her belly and pats it gently. How long has she been pregnant? Eight weeks? Ten? She's not showing yet, but clearly this is something she already likes doing.

"You don't *care?*"

There are many versions of this conversation I've had in my head, but the one that's taking place right now doesn't come close to any of them.

"*This* is all I care about," she says, hand still on her belly. "Lately, my relationship with Teddy revolved around the fact that it was never going to happen for us. He'd been tested and . . ." She stops, probably not wanting to share too much. "Anyway, there was tension around it. We spent a lot of time arguing." Her radiant smile returns. "But look at me now."

"*You?*" I say, almost shouting it. "Look at *me.*"

"I know, it's incredible. I only noticed it that night, after a few hours.

I mean, earlier? At the gallery? I was just too wound-up to notice anything. Then, at the hospital, I was confused. At first, I thought it was
some elaborate game. But later, when I realized I was pregnant? It
all seemed so obvious. What I have to keep reminding myself is that
with Teddy just about anything is possible . . ."

I stare at her for a second, not getting it. "What does that mean?"

"What else? This curious business of *you*. Whoever you are. Whatever your name is. But at the same time the perfect solution to our
problem. Who could have dreamt *that* up? Only Teddy."

I'm speechless. What does she think this is? Some advanced form
of designer natural insemination . . . and that Trager actually arranged
it for her?

Every day is an adventure . . .

"It's funny," she goes on, "that night at the restaurant? I told him
about you, I told him what I saw, but he didn't seem interested. I guess
I should have suspected something was up."

She smiles again.

Oh my God. She's so fucking *happy*.

But then it all loops back in my head. "Nina," I say, "if that's what
you think I am, just some carefully selected sperm donor . . . why am
I still here? Why am I running Paradime Capital? I mean, if you're
two months pregnant . . . *where's Teddy?*"

She holds my gaze for what seems like a long time. Then she stands
up. "I don't know." She says this quietly, and partly facing away from
me. Seeing her in profile now, I can make out a very slight bump, a
subtle curvature around the middle that someone like her, in normal
circumstances—I imagine—would probably feel compelled to work
off.

"I gave up trying to understand Teddy a long time ago," she says.
"So initially I thought . . . having found you, the perfect donor,
he wasn't just going to leave it at *that*. He'd be too excited. There'd
be too many possibilities, too many games to play—starting, I suppose, with the charade at the hospital." She walks over to the window.

"After a week, though? After *two* weeks? I don't know, Teddy could be self-absorbed, even a little crazy sometimes, but not a jerk . . ."

Could be?

It takes me a moment or two, from the angle I'm at, from how I'm sitting, from how she's standing at the window, to realize that Nina now has tears in her eyes. I stand up immediately. But what next? Go over and try to comfort her? Maybe in my dreams.

"Then," she says, composing herself, and turning around, "when I saw what was happening with PromTech . . ." She shakes her head. "It was ridiculous. It was clear that you were some kind of a . . . a *puppet*." She looks me directly in the eye. "So when I saw you down in the lobby just now, it was a little alarming. I didn't know what to think."

I drop back onto the sofa.

"What do you think now?" I ask.

Leaning against the window, she studies me for a while. "Well, what's weird is, you coming here like this, wanting to talk," she says. "It doesn't make sense. I saw you on *Charlie Rose,* and that didn't make sense either. So what I think is that when Doug Shaw first became aware of you—however that happened, maybe Teddy told him, in his excitement, I don't know—but he saw an opportunity, a chance to stop Teddy in his tracks, to replace him, and he couldn't resist, because that's something Doug has wanted to do for a very long time." She pauses. "But maybe he didn't know what he was getting into. Maybe he didn't know that when his partner chose *you*"—she points at her belly again—"for *this,* it wasn't a choice based solely on appearance, that maybe there were other, more complex factors involved. And maybe . . ." She leans forward a little from the window. "What's your name?"

"My *name*?"

"Yeah."

How can such a simple question feel so loaded, so dangerous? I hesitate, but then just say it. "Danny Lynch."

"Okay." She nods, considering it. "So maybe Doug didn't know that trying to control Danny Lynch would be just as hard as trying to control Teddy Trager. I mean, what you said on *Charlie Rose*? That was pure Teddy. Don't tell me Doug approved that, or had a say in it. And the idea of running for public office? Those thoughts were in Teddy's head too, no question about it. So I don't know who you are, Danny Lynch, but I don't think Doug Shaw knows either."

It's a convoluted theory, and I could shoot some holes in it, parts of it anyway, but what would be the point? If she believes in this notion of a grand romantic gesture on Trager's part, fine, I'm not about to take that away from her. Something important still needs to be cleared up, though.

"Nina," I say, "you do know . . ." I close my eyes for a second. "You do know that Teddy is dead, right?"

She gently taps the back of her head three times against the window. "Is that why you came here? To tell me that? Because I've been assuming it for some time."

I look up at her. "It was an accident, Nina . . . Teddy lost control of the car, he crashed it into that tree. I guess that was when Doug Shaw seized his opportunity and got me to take Teddy's place."

As an account of the events of that night, this is light on detail and extremely disingenuous. I try to prepare myself for a barrage of questions, a cross-examination that will expose the half-truths and misdirections and deliberate ambiguities here, but it doesn't come. She just stands at the window, staring at me. Eventually she says, "You really think it was an accident, Danny? Is that what Doug told you? Is that how he got you into this? How he persuaded you to keep it going?"

I don't answer. How *can* I without admitting I was actually there when it happened?

"One thing about Teddy," Nina goes on, "he couldn't lose control of a car if he tried. And especially not *that* car. It's something I was really puzzled about before I saw you, before I even got to the hospital. Teddy was an exceptionally good driver."

I feel a tiny twitch in my hand as I remember—as my hand remembers—how I landed that punch on Teddy's face.

"But once I accepted that he was gone, that he wasn't just going to show up some morning with coffee and bagels . . ." She stops and takes a deep breath. "Once I figured out that he'd been murdered—assassinated, actually—that Doug Shaw had effectively carried out a coup d'état at Paradime . . . well, *then* I started wondering how he'd done it."

I must have a look on my face.

"Oh, what, you don't think Shaw is capable of something like that?"

"But Nina, it was an acc—"

"Danny, *they hacked his car.*"

I stare at her now, moving my head very slightly from side to side. I have no idea what to say to this, but somewhere in my subconscious a sequence of controlled depth charges is being detonated.

"I looked into it online," she says, "which wasn't easy, believe me, but guess what? It's now entirely possible with Wi-Fi or Bluetooth to gain remote access to a car's ECUs and to do whatever you want with it, to turn off the AC, to lock the steering wheel, to accelerate, to *crash* it. I knew this in theory, but to see demonstration videos was pretty shocking. Then I went back and got some details on Teddy's supposed accident, which was even harder to do . . ." She takes another deep breath. "I don't know if you realize it, *I* didn't, but there are already conspiracy theories out there about what happened that night. On the deep web there's this one site that keeps track of suspicious accidents—you know, car crashes, plane crashes, helicopters, whatever, people who get killed or injured and the timing is weird, or the details don't add up—well, Teddy's crash is on there, and I don't know how they gather their info, what their sources are, but they make a couple of very serious claims. One, they say the airbag didn't go off—now how *that* could have happened without some kind of interference, I don't know—and, two, they say that if you take stuff like throw weights and friction coefficients into account, the damage to the car clearly shows there was no *way* the driver could have survived, let alone escaped with minor injuries." She pauses. "So I think it's pretty obvious what happened."

As I continue to stare at Nina, my insides are churning. Everything she's saying is plausible and makes sense. At the same time, my brain is spooling back through those last few seconds with Teddy. I know he was angry, and with good reason, but his actions *were* strange. I mean, banging the steering wheel like that . . . was he not able to turn it? Was he not able to slow the car down? In retrospect, I suppose, it *could* seem that way. And there was the second vehicle. Did I imagine that or not? So, here's the real question: is it possible that when Teddy was pushing me out onto the road he had just realized he was no longer in control of his car? That that was *why* he was pushing me out? That he was actually trying to save my life?

I stand up, feeling unsteady, dizzy, a bit like I'm out of my mind on something, bad acid or too much cheap tequila. I want to get out of there now, and fast. I want to escape, but something is holding me back. I look at Nina. "If all of this is true," I say, "what are you going to do about it?"

She shakes her head. "Nothing."

"But . . . I don't . . . *nothing*?"

She steps forward a few paces and stands right in front of me. "What *can* I do? I can't prove anything. Besides, I'm pretty sure I'm being closely monitored, so if I cause any trouble, if I rock the precious boat, how long do you think I'll last?" She lifts a hand up and gently strokes the side of my face with it. "And Danny, you know what? To be perfectly honest, forget about me, I really can't see *you* lasting very long at all."

I look into her eyes. I'm not sure what she means. "No?"

"No." She glances down for a moment, then back up. "You should consider what you're doing very carefully. Because the more you act like Teddy, the sooner you'll end up the way he did."

"So . . . what, I just go on being a puppet?"

"I don't know. Why not? They're *paying* you, right?"

She's so calm, so controlled—it's impressive. And then it hits me again, what she said earlier. She's pregnant. She doesn't *care*.

I look down and place my hand—slowly, tentatively—on her belly. Because when will I ever get the chance again?

She doesn't stop me.

After a couple of seconds, I look up, feeling very self-conscious. I withdraw my hand. "I have to go."

"You know," she says, "I miss him every day. I grieve for him. So this is not easy for me . . . standing here, looking at *you*." She studies my face for a moment, carefully scanning each feature. "It's really quite extraordinary."

Her gaze is intense.

I look away and move across the room.

When I get to the door, I turn around. "I'm sorry, Nina."

"Don't be," she says, patting her belly once more. "Really. I *have* what I want."

14

The next week is something of a blur. I show up at the office but do no work. I cancel things at the last minute and refuse to see people or take any calls. I spend most of my time standing at the window, staring out over Midtown. If Nina is right, then I'm little more than a puppet here at Paradime, so what difference will it make? None. The work of the company won't be impeded in any way. And if I persist in trying to be more like Teddy? Then . . . I'll just end up like Teddy.

It's remarkable how quickly I get used to the idea that his death wasn't an accident. I resisted at first, because it seemed so preposterous. But what seems preposterous *now* is that Shaw would wait around for some random act of chance to move things along when he already had an elaborate arrangement in place that would do it for him on command.

I'm prepared to concede, therefore, that my blow to the side of Teddy's face wasn't the cause of the crash. But doesn't that mean, in turn, that when I signed those contracts—here in *this* office—I was effectively signing his death warrant? Because wouldn't that have been the obvious trigger for Shaw?

These questions play on my mind, but they're not the only ones.

Why, for example, did Shaw want to replace Teddy? What was the *real* reason? A clash of cultures within the company? A disagreement over which direction Paradime should take? A contentious deal even? Whatever. These are all legitimate sources of conflict, but . . .

Car hacking and murder? Seriously?

Say Nina is right, though—about this much at least, that the opportunity *I* presented was simply too much of a temptation. Fine. *Where is Shaw then?* MIA in Florida? That doesn't make any sense. You'd imagine he'd be up here micromanaging my every move. Instead, it seems, I'm free to do as I please and am only limited by . . . what? My own lack of imagination?

I don't get it.

I probably should have asked Nina if she knew anything about Dr. Karl Lessing, but I didn't, so all I can do now is follow my nose.

Near the end of the week, in something of a fluster, Nicole informs me that six months ago I was invited to speak at a tech and innovation conference in Ireland and that I apparently accepted. It's happening next week, and she apologizes for reminding me about it so late—somehow the event slipped through her scheduling grid—but she can cancel if I like.

"No," I tell her, "that's fine. Make the arrangements."

I've never been to Ireland, even though I have family there, or so I understand—it's hardly surprising with a name like Lynch. I go through Trager's notes from the cache on the flash drive and find a couple of files relating to the conference, including a sketchy outline for his keynote address. I spend most of the weekend working on this, fleshing it out, reading up on stuff, and generally keeping myself distracted.

The event is in Dublin—an annual affair called ExpoCon—and it draws all the big names in global tech and investment, so if Shaw or

Lessing or whoever it is don't want me getting my Trager on in front of all those people, they're going to have to intervene.

And I wait, expecting up to the last minute that they will, but it's only when I'm crossing the Atlantic in a Gulfstream G650 that I realize just how much latitude I have here—or maybe it's not even latitude, maybe it's actual freedom. As I sit gazing out the window at the billowing sea of clouds below me, I speculate—or fantasize, really—about what it'd be like if both Shaw and Lessing were somehow to be eliminated from the equation. Who else would then know for sure that I wasn't the real Teddy Trager? More to the point, who would have the authority or the balls to call me on it and expect to be taken seriously? And in *that* scenario, with all of Trager's resources, what could I not achieve?

Dublin is small and has lots of local charm, but the convention center where ExpoCon is taking place could be anywhere, Seattle or Frankfurt or Kuala Lumpur, a neutral, streamlined international "space." I meet a lot of people, and I expend no psychic energy whatsoever angsting over whether or not I actually know any of them. Have I met them once or a thousand times? Have I rejected their pitches or vacationed on their islands? I don't know, and I don't care. I maintain a steely demeanour, an aloofness, and, far from silencing people, this tactic renders most of them helplessly garrulous while at the same time laying bare certain familiar and unattractive insecurities. I attend seminars, workshops, and panel discussions. I have coffee with people, engage in whispered confabs on the "sidelines." By the time I'm waiting to step out onto the main stage that evening to deliver what is now very definitely *my* keynote address, I feel—to use Karl Lessing's word—"bulletproof." I've done a run-through with the production people, approved the music cues, and scanned a version of my speech on the teleprompter. The speaker before me was showcasing an amazing new piece of technology, but his delivery was flat and uninspiring, so he's not exactly a hard act to follow. I know it's one thing to appear on TV in a controlled studio setting and that it's quite another to walk out in front of two thousand pumped delegates in an auditorium, but as the host announces me now, and the music surges, I experience no real fear or even nerves . . .

I head back to the States the following day and spend most of the flight time reading e-mails and blog reactions to my speech. A hefty percentage of these range from the sceptical to the dismissive: I'm naive, my ideas are ill thought out, they're derivative, the speech was quixotic, it was dangerous, I'm a crazy person. But some of them give it a fair shake, with a select few going all out for the Kool Aid. "Teddy Trager," one of them writes, "is a true visionary in a time when the vision thing has been debased beyond recognition. We may not deserve this man, but we certainly need him."

When I get into the office early the next morning, Nicole is dealing with a torrent of interview requests from various media outlets. At one point I sit down with her and we go through a list, quickly rejecting most of them out of hand. Nicole has a good grasp on this stuff, she knows what's worth pursuing and what isn't: which shows or podcasts are popular, which sites run stories that get picked up by the aggregators, that kind of thing. As I'm scanning the list, I spot a name that I've seen before and point to it.

"Who're they?"

"Oh . . . no," she says. "I wouldn't bother with them, they're too niche." She pauses. "Weirdly enough, though, they *are* persistent. I've had repeated requests from them over the past month, three or four I'd say, at least."

It's a political web site called Pivot, and I'm pretty sure it's the one that Kate interviewed for and got that job with. I ask Nicole for the name of the contact person there, the one who made the request.

She checks. "Pete . . . Kettner."

I google him and go straight to Images. The page that opens up contains a lot of different possibilities for Pete Kettner, but I spot the one I'm looking for almost immediately, in the second row of the first page—and that's because I recognize him. He's the beardy hipster guy I saw with Kate that night. I stare at his picture for ages—it's small, like an ID photo—and several things race through my mind at once.

He's a colleague. They work together. It's a small world. This is a *coincidence*.

Then I point at the list and say to Nicole, "That guy, Pete . . . whatsit, arrange something with him, will you? As soon as possible. Today, if you can." I stand up from my desk. "We'll look at the others later, okay?"

"Oh . . . yes, of course, if . . ."

"What?"

Her eyebrows are furrowed. "If you're sure?"

I nod, *yes*.

Nicole stands as well, gathers up her stuff, and leaves.

I wander over to my default position at the window.

Fifteen minutes later, Nicole reappears. "Lunch with Pete Kettner today, twelve thirty, at Soleil."

I arrive early so I can see him enter the room. He's young, probably midtwenties, if that. He's fairly scruffy and may well be wearing the same jacket and T-shirt he had on the night I saw him with Kate. As he approaches the table, he has that defiant air of someone refusing to be fazed by unfamiliar surroundings—in this case the opulent decor of a slightly stuffy high-end Midtown eatery.

I don't know why I'm doing this, other than from some perverse need to check the guy out, to put my mind at rest on the question of whether or not Kate could possibly be interested in him, or he in her. Probably, *he* is, but it's less likely that . . .

Oh God.

This was a bad idea.

"Pete?" I say, half getting up and extending my hand. "Hi. I'm Teddy."

"Hi, Mr. Trager, uh . . . *Teddy*," he says awkwardly, and sits down. "Thanks for agreeing to meet with me."

"Finally."

He smiles. "Yes. I was beginning to wonder how else I could get your attention . . . without . . ."

He stops, and fumbles for a moment with his phone and a small notebook, placing one on the table and the other in his jacket pocket, and then switching them around.

"Without *what*?" I say.

He stops fumbling and looks at me. "Without going some other route, I guess . . . the legal route maybe."

I express surprise at this. "Oh?"

He nods. "Yeah, well . . . let me explain why I wanted to see you."

Before he can start, the waiter arrives. I order something simple, and Kettner surrenders his menu saying he'll have the same. He then launches into a quick spiel about Pivot, the kind of stories they run, what they stand for, the kind of change they'd like to bring about, ". . . oh, and by the way," he says, interrupting himself, "that was a *great* speech at ExpoCon the other day."

"Thank you."

"You're welcome." He pauses, clearly nervous now. "Okay, so . . ."

It turns out that there's this other issue Kettner wants to raise with me, it's not strictly a Pivot story, not yet anyway, and he wants to be both thorough *and* fair. He wants to give me a chance to respond before he takes the story any further.

I'm intrigued. But also starting to get a little worried. Does Kate come into this? Is it *not* a coincidence after all?

"So," Kettner says, "I'll just get straight to it. I have this friend at the office, okay, and her boyfriend died a couple of months ago. He was found in the river, over by Pier 81, they think it was probably suicide, they don't know, but the thing is . . ." He hesitates, and as he looks down at his place setting for a moment, I stare at the top of his head in disbelief. Then he continues. "I'm sorry, it's just that this is going to sound very weird."

"No need to apologize," I say, trying to be reassuring. "Go on."

"Okay. Well, for a while before he died, her boyfriend, whose name was Danny Lynch, had become more or less fixated on *you*, but for a very good reason, as it turns out."

I might be expected to show curiosity here, even irritation, but I remain impassive.

"Which is?"

"He looked *exactly* like you." Kettner takes something out of his pocket and slides it across the table in front of me. "This is him."

It's a photo, naturally. But it's of *me*, standing next to one of the grills at Mouzon. I remember the day it was taken. I assume he chose this one because it's both very clear and very clearly *not* Teddy Trager.

"Oh my God."

"Yeah."

The waiter arrives with water and bread. I pick up the photo, as though to examine it closely. When the waiter leaves, I hand the photo back to Kettner. "I don't know what to make of this, Pete."

"I understand," he says, putting the photo away again. "But the thing is, Mr. Trager, after Danny died, Kate—that's the woman I work with, Danny's girlfriend—she was so cut up about it, naturally, that she couldn't bring herself to go through his stuff, and didn't for quite a while afterwards, a few weeks. But then she did." He takes a sip of water. "The night he died, Danny had been working on his laptop, and when Kate finally got around to checking his browsing history, it was all to do with *you* . . . your business partner, Paradime Capital, a Ms. Schlossmeier. It was just Teddy Trager, Teddy Trager, Teddy Trager, columns and columns of searches going back days. Now fine, that wouldn't be . . . it wouldn't *mean* anything if Danny and you weren't so physically alike, and it wouldn't—"

"But what does it mean *anyway*?"

I'm feeling very uneasy now.

"I don't know, that's the thing. Danny was troubled, in certain respects, and he'd been behaving strangely, there's no other way to put it, but . . ." He looks around, as though searching for the right words. "Kate is trying to understand why he took his own life, if that's actually what happened, and she can't help wondering if Danny may have . . . approached you, if there wasn't some form of contact, if—"

"Why doesn't she ask me this herself, why send—"

"Oh, she's tried. She's called your office multiple times now, left messages, sent e-mails, but she's never heard back. You see, as a blogger, as a *journalist,* I get to knock on a few more doors. I get to push a little harder." He smiles sheepishly, almost apologetically. Pete Kettner is doing this because he likes Kate. No other reason. He thinks he might get lucky.

"What does Kate do at Pivot?"

"Oh . . . she's a production assistant."

I nod. "What you said there, 'if that's actually what happened.' What does that mean?"

Kettner squirms a little. "Well, in the absence of any response from you, at least up to now, Kate hasn't been able to keep herself from speculating." He looks me in the eye. "To put it bluntly, she wonders if you maybe had something to do with Danny showing up dead in the Hudson."

I hold his gaze, but don't speak for a few moments. My whole body is tense, my insides are churning. All I want to do is get up from the table and walk out of there, *run* out.

"Okay, Pete," I say, "what you're suggesting is ridiculous, you do know that, right?"

"Probably, yeah, but I don't know it for sure. Nature abhors a vacuum, Mr. Trager."

Teddy, it's fucking *Teddy.*

"And what does that mean?"

"Look, this isn't about chasing a story. Because, believe me, there's *already* enough of a story here . . . the physical likeness, the tech mogul, the body in the river, are you kidding me? If Pivot ran this thing it'd trade up the chain and go viral in minutes flat. But that's not what Pivot is about. We don't do unsubstantiated, we don't do tabloid *non*-stories, that's why we're so small and why no one's heard of us." He leans forward. "This is about someone trying to get answers, someone who wants to be listened to."

"But I don't *have* any answers, Pete. I didn't know this Danny Lynch, I never saw him, never heard from him, never had any contact with him. What you're saying here? It's all news to *me*."

Kettner leans back in his chair. "Well, that *is* an answer. And that's all Kate wanted to hear, or *needed* to hear. She's grieving, you know." He looks away. "It's . . . it's a process."

I nod, and then look away myself, feeling like a piece of shit.

The waiter arrives with our food.

A moment later, as Kettner is unflapping his napkin, he says, "Look, thanks for hearing me out on that, Mr. Trager, I really appreciate it." He nods down at his food. "But hey, since we're here, could I maybe ask you a couple of questions about your speech?"

On my way back to the office, I experience a horrible, gnawing sense of guilt, mainly for what I've put Kate through. I'd forgotten about the laptop, and it never occurred to me that she might end up raking over my recent search history. I suppose it was likely that sooner or later she'd come across Teddy Trager, but not that she'd ever suspect there was an actual connection between us, or that one of us could in any way be responsible for the death of the other.

Soon, though, guilt is replaced by paranoia.

Because . . . what was that Pete Kettner said? Kate contacted my office *multiple times*? Why did I never hear about that? Why was it filtered out? And Pete Kettner himself . . . he seemed reasonable enough, I even sort of liked him, but was he on the level? Was he just clearing up that one point—confirmation for Kate that I'd never had any contact with Danny Lynch—or was he initiating a campaign of some kind that would lead to, as he called it, "the legal route"? Meaning what? A perp walk at some point? An indictment, an eventual conviction? Or maybe it's a different route he has in mind altogether, a shakedown, blackmail—something along those lines.

If guilt is followed by paranoia, what comes next?

I start by thinking that Pete Kettner and Kate need to be warned off the idea of pursuing, in any way at all, this suspicion they have—but how do I do that without it sounding like a threat? Back at my desk, I make a couple of calls, first to Paradime's head of corporate security, Jerry Ellis. I ask him to recommend a private investigator and tell him I need someone discreet, that it's not a corporate matter but that it's fairly urgent all the same. He gets back to me in ten minutes with the name of an agency, McNicoll Associates, and a contact, Leonard Perl.

"He's very reliable, Mr. Trager. I've known him for years. You want me to give him a call?"

"No, that's all right, Jerry, I'll do it, thanks."

I arrange a meeting with this Leonard Perl for the next morning, and, just after ten o'clock, Nicole ushers him into my office. He's tall, slim, midforties. He's wearing a dark-blue suit and could be a corporate executive. I invite him to sit down. I ask him about the kind of work he does.

"Well, sir, we're involved in a lot of areas: insurance claim verification, credit reference reporting, tracing of missing persons, personnel screening, company searches. We offer these, as well as a range of surveillance packages."

I nod along and then tell him exactly what I need: eyes and ears on the offices of a web site called Pivot and on two people who work there in particular. Put baldly like this, the whole thing sounds pretty creepy—and the irony of it isn't lost on me either, but Perl reacts as if I've asked him to put a trace out on an antique piece of furniture I'm interested in acquiring. We discuss budget parameters and time frames, and he says he'll get on it immediately.

He's as good as his word, and pretty soon I'm receiving daily reports on what Kate is up to, her routine, who she meets with, what's happening at the office. I get audio, video, e-mails, transcripts—more material than I know what to do with, most of it tedious, none of it revealing. There's nothing about what Kate is thinking in relation to Teddy Trager, and there's nothing about what Kate is just . . . *thinking*. Nor is there any evidence that she's in any kind of a relationship with Pete Kettner, but apparently a breakdown of the data shows that she's spending more time, minute for minute, in *his* company than in anyone else's. What does this mean? Nothing, necessarily. It's just data. But not everything they say to each other is retrievable, so what if, in their more private, secluded moments, they're talking about the very thing I'm paranoid about, the very thing I'm spending all this money trying to identify and inoculate against? It seems like a stretch, but if I let my imagination run with it, I can see the whole thing unfolding before me, and where it leads is to some kind of twisted nightmare: Teddy Trager being indicted for the murder of Danny Lynch.

Factor in DNA, of course, and it all pretty quickly gets reversed, but what you end up with then, as far as I'm concerned, is equally nightmarish: PTSD-addled Iraq vet indicted for the murder of visionary tech billionaire . . .

So I need to get way out ahead on this, and fast. The encrypted files I'm receiving on a daily basis from Leonard Perl are great, but they're not enough—even though in a sense they're *too* much. Plus, there's a real danger here that I'll get distracted, seduced by the streaming video feed from various surveillance points Perl has linked me to—one a plant in the Pivot offices, others random CCTV security cams in the immediate neighborhood. Over the course of a week, a week and a half, being able to watch Kate in real time moving around rooms and streets like this takes its toll on me, and not just in terms of focus but emotionally too. I'll replay a section multiple times just because I like how she moves in it. I'll find myself watching clips at four in the morning, freeze-framing her at different moments.

But with all of this I'm no closer to finding out what's going on in Kate's head or even if she's given the whole business another thought since Kettner reported back to her on our conversation.

That's when I get an idea for a more efficient way of dealing with the problem.

I decide to buy Pivot.

With no Doug Shaw around to consult, I get Lester to call a meeting of the relevant personnel, and, when we're all seated around the table, I ask them for ideas about how we should proceed. I tell them we can't buy Pivot directly, or be openly associated with the acquisition, and that what I envisage instead is some mechanism whereby we do it at a few removes, through a series of dummy or shell companies, or by getting a company we're already affiliated with to do it.

But at the meeting there is strong opposition to all of this. It starts out more as confusion, incomprehension even, than any coherent argument, but then the objections come thick and fast. Why Pivot? It's small, it's niche, there's no business model to work with. A successful web site is all about traffic, all about clicks, page views and ad revenue, all about manufactured urgency and polarizing headlines—and Pivot is pretty much a textbook example of how not to do any of that stuff. So how would you value it? And where's the growth potential? And just what would you *do* with it?

Most of this comes from Dick Stein, one of our senior investment analysts. The thing is, my idea, which I can't advertise to him, or to anyone else here, is that by owning Pivot I'd not only be able to keep a close watch on what Kate and Pete Kettner are doing, I'd be able to exert a certain amount of influence over them as well. Pumping additional money into the operation would generate new activity, and that, in turn, would redirect their attention and, with any luck, distract them.

That's the idea anyway.

The meeting gets testy. Most people agree with Stein, whether or not they say so out loud. I can see it. And Lester looks uncomfortable too.

I stare at the glass of water in front of me for a few moments and have a small epiphany. Of *course* these people all agree with the professional investment guy, because that's what he *is*, a fucking professional investment guy. He knows what he's talking about. *I* don't. *I'm* being irrational. *I'm* being a jerk.

And I understand this.

Nevertheless, I end up shouting at them. I end up telling them to just do it anyway before storming out of the room.

The next day I'm at Jean-Georges having lunch with Oberon Capital Group CEO, Dessie Litchfield, when something extremely weird happens. I look up from my truffle salad and see, approaching us from across the room, the unmistakable figure of Bill Clinton. We have a table by the window, and I glance out for a second to gather my wits. I have no protective blanket of morphine this time, but I'm sure it'll be okay. He'll probably do all the talking anyway. As he gets to the table, I'm about to extend my hand and greet him warmly, but Clinton isn't looking at me. Instead, and with a grin on his face, he gently slaps Litchfield on the back and says, "Dessie, my main man, what's up?" Litchfield turns and laughs, "Bill!"

The two men go at it for a minute, Clinton pointing over at his table and saying he's here with some friends from Paris, Litchfield mentioning something about his wife. This is followed by a brief exchange about the *weather*, and then, turning to me, Litchfield says, "Bill, I'm sorry, have you met Teddy Trager?"

I'm about to extend my hand again and make some lame joke about this when Clinton shakes his head. "No, I don't think I've had the pleasure, Teddy." Then he extends *his* hand.

We shake.

In disbelief, I look into his eyes. Familiar and searching as they are, I see no sign of recognition in them whatsoever.

"Paradime," he says, "right? Paradime Capital?"

Unsure whether to call him *Bill* or *Mr. President* I end up just nodding.

"Great company," he says. "Doing some great things. Yes, sir."

And that's it.

He and Litchfield engage in another few moments of banter, during which I stare up at Clinton, at his florid complexion, at his silver hair. I listen, uncomprehending, to whatever words he's saying in that whispered, husky, conspiratorial drawl I remember so clearly from the hospital.

Afterward, I try to make sense of what happened, but I can't. As I cross the lobby of the Tyler Building and go up in the elevator I feel increasingly strange and a little nauseous. In reception, Nicole approaches with a note in her hand, but I wave her away. I sit at my desk and swivel for a bit. Then I turn to my computer and look up Bill Clinton. I hop around aimlessly, from his Wikipedia page to the Foundation web site.

What's going on? It's not just that this man with legendary recall powers didn't remember visiting me in the hospital two months ago, it's that he claimed never to have met me at all.

Maybe it was the morphine.

But if so, what else did I hallucinate? Clooney too? You don't really hallucinate on morphine though, do you? Not with the low dosages I was on. And not like that anyway.

Then something occurs to me.

I work out the dates that I was in the hospital and compare these to *NYT* search results for references to Clinton on those same dates.

It seems that on the very morning Bill Clinton spent ten or fifteen minutes sitting at my bedside in New York, he was attending a regional-aid conference in Lisbon, Portugal.

Fuck.

I slump forward on the desk and, for a few seconds, feel as if everything around me, every solid object—the chair I'm in, the desk in front of me, the office itself, the seventy floors of steel and concrete stacked beneath it—as if all these things are on the point of crumbling suddenly and falling in on themselves.

But the room remains solid. There's no trillion-particle dust storm blowing up around me. No understanding of *this* either, though.

I'm about to look up Clooney when an anxious-seeming Nicole appears at the door. I raise my head.

"What?"

She holds up the note she had in her hand earlier. "A message," she says, "it's urgent, apparently . . . from Dr. Lessing?"

He wants to meet and suggests a coffee shop four blocks away. This seems weird to me, but on my way down I realize something. I've only ever met Karl Lessing in the apartment, never here at the Tyler. I've never spoken to him directly on the phone. I could spend time wondering why this might be and devise some workable theories, but I'm too consumed with the other matter to really think about it.

The coffee shop is very ordinary, even a little shabby. I spot Lessing at a table near the back, occupied with his phone.

When I get to the table, he looks up and nods at the chair on the other side. "Sit down."

An impulse to upend the table and punch Lessing in the face ripples across my brain, but I have a question I want to put to him.

I sit down.

He has a question too, and manages to get it in before mine. "What the hell are you doing?"

I don't answer at first. I look around. It's as if I'm impatient for someone to come over and take my order. But I'm not. I've just had lunch. I do it because I'm confused. Every new thing that comes along now is confusing, and they're all piling up confusingly inside my head. I look at Lessing again. "What do you mean?"

He makes a huffing sound. "What do you *think* I mean? This Pivot thing. You're trying to *buy* it? And Leonard Perl, the surveillance? What's that all about? We had an agreement." He leans across the table and locks eyes with me. "No contact with your old life, no crossover."

Lessing is wearing a suit, but there's something shabby about it, and about him too. Who *is* he?

That's another question I want to ask him, but I'm afraid of what the answer will be. While we're at it, here's another. Does he know why I want to buy Pivot? And if he doesn't, do I tell him?

He's waiting for me to speak when a waitress comes over.

"Two coffees," Lessing says without looking at her.

When she leaves, I say, "Karl, I don't have to explain myself to *you*."

He adjusts his glasses, then takes them off, fiddles with them, and puts them back on again. For the few seconds he doesn't have them on, he looks strange, like an outsized fish. "No, you don't," he says, "about most things, that's true. It's the way we want it, and it's working out great. Look at ExpoCon." He throws his head back. "Fabulous. And before that, asteroid mining? Running for public office? It's all *very* exciting." He lowers his voice. "But *this*? I don't get it. Basically, we make one request of you, we have *one* simple condition. And that's only because it makes sense. I mean, how is this thing going to work if you get entangled with your past again?" He shakes his head. "If you get entangled with *her*?"

Okay, at least that answers my question. It's clear to me now that he doesn't know. He thinks I've lost it. But I haven't. And I'm certainly not trying to get entangled with Kate again. I'm trying to save her.

From *me*.

But I don't see how I'm going to be able to do it alone, not anymore.

Our coffees arrive. I don't touch mine. Lessing doesn't touch his. "Well?" he says, drumming his fingers on the tabletop.

So I explain it to him: the laptop, the search history, Kettner, everything. I explain my motivation in hiring Leonard Perl and in trying to acquire Pivot. I tell him I need help in bypassing people like Dick Stein. I tell him we just need to get *on* with it. "Look," I say, "when we control Pivot, we'll be in a position to control, you know . . . the narrative."

Lessing stares across the table at me. He's taken in all I've said, he's processed it, but behind his eyes now—I can sense it—various cortices have flared up and are going into hyperdrive. And suddenly I'm scared. Suddenly I'm thinking I should have kept my mouth shut.

He mumbles something.

I lean forward a bit. *"What?"* This comes out a little louder than I intended.

Lessing shakes his head. "Nothing. I just . . . I need to give this a little thought."

Before I know it, he's peeling a ten off a roll of bills and making to get up out of his chair. He puts his phone into his pocket.

"That's it?" I say, looking up at him now.

"I have a thing." He adjusts his glasses. "But let me get back to you on this, okay?"

There are so many questions I want to put to Dr. Karl Lessing. Who are you? Where is Doug Shaw? Who hacked Teddy Trager's car? Do I really know Bill Clinton? Are Kate and Pete Kettner now on some kind of . . . *list*?

"Sure," I say, "yeah."

I pick up the cup of coffee in front of me to indicate that I'm staying.

"Okay, Danny."

When he moves off, I put the cup down again and stare at it for a moment.

Right now, if I had only one question, I guess it would be this: if you're so fucking happy with what a good Teddy Trager I make, what was wrong with the original?

I stand up from the table and turn around. Lessing has already gone. I make my way out of the coffee shop and onto the sidewalk. I look left and right. Nothing. Then I spot him across the street, on the far corner—and again, in a glimmer, he's gone. I cross over, move along the block and make the same left turn he did.

It takes me a moment to focus, to filter out what's not relevant in my line of vision—the two old ladies chatting by the newsstand, the delivery guy hauling a large crate across the sidewalk, the approaching group of tourists—but I see him. He's directly ahead, about half a block away. We're on 52nd Street, going east. I keep walking and could easily go faster. I could catch up with him no problem. I could tap him on the shoulder, pin him against a storefront window, *make* him answer my questions.

But I hold back, and follow him.

This reminds me of how things were before, at the beginning, with Trager, when I was following *him* around, and somehow it feels wrong, like a misstep. I'm about to ramp things up a bit when Lessing takes out his phone. He holds it at arm's length for a second, either to check who's calling, I guess, or to make a call himself. Then he brings the phone up to his ear. Whoever he's talking to, the conversation carries him all the way over to Third Avenue. He turns right and keeps going. At the corner of 49th, he comes to a stop. He's in a huddle of people waiting to cross, and I back up behind him—almost right up against him. He's still on the phone.

"Okay," he's saying—and with the sound of traffic and other people talking I can just barely make this out—"I'll see you there, outside, five minutes."

The light changes.

As Lessing is stepping off the sidewalk, he puts the phone back into his pocket. I wait to let him get ahead a bit and then step forward myself. We move in unison, half a block apart. There's almost a rhythm to it.

But after a while, certain angles and contours of Third Avenue—of this stretch of it, anyway—start to shift in front of me, sliding and subtly realigning. A specific formation I recognize then clicks into place, and that trillion-particle dust storm blows up right inside my skull. Because over to my left, on the other side of Third, is the Wolper & Stone Building, where Gideon Logistics has its headquarters. And just up ahead here, on my right, is that cocktail lounge with the great olives—what was it, the Bradbury?

I slow down.

Holy fuck.

There's a newsstand on the corner, just to my left, and I stop at it. I use it for cover but also for something to lean against, because, right now, I can't breathe.

I tilt my head at a slight angle and watch as Karl Lessing moves along the busy sidewalk. He veers towards the entrance to the Bradbury. And approaching from the opposite direction, veering towards the same point, is Phil Coover.

15

When *I* met Coover, and we were crossing Third to go to this very bar, I remember thinking I could short-circuit my rising sense of panic by just taking off at a run and making for the nearest subway stop.

It's what I do now, but I no longer have the expectation that it's going to cause my fear index to drop by even a single point. All movement there, I can tell, will be in the other direction.

Because Phil Coover . . .

Who is he? *What* is he?

A train rushes into the station now that matches the speed and roar of my thoughts.

Is he a consultant, as he said when we met? Is he a private-security contractor? Is he an executive at Gideon? Is he US military? Is he NSA? Is he CIA? What's his interest in me, and how far back does it go? Did *he* have Trager's car hacked? And the prep cook at Barcadero, the one I replaced, Yannis . . . holy fucking *shit*, was that Coover too?

Somehow?

And what about Sharista?

I get on the train, shaking, maybe muttering to myself, only a step or two removed from being *that* guy—the central-casting crazy person, the one who makes you wish you'd gotten on the next car.

Hey, you!

Hey, buddy!

Hey, gorgeous!

I stand, leaning back against the door, and try to remain calm. Then I look up suddenly, and around, scoping out the other passengers. Am I being followed? *Watched?* That's what Coover said, at the beginning. But did he mean watched all the time, or is it more like what Trager said when I mentioned surveillance to him? *Not twenty-four-seven, Jesus, don't flatter yourself . . .*

I don't know what to think.

Except that I've presumably just put Kate into a very dangerous position. It was obvious from his reaction that Lessing was freaked out by what I told him, and he reported it back to Coover almost immediately. So what's Coover's reaction going to be? And how long before they realize I've cut loose? If they don't already know?

I look around again.

I have no idea where I am or where I'm going. I just ended up on this train . . . which is . . . an uptown 6. It'll soon be pulling into 59th Street. What good is that to me?

None.

When it stops, I get off. At street level, I wander for a block or two and then head into Central Park. Not wanting to go too far, I walk down by the pond and find an empty bench to sit on. Huddled now in this oasis of calm (though watched over by the steel and granite monoliths behind me and to my left), I close my eyes for a while and think.

Maybe cutting loose is the wrong move. Maybe I shouldn't be panicking at all. Maybe I should just go back to the office and act like nothing happened.

Or back to the apartment.

Because where else would I go? How else would I function? At this point, who else would I *be?*

In any case, Kate and Pete Kettner aren't a real threat. They don't have any incriminating evidence. There's nothing they can actually do.

I open my eyes.

The reason I told Lessing about them was to explain *my* behavior, to demonstrate how cautious *I* was being. This is a rationalization, I know, and just as I'm about to tie a nice little bow on it, my cell phone rings. I take it out and check the screen. It's a private number. I think about not answering it, but I don't want to set off any alarm bells.

"Hello?"

"Teddy. It's Karl."

I focus on the dark pool of water in front of me, people gliding by, insubstantial, like shadows.

"Hi, Karl."

"I've been thinking, Teddy, and, you know what? Your instincts were right. Easy to see how it could happen, with the laptop. And she was bound to get curious, which is probably all this is . . . but better to be safe too, better to be inside the tent and all of that. For now, at least. So . . . yeah, we're going to put some money into Pivot. In fact, we're going to try and buy it, like you suggested."

We?

A little dart of pain shoots up the back of my neck.

"What does Doug have to say about all of this?"

"I wouldn't worry about what Doug thinks."

"No?"

"No." He pauses. "Look, Doug is having some issues right now, health issues. He's not really in a position to weigh in on stuff like this."

I remain silent as I try to process what I've just heard.

"Teddy? You there?"

"Yeah." I crouch forward. "I'm here. So . . ."

"So, yeah, that Pivot thing will be taken care of. Better that you keep a little distance from the whole thing anyway, right?"

"Yeah."

"And by the way, listen, I should tell you . . . you're doing a great job, and, uh . . . keep it up." It sounds like he's reading this from a card or off a screen or something.

I say a mumbled thanks, and then he hangs up.

As I walk out of the park, I'm tempted to let myself think that I've dodged a bullet here, that I could easily rewind a bit and pick up from where I left off . . . but where would that be, exactly? At the office, before I went to lunch at Jean-Georges? Before I hired Leonard Perl? Before that conversation with *Nina*?

I cross at the light and walk south on Fifth.

What does it matter, though? There *is* no rewind option, so if I'm going to pick it up, it has to be from here. It's just that . . . everything has changed, and this is no longer just about me. If Phil Coover is the one buying or putting funds into Pivot, he will have a window into Kate's life and will be in a position to exert a degree of control over her. It's bad enough that that's what *I* was proposing to do, but this is a lot worse.

I keep walking, and a few minutes later I'm at the Tyler Building. But on my way in I have this overwhelming sense of dread. For the first time, I feel like an actual fraud. I certainly don't feel like someone who's doing "a great job," or even someone who knows what their job is. I'm also unsure of what to expect when I step out of the elevator and into reception. Everything seems normal, though, and as I approach my office, Nicole appears, tablet in hand, as usual. I shake my head.

"But—"

"Later," I say without looking at her.

I go inside, close the door behind me and head over to my desk. I need to find out who Phil Coover is, and I spend the next couple of hours searching for information about him, a reference, an image, anything. There are plenty of people called Phil Coover, but none of them quite fits the bill. I trawl through all things Gideon, I go to DoD and CIA web sites. I look up work by investigative journalists who operate on the fringes and have written previously about PMCs and the intel community.

I come up with nothing.

Then I remember what Nina said when she was talking about Teddy's car being hacked and where she'd come across information on the crash forensics.

I get on the phone and call Jerry Ellis again. Now, clearly this shit-head can't be trusted, because if *he* didn't tell Karl Lessing about my dealings with Leonard Perl, then I don't know who did. But I reckon he can still be useful. Without going into specifics, I say I have an IT issue and ask him to send me over someone who knows their way around computers.

An hour later, an intense young guy called Billie Zheng shows up, looking eager but also slightly apprehensive. I tell him to sit, and I chat with him for a few minutes. Then I square up to it. "Okay, Billie," I say, "I need to get onto the deep web . . . or, uh, the dark web, or the deep *net,* whatever the fuck it's called." I pause. "Can you get me down there?"

Billie Zheng looks simultaneously relieved and puzzled—relieved, I'm guessing, because this won't be a challenge as far as he's concerned, and puzzled, I'm pretty sure, for the same reason—because if it's no challenge for *him,* how can it possibly be something that tech visionary Teddy Trager needs help with?

He hesitates, as if there might be a punch line coming that he should wait for.

I lean forward. "Well?"

"Yeah," he says, "sure, of course."

So we get into it. He explains stuff to me about encryption and randomized peer-to-peer relay channels. I ask him questions and take notes. My obvious lack of basic knowledge here continues to puzzle him, but I don't care. I'm focused on what he's telling me. Within an hour we have downloaded TOR, the deep web browser, and he's giving me tips about how to maintain anonymity: turn off cookies and JavaScript, for example, and put some duct tape on the webcam. He then shows me the basics of how to navigate my way around and how to locate specific sites. He mentions Hidden Wiki, a reliable deep web link directory for newbies and a couple of real-time chat rooms where experienced denizens of this shadow realm can steer me in the right direction.

When I have what I need, I send Billie on his way. If he ends up getting quizzed by Lessing or anyone else, there isn't much he can tell them about my intentions, because I didn't tell *him*. And I'm not even sure I know what they are myself. In fact, it takes me a few days to really get my bearings here, to swim around all the drugs, guns, porn and human organs for sale and find what I'm looking for, which is the kind of site that Nina mentioned, a place where investigative journalism and public interest accountability can operate without fear of restriction or censorship.

There's no doubt that some of the material I manage to see is insane, hardcore conspiracy stuff, but not all of it. There are plenty of sites on the surface web that track corporate corruption and malfeasance, but nothing like a thing down here called Soul Trader Inc. This is where I find the details of every single whistle-blower allegation that has ever been levelled at Gideon Logistics—and not just the nine cases that Kate did her best to tell me about, the ones that went to trial, but *all* of them . . . including what may be a reference to the incident *I* witnessed at Sharista.

Through a Nepalese lawyer, the family of a Sajit Pradhan has apparently been trying to establish the whereabouts of their son, a so-called TCN, who went to work for the company in Afghanistan months ago and now appears to be missing. This is one of several similar cases, some of them going back years, but in all of them the families have met with resistance and obstruction leading to prohibitive legal costs and, in many instances, financial ruin.

Extremely uncomfortable with this, I move on to another site and read about Gideon's legal battle with the Pentagon. The level of detail here is staggering and would be unimaginable on any normal news outlet. But what's really shocking is the revelation that Gideon Logistics, one of the world's largest private military and defense contractors, was started in the mid-1990s with seed money from a CIA-fronted VC firm called Silo, which was itself a forerunner of the agency's official VC arm, In-Q-Tel. Apparently, the connections and links between these companies are labyrinthine and ongoing, which makes the multi-billion-dollar fraudulent billing case something of a joke.

But there's a trail here, and I follow it all the way to what emerges slowly—to me at least—as some kind of logical conclusion. Because it transpires that what I discovered about Gideon Logistics is also pretty much true of Paradime Capital. The exact details are way too knotty to unravel, let alone retain—I can just about understand this stuff as I'm reading it—but the basic point is the same. The seed money for these companies, the funding, the patronage—it all came from the CIA.

If this were a Venn diagram, it occurs to me, I'd be at the intersection, and so would Phil Coover.

It takes another couple of days before *that* name elicits a response. I throw it out there on a corporate-watch forum, and someone with the user ID *fg63br7iyzg* chimes back with: "Oh shit, is that Project Mandrake Phil Coover? Haven't heard HIS name in years."

I ask a follow-up question, and wait. There's no reply.

The next day, I try to go onto the forum again, but it appears to have been taken down.

I've seen all I want to see anyway. I may not fully comprehend everything that's happened to me, or why it's happened, but I have enough of a sense of it to understand one essential thing: this is no longer a dream, no longer a weird, extended, solipsistic trance. Whatever spell I was under has broken, whatever edifice of delusion I was occupying has crumbled. As Nina suggested, I am, in fact, and have been all along, a puppet. And is there anything more pathetic than that? A puppet who believes he is a free agent?

A marionette with a soul?

Outwardly, over the next few days, I carry on as normal. But really, I'm just floating along in another trance, a different kind of trance—this one fueled by guilt and dread, by images of the past and visions of the future, by the now-spectral face of Sajit Pradhan and the yet-to-be-seen face of Nina Schlossmeier's child. And as for the great job I'm supposedly doing, by the end of another week it really couldn't be said—unless staring out the window counts—that I am doing any job at all now.

So how long can *this* last? How long before I feel a gentle tug on my pull strings? Not long at all, as it turns out. The next morning, I'm in the back of the limo, we're on the way to the office, Ricardo driving, when I feel it. Instead of going his normal way, Ricardo heads for the Lincoln Tunnel. As soon as I notice the change of route, I reach over to the intercom to say something, but . . . I don't know what it is, I hesitate. I hold my finger over the button and let it hover there for maybe fifteen seconds. Then, just at the entrance to the tunnel, I sigh loudly, flop back in my seat, and proceed to gaze vacantly out at the oncoming rush of flickering lights and vitreous white tiles . . .

After a while, I look at the back of Ricardo's head through the thick glass of the divider. I'm not going to give him a hard time. What would be the point? He hasn't lost his mind. He hasn't gone rogue. He's just doing his job.

By the time we get onto the New Jersey Turnpike I have a fairly clear idea of where we might be headed: the Gideon training facility where I did my orientation sessions before shipping out to Afghanistan. It's in Pennsylvania, not too far from a place called Doylestown.

It takes us a little over two hours to get there, and I spend most of this time lost in thought, in loops of anger and regret, but also moving, slowly, I suppose, to a state of resignation and acceptance. Whatever reason they have for bringing me out here, it isn't to do further training or orientation, that's for sure.

We drive through the gates of the facility, which is in a fairly remote, wooded area, and park directly in front of a plain, single-story building. That's when I start to feel a little sick. I get out of the car and look around, avoiding eye contact with Ricardo. The contrast of the sleek black limousine with the dusty, sunbaked, almost ram-shackle surroundings is quite stark. As I remember it, there are several similar buildings to the rear of the one we're parked in front of.

There doesn't seem to be anyone around.

I look over at Ricardo, who's leaning against the side of the car. I'm about to say something to him when a figure emerges from the building, a guy in his twenties wearing fatigue pants and a black T-shirt.

He approaches me and says, "Sir, come this way, please." He then turns around and goes back inside. I follow him into a small, sparsely furnished office. "In there, sir," he says and points to a door in the corner.

I nod in acknowledgment, wondering if there's any way I can delay this. There isn't. I take in a deep breath, hold it for a few seconds and release it slowly. I head for the door. What's behind here? I quickly visualize a large empty room, blacked-out windows, a single light bulb, and then . . . after the bullet has entered the back of my head, and I'm falling forward, a spray of blood hitting the bare floorboards just *inches* in front of me . . .

The room *is* large, and pretty much empty, except for a pool table in the middle and several rows of stacked plastic folding chairs over to the right. The floorboards are bare and worn. To the left there are two windows, both of them grimy, probably from a combination of dust and rain. These are the only sources of light here, making the atmosphere dim and oppressive, and for this reason it takes me a couple of moments to realize that there is a man standing at the far side of the room. The fact that he has his back to me isn't helping.

I take a few steps towards him. "Hello?"

He's wearing a suit, a well-cut one, and is about my height and build, and—

He turns around.

I remain calm.

Controlled breathing helps, short ones—in, out, in, out. Because it's Teddy Trager. Standing there in front of me now. Ten feet away, and smiling.

It's Teddy fucking Trager . . .

Except that . . .

I take another step forward.

Except that it *isn't*. He looks like Teddy Trager, but there's something off . . . the cheekbones, the eyes, I don't know what it is . . . *something*. He also has a visible scar below his left ear. As I get closer, he takes a step forward too and holds out his hand. "Hey," he says. "Pleased to meet you."

And he doesn't sound a fucking thing like Teddy Trager.

I ignore his outstretched hand and study his face for a moment instead, the lines, the proportions.

That scar is really distracting.

Is this guy meant to be a replacement for me? They can't be serious.

I'm about to say something to him when I hear a sound behind me—the door opening and then footsteps. On these floorboards, the footsteps are loud and firm. I swallow hard and find myself wondering, as I turn around, where the nearest subway stop might be.

"Danny," Phil Coover says, striding towards me. "Danny, Danny, Danny."

In green khaki pants and a black turtleneck sweater, he looks a little older than I remember. He radiates a similar vitality and presence, but his face seems heavier, more lined, his eyes less intensely vivid.

We shake hands. His grip is just as firm as before, and, as before, when we're done he places a hand on my shoulder. "So, how's my favorite cockroach?"

No change in style, either.

It might be a little soon to say *fuck you,* but nor do I want to waste any time being polite. I flick my head back to indicate the guy stand-ing behind me. "You're kidding with this, right?"

Coover removes his hand from my shoulder. "Say what?"

"Oh, come on, *look* at him."

Keeping his eyes on me the whole time, Coover seems to consider this. Then he says, "Leon here is a work in progress. The scar is un-fortunate. We need more time for things to settle in."

"And for a little *voice* work, maybe?"

"Yes. Obviously. We can't all be perfect like you, Danny."

My stomach flips, and I feel weak. "So why show him off like this?"

"Why do you think?"

Oh God . . . "Well, let's see . . . you want to make a point? You re-placed Teddy Trager, you can just as easily replace me? Is that it?"

"Not *just* as easily, but . . . yes."

"So then . . ." I look down at the floorboards, frustration mounting, a part of me wishing there really had been a bullet waiting on the other side of the door. I look back at Coover. "I don't get any of this. None of it makes sense. What are you running here, some kind of pro-gram? Or *project*, I don't know . . . Project Mandrake?"

Coover holds my gaze for a moment, then looks over my shoulder. "Leon," he says, "thank you."

Leon moves immediately. He walks around us and leaves the room.

When Coover hears the door closing behind him, he says, "Okay, so . . . no, Project Mandrake, that was"—he clicks his fingers—"that was the late seventies, after the Church Committee hearings, in fact. So I doubt very much, quite frankly, if you know anything more about it than the name." He turns and walks over to the pool table. Resting against the edge of it, he folds his arms. "Things are different today. Well, the *names* are certainly different, but I suppose they all lead back in one way or another to the great fountainhead, MKUltra. That was Allen Dulles, in '53. And even before that, I suppose, to get the ball rolling, there was Operation Paperclip." He seems quite wistful about all of this. "So you see, Danny, we're part of a great tradition here."

I shake my head. "I'm not part of any fucking *tradition*. I didn't choose this—"

"Well, none of us *chooses* it—"

"Oh please." I feel another wave of exhaustion. "I need to sit down."

He holds out a hand, indicating the stacked chairs. "Be my guest."

I walk over and pick out two of the folding chairs. I set them up a few feet apart and take one of them. "Okay," I say. "This program I'm apparently taking part in, what is it, Operation Doppelgänger? Project Lookalike? What?"

"Something along those lines," Coover says, coming over and sitting down in the second chair. "Understandably, it's classified, but yes, the idea is essentially that . . . to harness this opportunity nature provides, albeit rarely. Though not as rarely as you might think. Leon there, for example—okay, he needs work, I'll admit it—but he comes from an area of Russia where for some reason we have found there's a higher statistical probability of being able to find a lookalike, for *our* purposes, at any rate, than anywhere else in the entire world. And believe me, we've looked. This program goes back twenty-five years."

"Holy shit."

"Yes, the thing is, you see, in most cases, there's an initial *wow* factor, and then you look closer—like with Leon, I guess—and maybe it's not such a close match. But there are enhancement options . . . surgical procedures, for example, prosthetic implants, genetic manipulation, and new areas are opening up all the time. It's a regular Pandora's box." He leans back in the chair. "But then, once in a while . . . *man* . . ."

"What?"

"We get a live one . . . a ninety-seven, ninety-eight percent match. Almost too good to be true."

"And that's *me* you're talking about?"

"Damn right. You're the jewel in the crown of this program, Danny."

I shake my head, struggling here. "So . . ."

"Yes?"

"What about Bill Clinton?"

"Ha. That's another Russian guy, and he's *very* good, but he doesn't have anything like your numbers."

"Clooney?"

Coover shakes his head. "No, no, that was George. He and Teddy go back. It was Ray too. We put Bill in there to mix it up a bit."

"Look, what *is* this program? I don't understand."

Coover clears his throat quietly, then sits up straight in the chair. "Okay, like any of these programs, it's a form of unconventional or asymmetric warfare. It's an attempt to weaponize something that you wouldn't usually think of in that context—so . . . psychiatry, LSD, sleep cycles, sex, the media, video games, consumer technology, or *whatever*—and it's all done in the interests of protecting national security. In this case, it's the strategic use of political decoys or body doubles. At least that's how it started out, and you can see the appeal of it, being able to replace key figures, and then influence decision-making, reverse policies, and, ultimately, shape events. But the limitation of it has always been this: how do you control the decoy? How do you control the double? Do you pay them? Or do you coerce them? Is it a suitcase full of money or a baseball bat? It's all a little crude, I'll admit, and more often than not it ends in tears. Or a goddamned book deal." He pauses. "Because the double, usually, is a nobody, a loser."

"A cockroach."

"There you go. But what *if*,"—he holds up a finger—"what if you could engineer it so that the decoy doesn't really know what's going on, so that the decoy thinks this is all happening to *him*, that he's got the chance to become this other person all on his own . . . and then he does, and we just watch. What if you could engineer a sense of destiny for someone and then install it in them like a piece of software?" He lets that hang in the air for a moment. "You know, at one time we had whole research departments working on it, in labs, in universities, looking at this deep-seated desire we all seem to have for personal transformation and what we'll do to achieve it, the lengths we'll go to . . . as well, of course, as our capacity for denial and self-deception. This stuff is all there in the literature. You can read it. Also, go talk to Karl—really, he's fascinating on the subject." He clears his throat again, loudly this time. "Now, there's a wild-card aspect to it as well. There's unpredictability, there are variables—in this case, getting you in front of Teddy, for example, or trying to keep Doug Shaw in line, to convince him this was bigger than just protecting Paradime—but once the subject is embedded, sort of like a sleeper agent, then that's a solid asset we have in place that we can activate further down the line, if and when we need to."

I shift in the chair, partly because it's uncomfortable, partly because I may be about to get sick. "And then?"

"Well, at some point we have a version of *this* conversation. But, you see, the theory is that the decoy is now so entrenched in his new identity that there doesn't need to be much persuading. The old life has been left behind, we're all set, and, as for money or coercion, neither of those things is actually required. To be frank, though, Danny, I'm a little disappointed that *we're* having the conversation so soon. Things seemed to be going pretty well, and then . . . I don't know . . ."

He lets that trail off. But what does he mean? Is he referring to *Kate*?

"What about Teddy?" I say, in a blatant attempt at deflection. "I don't get it. How is *he* such an asset? Where does national security come into it with him?"

Coover shrugs. "Maybe it doesn't," he says, after a moment. "On the other hand, maybe it does. Maybe Teddy runs for public office, and crushes it. Then we have a glittering prize in our pocket. In any case, he's on the board of all the major tech companies, and *that's* certainly valuable. But you know, none of that really matters, because the point is, Danny, you're an experiment, a trial we're running. This is now a big program, and we're taking the long view. We've secured a *lot* of funding."

I take in a deep breath. "There are others? In the program?"

"There *will* be," Coover says. "So this trial, in terms of future budget allocations . . . it's very important." He pauses. "Look, since 9/11 the whole national-security apparatus has mushroomed, it's out of control. There are now thousands of programs and initiatives, and this is just one of them. But I'll be honest with you, Danny, you revived it. Single-handedly. I'm serious. The program was more or less dormant, had been for a while. I was involved in other things—I was with Gideon, consulting, liaising . . . and then *you* showed up on the radar."

"At Sharista."

"Yeah, after the incident that night, the riot. I'm looking through the reports, there's video footage, there are photos, and, holy shit, if I don't see this . . . this *face*."

More questions arise here than I'll ever be able to put to him, but as I go back in my mind to that night, and fast-forward through the subsequent days and months, only one of them forms coherently in my head. "What about the cost?"

Coover shakes his head. "I don't . . . what do you mean? Our budget is—"

"The *human* cost, Phil. Sajit Pradhan? That prep cook at Barcadero? Trager himself? You hacked his car, you *killed* him. Then all the surveillance, the invasion of privacy, the denial of . . . I thought we had a constitution in this country."

"Danny, that's a bit naive, isn't it? Don't you see that what we *have* in this country, what we're facing, is an existential threat? Nothing less. Now that's not anything the Founding Fathers ever could have imagined. So what I reckon is"—he shrugs his shoulders here—"we're no more than a terrorist incident or two away from pretty much having to let that thing go."

"Let what go? The Constitution?"

"Yep," Coover says, nodding solemnly, "I'm afraid so. I mean, the argument has been used before that conditions in the country have changed . . . in relation to the Second Amendment, for example. But this is different. This is a whole new ball game."

I stare at him. "What do you want from me, Phil?"

"I want you to stay in place, Danny. I want you to go on being Teddy Trager, but to play by the rules, and we both know there's only *one* of those." He gets up from his chair and stands, towering over me. "Okay. We've had the conversation. We're beyond that now. As for incentive, well . . . you're already rich, far richer than I'll ever be, so I'm obviously not going to pay you, but please—and I mean this—don't put me in a position where I have to coerce you."

16

The next few days have a strangely calm, dreamlike quality to them. I sleep better, I swim in the pool every morning, I eat properly, I'm not on edge all the time. At work, I pay attention in meetings and engage with people. I listen to their ideas. I even start to hatch some of my own. For example, if developing and launching the LudeX game console is going to tear PromTech apart, why shouldn't Zabruzzi and a couple of those other guys out in New Jersey form a separate company with a more hardcore R&D emphasis? I get Lester to draw up a proposal, and I meet Zabruzzi for a drink at Sakagura, a Japanese place on 43rd Street. Another thing I do is sketch out some notes on how to get a political campaign off the ground—raising funds, hiring staff, shaping policies—and I attend a DNC Roundtable event at the Waldorf Astoria. Premature maybe, but I'd like to be a little more informed and coherent on the subject the next time I end up having to talk at any length about it.

It feels for a while as if a weight has been lifted from my shoulders. I know where I stand now. I know who and what I'm dealing with. I know the rules.

Or, the *rule*.

No contact, no crossover.

Except . . . I always knew that, didn't I? And I never broke it. I came close one time, on the street that night, very close, but nothing actually happened. And the more elaborate infringement later on—Leonard Perl's surveillance package—that was a defensive measure in response to repeated requests for contact from the other side.

And there it is, the essential problem.

How can I ever control that? The other side? I can't really, and if that's the case, how can I ever protect Kate? Which is what I've been trying to do on one level or another from the very beginning. Talk of buying Pivot is all very well, but that's no solution either. It wouldn't be a movement away from this, it'd be a slow, progressive, creepy entanglement *into* it—and with no guarantee of a satisfactory outcome.

But within a few days, there is, unexpectedly, an outcome of sorts. I'm on my way back from a long and fairly demanding lunch with Ray Dalio at the Four Seasons, so I'm eager to get back upstairs now to my office, to that space by the window where I can just gaze out vacantly on the geometric swirl of Midtown and flush everything out of my head. I'm crossing the plaza, heading straight for the revolving doors, when I hear it. And I'm not even sure at first that I do.

"Excuse me . . . Mr. Trager?"

But I turn around anyway. Standing there in front of me, a few feet away, is Kate.

I feel an immediate tightness in my chest. What does she want? Doesn't she know that coming here is dangerous? That she's drawing attention to herself? That *she's* the glitch in this whole system?

But then, how would she know?

"Uh . . . yes?" I say, feigning confusion.

Her skin is glowing, her hair thicker, redder, glossier than I remember, her eyes on high alert, darting everywhere, scanning me up and down.

"My name is . . ." She hesitates, and I feel she wants to say, *you fucking know what my name is*, but she resists. "I'm Kate Rozman. My colleague, Pete Kettner, met with you recently."

"Oh, yes . . ." For a millisecond I consider extending my hand, taking hers in mine, but no good could come of that. There's *one* rule here. "Of course, yes, I remember."

I remember . . .

"Is there any chance that we could talk? Even for a few minutes?"

People are walking past us, around us, in all directions, busy, focused on their own stuff, and amid the voices, the noise, the traffic, *we* stand there, on a concrete plaza, face to face, Kate and I.

How can this be?

And how can it be that I have to walk away?

"Not this afternoon," I say, as cold as I can make it sound, as distracted, as Teddy-Trager aloof. "I have . . . appointments."

The look she gives me as I take a step backwards is bewildering in its complexity, a dense flip-book of irritation, disappointment, longing, and—no question about this one—determination. So I'm fairly sure that Kate Rozman won't give up. She may not push it here today—she seems a little nervous—but I know her, and she *will* regroup, she *will* insist on talking to me again.

"I'm sorry," I say, ending an encounter that has lasted barely twenty seconds, "I'm late."

I turn to move away, but something causes me to hesitate. As I glance back, I see Kate's hand slipping automatically into position over her belly.

In the elevator, I come close to another full-blown panic attack, but I wrestle this one down too. I make it into my office and close the door behind me. I sit at my desk and take a series of deep breaths.

Kate is pregnant?

But . . .

Is it scruffy hipster-guy Pete Kettner? Is it *me*? My hand is shaking as I click the screen awake to call up a calendar. We had sex the night I got back from Afghanistan—it wasn't great, it was awkward, it was tense (all my fault), but it's within the time frame, so it *counts*.

But maybe she's not pregnant. Maybe I was seeing things. Maybe she's just put on a little weight. If she is though, and it's Pete Kettner's, what is she doing chasing Danny Lynch's *ghost*?

That's going to get her killed.

Unless I stop her, and how do I do that without . . . getting her killed . . .

Is it too much to hope that my coldness during those twenty seconds, my rudeness, my seeming indifference, will be enough to put her off?

The answer—or at least *an* answer—appears on my screen as soon as I close the calendar page. It's a file marked "LP," and it's where all of Leonard Perl's reports are automatically downloaded and archived. It also contains links to the various live surveillance feeds he set up. It's been over two weeks since I clicked on this file, but it *was* an open-ended arrangement, and, although Karl Lessing was clearly informed about it, I have no reason to believe the account isn't active. It turns out to be *very* active, and I spend the next while scrolling through reports, one after the other, in sequence, feeling increasingly as if a noose is being tightened around my neck, because over the past week, and the past three days in particular . . . Kate has more or less taken to stalking me.

Subject left apartment at approx. 9 a.m., rode the subway to Rockefeller Center, and proceeded on foot to the Tyler Building.

Subject left work, took a cab to 45th Street, and proceeded on foot to the Tyler Building.

Subject walked vicinity of the Tyler Building for nearly two hours.

Subject waited outside the Tyler Building for forty minutes.

Subject followed client from the Tyler Building to Sakagura on East 43rd Street.

Subject followed client from the Waldorf Astoria Hotel on Park Avenue to the Tyler Building.

Subject followed client...

Subject followed client...

Subject followed client...

Once I've seen this, I know that whatever happens next has to happen really fast. I delete the entire contents of the file. I call Leonard Perl and instruct him to discontinue the surveillance immediately and to delete any relevant files he may have. I tell him I know that confidentiality has been breached, and I ask him straight out if any of the material his operatives gathered has been passed on to . . . a third party? He assures me that it hasn't, and from the slightly chastened tone of his voice, I decide to believe him.

Not that it'll make any real difference. This is just damage control. It's not the solution. *That* takes a little longer to emerge, but when it does I feel immense relief, and not just because it's so obvious, so simple, it's because I know it's the *only* solution.

I have to disappear.

As long as I'm around, Kate is in danger. And that's because she's a threat, a piece of unfinished business, what Phil Coover would no doubt refer to as an unticked box. But if I think about it for ten seconds, I also have to disappear for *me*.

I finally have to wake up from this.

Though in practical terms, who do I wake up *as*? It can't be Danny Lynch, and it can't be Teddy Trager.

The mechanics of this seem complicated, but once I set it all in motion, things happen with almost blinding speed. I hit the deep web again, and, within a couple of hours, I have set up a Bitcoin wallet, purchased what amounts to a new identity, and reserved an out-of-state PO box. My new documents—passport, SSN, driver's licence—will all be delivered to this PO box within, apparently, two to three days.

And addressed to one Tom Copeland.

I call Nicole in and tell her I need five thousand dollars in cash ASAP. I know I've pushed her hard recently, with my moodiness and unpredictable behavior, but this doesn't seem like the thing that's going to push her over the edge. Twenty minutes later, she reappears in my office and silently places a thick brown envelope on my desk.

That evening, back in the apartment, I have a long, slow swim in the pool. Then I spend a couple of hours in the kitchen. I cook an elaborate miso, shitake, lemongrass, and pork belly ramen. After that, I go around the apartment and gather up a few items—a couple of high-end wristwatches, some gold cufflinks, a platinum fountain pen, a silver money clip, and a Leica S2-P camera. I eye up the small Picasso again, but that still seems like more trouble than I need.

I get a few hours' sleep, and, at around 4 a.m., with bulging pockets and a wallet stuffed with cash, I leave the apartment. Walking out of the building, I nod at the doorman. A block down, I hail a cab, which I take to Chinatown. I walk around here for a while, through quiet streets, then take another cab, and another one after that. I'm probably not being followed, but by the time I find myself walking into the Port Authority Bus Terminal on Eighth Avenue just after 7 a.m., the city coming to life again all around me, I'm fairly sure that no one knows who I am, or where I've been, or where I'm going.

I think it takes about a month for Leon to show up. I'm not paying close attention, but I do check in online every once in a while, when I can. It depends on where I am, it depends on what Internet access I have. I'm moving around a lot, uncertain of everything and everyone, wary of my new identity. I manage to stretch the five grand, plus what I make on the stolen items, which is actually quite a lot, but I know it's finite, so I end up doing whatever work I can get along the way as well, usually in kitchens, dishwashing, prep if I'm lucky. It's at one of these places, a Tex-Mex smokehouse in Kansas, in the manager's office at the back, that I spot a reference on the computer to Trager. I click on the article, and when it pops up there's no doubt in my mind that the accompanying image is of Leon. Much earlier, I'd seen a mention on Forbes that Trager was possibly missing, and then that he was on an extended trip to Africa. Now this article is saying that he has embarked on raising a new VC fund.

Even from this distance I don't believe it.

Next time I check in, it's as if Trager has transformed into Doug Shaw. I come across a video clip on Fox News of an interview he does, and it's painful to watch. Phil Coover must agree and obviously decides to cut his losses, because inside of a year the experiment is over, aborted—at least this phase of it is. In a copy of the *Austin Chronicle* I find lying around a place I'm working at, I see a report that Teddy Trager has died suddenly of an aneurysm.

I feel weird reading this. First I'm killed in a car crash, then I drown in the Hudson River, and now a blood vessel in my brain explodes.

What's it going to be for Tom Copeland?

Now and again, I also check in on Pivot. When Leon first appeared, I was worried that Kate would simply pick up where she'd left off, but I sort of knew it wouldn't happen—she was pregnant and would be increasingly occupied with that. And, besides, it wouldn't have mattered, because Leon wasn't me, and the threat no longer made sense.

Kate posts regular blog pieces on Pivot, which I don't read, but at least it's a way of keeping track. These stop at around the time I reckon she's having the baby. Which is when I lose track of her, or when I stop looking.

Some of the time I convince myself that she wasn't pregnant at all, and when that doesn't work, I convince myself that the baby is Pete Kettner's, and I wish them both a good life. But as a sequence of thoughts, as a recurring preoccupation, as dream fodder, it never goes away—and never far behind it, though easier to suppress, is a shadow sequence featuring Nina Schlossmeier and *her* kid.

As time goes by, though, and I run out of money, and find it harder to get work, and harder to make the effort to even look for work, I feel my life fragmenting, losing definition, and these thoughts, these notions, these versions of what might be true, of what might really be out there in the world, also fragment and lose their definition.

Later on, when I need it, I'm unable to seek help as a veteran, because Tom Copeland isn't one; nor can I seek treatment for what—on certain days, I'll admit, after all—may be some creeping form of PTSD . . . because Tom Copeland can't claim to have it and therefore can't get a diagnosis for it. And later still, when I end up homeless on the streets of a city I'm not sure I remember the name of, well . . . I'm not surprised.

I *am* surprised one time when I stumble to recall, in my own mind, Kate's name.

That girl I knew . . .

And also struggle to remember her face.

Shit.

Is it all gone? My past, my present, my future? Is there nothing left to cling to?

It seems not, which is confirmed one day in a homeless shelter I'm staying at. This guy in the office is helping people out—filling in forms, getting information on various work and rehab programs—and he offers to let me use one of the computers. I mess around on it for a while, looking at job and employment web sites, but pretty soon I get demoralized. I'm about to walk away, when I think of something. I go to Google Images and type in Kate's name . . . and there she is . . .

I remember now.

There's only one photo, though—it's of her, and Pete Kettner, and a small boy, standing between them. He's about four years old.

Has it been *that* long?

I print out the photo. I keep it on me and look at it often. The little boy is cute. And I'm happy for them. I really am.

But the truth is I wanted him to be mine. I wanted me and Kate to make a kid together, to make a future together, or at least to give something of ourselves *to* the future—to restore the level of justice.

A secret retribution . . .

I'm closed off from that now, though—my identity erased, atomized, and my time limited. I'm aware that Nina Schlossmeier may have been lying to me in her apartment that night, but she may well have been telling the truth, and I may *actually* have a kid out there—but I don't want to know, I don't want to find out. Because it'd be the wrong kid, from the wrong me, and once again I'd be looking through the wrong side of the mirror . . .

I have this recurring dream. It's set in what could be North Carolina but equally could be Iraq or Afghanistan. There's this dark, windowless building; it's gigantic, the size of a whole city block, like a toppled monolith, but in a sunbaked, suburban landscape, or a desert. It's some kind of data farm, I guess. I'm in front of it, but also *inside* it, and I'm staring at these enormous servers, row after row of them stretching back as far as the eye can see . . . every machine clicking, whirring, terabytes spinning within petabytes. I turn at one point to see the flicker of graphics on a monitor, neural imaging, *faces*, one giving way to the next, slowly at first, then faster, then rapidly, hundreds of them, thousands, hundreds of thousands, millions, until the screen flashes, and an alert sounds.

And I wake up.

But at least I do *that*. I keep waking up. I keep going too. I keep moving. I even keep looking in the mirror.

And a couple of months after my time in that homeless shelter, I find myself gazing into a particularly grimy mirror in the restroom of a bus station. I'm gaunt, I have a scraggly beard, my eyes look tired—and I may have a fake identity that I bought with someone else's money—but it's still *me* in there, that's still *my* face. And *I'm* the one who decides what I do, and where I go.

And which bus I'm going to get.

With this little micro-dose of self-motivation sluicing through my limbic system, I head out to the main hall to have a look at the timetables. I glance up at the departures board and pick a destination, the decision quick and fairly random. But then something happens that makes me reconsider.

My eye gets distracted by a wall-mounted TV over in the corner. It's showing a news report, and on the screen a tall glamorous woman is being interviewed—door-stepped, it looks like—outside a Manhattan apartment building. She's smiling, and talking. The sound isn't good, and I can't hear what she's saying, but there's a caption.

Nina Schlossmeier, CEO, Treadsoftly.com

Holding her hand, tugging at it slightly as she talks, is a small boy. He's maybe four years old, and he's looking directly into the camera.

Without taking my eyes off the screen, I reach into my back pocket and retrieve the photo I printed out at the homeless shelter. It's torn and a little faded, but I hold it up and look at it closely. After a moment, and with my head—and the world—now starting to spin, I look at the screen again.

The two small boys are identical.

MORE FROM AWARD-WINNING
AUTHOR ALAN GLYNN

"Alan Glynn has created enough twists and thrills to keep readers up late—even without resorting to illegal and dangerous substances."—*The New York Times Book Review*

Limitless
ISBN 978-0-312-42887-7 / E-ISBN 978-1-4299-7363-2
WWW.PICADORUSA.COM/LIMITLESS

Winterland
ISBN 978-0-312-57299-0 / E-ISBN 978-1-4299-8463-8
WWW.PICADORUSA.COM/WINTERLAND

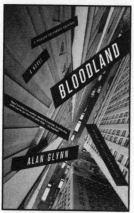

Bloodland
An Edgar Award Nominee
ISBN 978-0-312-62128-5 / E-ISBN 978-1-4299-2732-1
WWW.PICADORUSA.COM/BLOODLAND

Graveland
ISBN 978-0-312-62129-2 / E-ISBN 978-1-4299-4333-8
WWW.PICADORUSA.COM/GRAVELAND

PICADOR

www.picadorusa.com

www.facebook.com/picadorusa • www.twitter.com/picadorusa

picadorbookroom.tumblr.com

Available wherever books and e-books are sold.